# *Wild Night @ McKenzie's Bridge*

## AUSSIE TRUCKIE
## DENNIS LUKE

*Based on my life experiences*

First published as Aussie Fury by Dennis Luke 2019

This edition published in Australia by Aurora House 2022
www.aurorahouse.com.au
Copyright © 2022

Typesetting and e-book design: Cognition Technology
Cover Designer: Donika Mishineva | www.artofdonika.com

The right of Dennis Luke to be identified as Author of the Work has been
asserted in accordance with the Copyright, Designs and Patents Act 1988.

ISBN number: 978-1-922697-88-2 (paperback)

This is a work of fiction. Names, characters, businesses, places, events, locales,
and incidents are either the products of the author's imagination or used in a
fictitious manner. Any resemblance to actual persons, living or dead, or actual
events is purely coincidental.

 A catalogue record for this
book is available from the
National Library of Australia

Distributed by: *Ingram Content*: www.ingramcontent.com
Australia: *Phone*: +613 9765 4800 |
*Email*: lsiaustralia@ingramcontent.com
Milton Keynes UK: *Phone*: +44 (0)845 121 4567 |
*Email*: enquiries@ingramcontent.com
La Vergne, TN USA: *Phone*: +1 800 509 4156 |
*Email*: inquiry@lightningsource.com

With Adrian Tame & Margaret Luke

*In among all this chaos, comes an unexpected,
real-life hero…*

# About the Author,
# Truckie Dennis Luke

My life skills were learned, not taught. We all have our own way of digesting what we see and do in our lives.

Driving and working in many other occupations over my lifetime, and doing what I've been doing for so long, have taught me that you can learn a lot about yourself, as well as others.

Your life skills become your friends, and you can even pick them up unconsciously, not even realising you have them for later use.

I had to learn about the weather so I could meet my work commitments, especially over the past twenty years. Some of my friends could tell you I have an obsession with the weather.

Unfortunately, within a couple of weeks of leaving my gardening business, our house was destroyed by a fire at 5 o'clock on a windy Sunday morning. Gone in just seven minutes! The windy weather played a big part in helping the fire to destroy our house.

But driving around most of the country has also taught me a lot about being resilient when the weather and/or the road conditions have been horrible. Heavy rain, fog, wind, snow, narrow bridges, farms, city traffic—the list goes on. Not to mention dealing with all kinds of people and animals.

Worst of all was the long journey Cyclone Yasi took from Mission Beach in North Queensland until it left Victoria a few days later.

That's how I came up with this fictional story, and it is based on actual events over my trucking life.

I hope you enjoyed the ride.

**Connect with Dennis**

**Website:**     dennisluke.com.au
**Facebook:**    @dennis.luke.9237
**Twitter:**     @AussieDriving
**Youtube:**     Dennis Luke

# Contents

# Acknowledgements

I'm grateful for and humbled by the support and help of my wife, Margaret; my two kids, Elliott and Bellinda (Ell and Bell), for putting up with me for so long; and Lord Cardigan (Adrian), for your help and advice throughout this journey.

# Prologue

Death is inevitable. The problem is, no one knows when, where or how.

Do you know what's around the next corner?

Life can be inextricably linked to various forces. It's only when you find yourself facing death that you sometimes find the will to live—or not. Take Mother Nature's fury, for instance...

# 1

## The Calm Before

High above Far North Queensland, hundreds of floating satellites had their lenses focused on a monolithic cloud formation that would become known as Cyclone Yasi. It was currently heading west towards the north Queensland coastline.

Zooming in further on this sunny morning, you'd have seen a diminutive figure, a reporter, preparing for a live broadcast.

With the stunning beach setting around her, she was about to take her listeners into her world of impending danger. She meant to warn the world about what some would thrust aside as typical media hype. But was it?

"G'day Australia, this is Wendy Sinclair here on ABC Radio. I'm talking to you live from Mission Beach in Far North Queensland.

"Nestled in between Cairns and Townsville, it's a beautiful two-hour drive south of Cairns along a winding and sometimes treacherous coastal road. It's mid-morning, and what I can tell you is there's currently more than a hundred people here, strolling casually along this wonderful golden beach. They all seem mesmerised, looking out across the calm water, watching the approach of a dark and gloomy-looking cyclone in the distance.

"There are people here of all ages, including a mum holding her baby son while she takes snapshots of her family. There are teenagers who've never been exposed to a threat of this nature before, and older people who've seen it all in the past.

"It's an eerie feeling! The palm trees are swaying gently, all unprepared for what's coming."

As she stepped off the pavement, her feet sank gently into the golden sand. Her eyes were also fixed on the darkness out to sea. She stood on the shoreline of the Porter Promenade, with Dunk Island just visible in the distance. She knew everyone would certainly feel the full force of this cyclone if it continued on its predicted course. She walked over to her first interview with a young couple who were affectionately holding hands.

"Graham and his wife, Joy, are here from Tully, located just south of Mission Beach, and I'm speaking with them live."

She positioned the microphone in front of them both, then asked, "What's going through your mind right now, Graham?"

"I was on this coast… gee, must be twenty years ago now, before Cyclone Larry roared through, but this one's much more threatening."

He shrugged his massive shoulders and finished by simply saying, "I'm older now and perhaps a bit wiser."

"Well, you certainly look like you could withstand a cyclone!"

Joy, a tiny woman like the reporter, offered her take on him.

"He's a big bear on the outside and a big sook, all soft and cuddly, on the inside, and I wouldn't have him any other way." Joy's hands struggled to touch each other around his wide girth.

Wendy smiled at the affectionate gesture. "I see the romance is still there. Now, with this cyclone, when are you two planning on leaving? Are you going back to Tully, or have you made other arrangements?"

Graham nodded. "Now that we know more or less where the cyclone's heading, we're going south for a few weeks, down to our family in Melbourne. We'll stay with them until we decide to come back—if we have anything to come back to, that is."

Before moving onto the next person, Wendy added, "Thanks for talking with me, and I hope your home survives."

The next person was waiting for her.

"Now I'm talking with Casey. I've been watching you taking snapshots with your family. Your son, what's his name?"

Casey smiled. "Preston."

"What brings you and Preston to Mission Beach this morning, and shouldn't you be getting out of here?"

"We're up here on holiday from Melbourne, and in a few minutes we're off home. We're not waiting for the cyclone. We've had a great time here, and we were planning to leave tomorrow anyway, but we've moved that forward."

The tension in Casey's voice was obvious as she talked about the danger that everyone could see currently building offshore.

"You must be wondering why people are finding this so attention-grabbing, Casey."

"Yes! We've only ever seen cyclones on television. We have storms in Melbourne, and they're scary enough. But this is something else!"

"Thank you, Casey. I hope you and your family get home safely." Wendy smiled wryly, fully understanding that Casey wanting to get away. But it was still hard to imagine just how much things could change within a few hours, at the picturesque holiday spot.

"Now I'm with Bellinda and Elliott, who are also from Melbourne. Seems like half of Melbourne is up here. Can you explain why that might be?"

"Elliott and I are here for a Scout conference, and we were hoping to get some down time on the beach for a few days. But I guess we'll have to ride out the cyclone like some of the other guests and help with the clean-up afterwards."

Elliott took up the story. "We didn't realise it's so cheap to stay up here, whether you're on your own or with a family or group, and that's one of the reasons why we came. But also, the Scout philosophy is to help other people, so it's second nature to us."

Bellinda added, "I'm not sure how it's going to affect the conference, so we'll just stick it out and entertain the kids like we do on Scout camps."

"If Bellinda and I weren't in Scouting, then we wouldn't have learned some of the life skills that we know we'll need soon. So, we urge anyone listening that has kids, do yourself and them a favour and join scouting. It's an adventure they'll never forget."

Wendy was slightly taken aback by the enthusiasm and maturity shown by Elliott and Bellinda, wondering why she missed out on all that adventurous spirit.

"Good luck riding out the cyclone, you two, and I hope the conference goes well.

"And finally, I'm talking with Chef Jasmine here at the Castaways Resort & Spa at Mission Beach. Hello Jasmine, how have the guests responded this week to the news of the impending cyclone?"

"Well, we have over a hundred guests who've decided to stay and weather the cyclone. Others, though, who weren't terribly impressed by its timing, have already left. So those guests who've chosen to stay know their safety is up to them."

"What about supplies for the residents in the community at large, Jasmine?"

"Over the years, most communities along this coastline have stuck to one simple idea, 'Stock up and shut up.' Everyone knows it's vital to be ready."

Wendy noticed the surrounding area was still teeming with holidaymakers.

"I'm surprised to see so many people still on the beach. Aren't they concerned?"

"Most of them will probably enjoy the day, and some will stay into the evening and then come inside around dusk. Then we'll all get together to support each other to get through the night, especially some of the older guests and children."

"Does anything out of the ordinary happen along the coastline before a cyclone? I'm guessing you have experienced or heard of a few strange things over the years."

Jasmine nodded. "Yes, at a place called Bingil Bay. It's just five minutes up the road. That's where all the action is when a cyclone is about to arrive. You can bet many surfers, windsurfers, kite-boarders and kayakers will be out in the giant swells until the last moment, riding for as long as possible."

Wendy wrapped up her interview. "Gee, thanks for that great insight, Jasmine. I'm heading back for my late breakfast, and then I'm outta here too. This is Wendy Sinclair, reporting live on ABC Radio from Mission Beach, up here in Far North Queensland."

As Wendy and Jasmine made their way quickly back to the resort, they saw everyone was still happily enjoying the morning sunshine, but their eyes couldn't dismiss the increasingly dark and ominous clouds out to sea.

# 2

# Far North Queenslander Times

The cyclone advanced towards them, a massive, black cloud-monster showing nature at its most threatening.

Children, too young to realise the enormity of what was coming their way, continued playing. Their worried parents insisted they stop, as this was neither the time nor the place. They were also conscious of what others might think of their parenting, when, in reality, few could care less.

But most children only seemed bewildered. Instead of obeying their parents, they continued cavorting happily in the shallow surf, running away from the advancing waves to avoid getting their clothes wet.

Before long, they were whisked away to a safer place, or so their parents thought.

Once inside their havens they hoped would protect them, they became frightened by the unfamiliar sights and sounds assaulting their senses.

Few could grasp the scale of this advancing catastrophe until they heard houses shattering and buildings being ripped apart.

As this massive category-five cyclone roared ashore, the meteorologists suggested that the warnings would soon be for a category six or even seven.

Around the world, the story broke that Cyclone Yasi had hit Far North Queensland with a vengeance.

Yasi destroyed homes, shredded crops, uprooted trees, decimated marinas and resorts, brought power lines down and, worst of all, left people missing.

Many people were saying things like, "It was bad enough that we lost our house to a fire more than a decade ago, and now this? I thought it couldn't get any worse. This is too devastating even to think of a future. Will there be anything to go back to?"

The aftermath brought with it a feeling of numbness, a feeling that the old life was over, and everyone would have to begin again. For those who survived, everything had changed.

Nothing remained as it was.

As the days went by, news filtered through of houses and lives lost, and, for many, the sudden shock of not knowing about the fate of their house, their family and friends, or what life would be like after this catastrophe. People felt numb.

The Red Cross in Tully described how one of its workers moved a group of elderly people from one shelter to another. She was concerned the first location was unsafe. Her instinct saved their lives, as the first shelter was completely destroyed.

Was this woman commended for her efforts, or was she overlooked in the chaos?

Tully residents Margaret and her husband William were huddled together in their bathroom, petrified by the cyclone's menacing roar.

"The noise! It was like a train coming, it was absolutely terrifying and unbelievable when the windows popped, with glass flying everywhere. Forget Cyclone Larry and all the other cyclones. They were nothing compared to Cyclone Yasi," they said after.

Tully was decimated, and it was estimated that up to half the town's homes lost their roofs to the 140-knot winds. The landscape looked like a war zone—only there were no bombs, just Mother Nature's fury.

# 3

## 6pm, Thursday, 3 February 2011

Somewhere in a north-western country town in Victoria, Australia, a young radio host prepared to read the evening news, the only piece that the station would broadcast.

"G'day, this is Michael Scanlon here on your outback's own radio station, ABC Crazy FM, and here is the latest news.

"Cyclone Yasi arrived late last night in Far North Queensland, just before midnight. It crossed the east coast of Australia between Innisfail and Cardwell, affecting areas from Ingham to Cairns. Residents experienced winds of up to three hundred kilometres per hour. It lasted three to four hours over a five-hundred-kilometre radius. The eye of the cyclone crossed the coastline at Mission Beach just after midnight, passing over the town of Tully sometime after.

"The prospects of it continuing as a large and intense system are high. Astonishingly, Cyclone Yasi maintained its intensity further inland, more so than what is considered normal, before it decreased slightly to a category-three system near Georgetown, 450 kilometres further inland. It also affected the mining town of Mount Isa.

"On the phone in Tully is ABC reporter Wendy Sinclair. Good afternoon, Wendy, can you update us about the damage?"

"Hello, Michael, the conditions are quite devastating around me, as you can imagine, with so much debris strewn across roads that they've become impassable. It will be some time before any traffic will be allowed on most of the roads, especially in the short term.

"Even as I'm talking to you, I'm receiving reports of ten-metre waves crashing into the coastline of Innisfail last night. Huge rainfalls have brought an area hundreds of kilometres to the north, west and south of Innisfail to a standstill. The howling winds uprooted one hundred year old trees as though they were sticks of wood. According to reports, all types of vehicles were being tossed around in the air like leaves. Some vehicles have ended up in trees, a couple on rooftops, and, because of the enormous strength of Cyclone Yasi, a bus is sitting precariously in someone's swimming pool.

"I was here only yesterday after leaving Mission Beach in Far North Queensland, and these pools were filled with happy families enjoying the hot sunshine, oblivious to the approaching cyclone.

"Many families who took refuge from the overnight destruction awoke this morning to complete devastation.

"Some residents who spoke with me earlier said they felt powerless and numb. I spoke to several others as they were coming out of their unaffected homes, and they said they'd lost confidence over time in the government's weather updates. So as a result, they'd mostly ignored the weather warnings, which kept changing when and where the cyclone would hit."

Michael asked, "Were many of those hundred year old trees still intact? Or do you think they were infected in some way?"

"Funny you should ask that, Michael. Only a couple of weeks ago, some residents and local council representatives were discussing this very thing. They were going to get someone to inspect the trees for infections. But now, I guess they'll have to rethink that and just cut them down, what's left of them, of course."

"Wendy, I heard your podcast when you were talking with Jasmine, the chef at the Castaway Resort on Mission Beach, what did she have to say?"

"I asked her what went through her mind when she saw the devastation this morning. She didn't say anything for a few moments. Then she replied, 'Raw and broken.' I thought that was chilling. She nailed it."

"Wow, some awesome words there. Thanks, Wendy. We now go to Cardwell and talk to our reporter Roger Aldridge. Hello Roger, tell us what you know about last night's cyclone. I'm guessing that you're seeing the same as Wendy ?"

"Good evening, Michael. Yes, much the same here. It's a mess, all right. Reports have been coming in throughout the day about wild seas and damaged boats. Many of the large and small boats moored along the jetties or offshore were tossed about like cardboard, landing on top of one another, creating heaps of squashed and mangled wrecks. I've never seen anything like this before. These once-pristine sandy beaches are now cluttered with pieces of broken boats and heaps of debris scattered all along the shoreline.

"They're lying alongside the remnants of kitchens and other fittings like outboard engines, canopies, eskies—even food.

"Discarded clothing is spread out on the sand, giving the impression that someone has washed up on the shoreline or drowned.

"Driving rain has flooded the low-lying areas along the coastline. It continued its devastation in other towns on its way to Mount Isa last night before it turned south this afternoon.

"Authorities have received calls today from many residents who were terrified by the howling winds as they cowered inside their houses. Some people told me it was pure luck that they're still alive. Their children were too frightened to sleep, unsure if they would survive the night.

"Waves higher than ten metres destroyed some of the smaller buildings along the coastline. And areas further inland, that is, areas located at the bottom of the many deep valleys, have continued to flood over the past twelve hours."

"Thanks, Roger, I've seen some of the photos on your station's website, and it looks like you also have a long clean-up ahead, especially along those pristine beaches you spoke about."

"Yes, thanks Michael, and I'd like to add there are probably journalists older than I am who've seen this kind of devastation before. But, for a newbie like me, it's just overwhelming. I have to say I'm feeling quite emotional about all this.

"As for the reactions from most of the community, they're not dilly-dallying. They're focused on getting on with this huge clean-up operation."

The interview wound up as an obviously emotional Roger said, "Take care with what's coming your way, Michael."

In an outback area of the Australian bush, events were unfolding that would have a catastrophic effect on the lives of thousands of people—particularly those in the small country town of Steering.

# 4

# A Battle of Wills

In the early afternoon the day before the cyclone, Jack, a stockman, leant on a cattle stockade, gazing out across the parched landscape. With his left foot resting on the bottom railing of the fence and his arms folded across the top railing, he squinted against the hot sun beating down on him. A small group of people was also standing close by.

Jack recalled the recent deaths of his parents, thanks to a reckless driver. Sorrow clouded his vision. Angrily, he frowned and clamped his lips together hard, thinking of the callous way they were taken from him, both in their early fifties, too young to die like that and still so full of life. He and his brothers would never forget them, ever.

The little group was dwarfed by the flat and dusty land, which had been brought to its knees by the prolonged drought. Jack and his brothers, Jim and Sean, were preparing a stock transfer in a far north-eastern part of South Australia.

The flies, brought in by the weathered animals, were annoying everyone. Most of the group was giving the great Aussie salute, attempting to repel the annoying blowies. The temperature, then 45 degrees Celsius in the shade, added to their discomfort.

Jack and his brothers were from a family of tough stockmen. He was in his late twenties, six foot four, broad-shouldered and tanned. His brothers shared his build and blue-eyed good looks. Only Sean had a dimple in his chin.

They all wore wide-brimmed Akubra hats and, on hot days like these, light shirts and shorts with heavy-duty boots. The three brothers had left the family property after their parents' sudden deaths. They now roamed the country, working where and when it suited them.

Robyn Hunt produced a regional ABC Radio program for a station called Crazy FM and was at the cattle property to interview the three stockmen.

She was unprepared for the striking trio. As she turned on her recorder to start the interview, Robyn looked up and was struck by Sean's stunning looks. She'd seen many good-looking men in her job, but not like Sean.

Maybe it was the piercing, deep-set blue eyes, partly closed against the sun. At any rate, his presence mesmerised her briefly. Jack put a hand on her arm, snapping her out of her trance.

Robyn was about to begin her introduction but was still distracted by Sean's charms, so she fluffed her first interview attempt. At last, she cleared her throat, but it took a few words before she settled into her familiar rhythm and deeper, more confident tone.

"The stockman has often been celebrated in various forms of media for his ability to bring down a bull—or was it for his cheeky, sharp wit?" She turned and smiled at the brothers, especially Sean.

Jim chimed in, "Early stockmen were carefully selected and highly regarded men. This was because of the value and importance of livestock in the early days of the last century. They needed to be able to handle animals with confidence and patience and to make accurate observations about them, while still able to enjoy the great outdoor life."

Jack moved away slightly as Jim and Sean continued with the interview. He watched as a semi-trailer reversed up to the old wooden loading dock where Texas Longhorn bulls stood motionless inside the fenced-off area, their flicking tails the only sign of life in this withering heat.

The semi driver, Ron Williams, was strong-looking and just shy of forty, not something he was looking forward to.

His large frame had conditioned him to winning life's confrontations, whether with man or beast, but after the long drive in almost unbearable heat, even with air-conditioning, he realised he was exhausted as he climbed down stiffly from the cab.

Despite that, he still smelled reasonably fresh. He'd been told in no uncertain terms by the missus to use deodorant, whether he thought he needed it or not.

"Don't be like other people who don't bother," she'd warned.

Sweat immediately formed on his forehead and started dripping down his face, almost as if he were crying. He wore his customary heavy boots, dark blue shorts and singlet, which did nothing to hide the impression he liked a beer or three.

Up until a couple of years ago, after he was persuaded by his wife Dianne to stop, he'd often have a few beers. Now, he didn't touch a drop unless he wasn't driving for more than a couple of days.

In his younger days, he'd never worn a hat, but after Dianne worried him about the dangers of melanoma, he usually remembered to wear it. She'd lost her father the previous year because he hadn't covered up in his younger years, so she worried about Ron out there in the sun.

Groaning softly, he limped back to the loading area, then caught a glassy-eyed, menacing gaze from one of the waiting Longhorn bulls. Unexpectedly, it sent a shiver down his spine. After all the years of moving large beasts, this was something new to him. Ron had never dealt with Texas Longhorns before and felt this could be a little bit more than an average run to the abattoir. He took a clumsy step backwards, frowning and eyeing down this one particular bull.

"First time with Longhorns, mate?" a voice asked. Ron picked up on the rough, friendly tone born of years outside in these dusty surroundings.

Ron turned and nodded, putting out his right hand. The stockman did likewise, and they exchanged names.

"Well, at least ya only have to take 'em to the abattoir, mate. You don't need to lay a hand on 'em compared to the rest of us, so relax, mate, and enjoy the show," Jack said, even though he clearly knew how things could quickly turn sour, especially when one of these Longhorns was on its own and agitated.

"Brought the wife and kids along for the trip," Ron said to Jack. "Okay if I get 'em to stand somewhere so they can watch, as you say, the show?"

"Yeah, sure Ron." Jack pointed to Mrs Wilson, the wife of the farmer who owned the beasts. She was standing next to Jack's wife, both of them ready to watch the loading.

"Stand over there near the shed, out of harm's way. I'm actually about to go back to a radio interview," Jack explained.

Jack and his brothers had been helping the Wilsons sell up and move on after fifty years of hard labour. The past decade's severe drought, which had affected the whole continent of Australia and been caused by the El Niño phenomenon, had been the last straw.

Graziers had been watching the supply of grass dwindle. Vast areas across the world, not just in Australia, dried up so much so that some of the resulting cracks in the earth were quite deep.

Texas Longhorns and other varieties of livestock were being loaded into semi-trailers, to be sent to other farms across various parts of the country or to abattoirs.

Robyn had already learned some facts from the Wilsons' experiences of life on their farm. She knew they loved the open air and the beautiful country where they'd spent so much of their life. But she also found out how they'd finally understood the toll that it had taken on their ageing bodies, with no public holidays, working over Christmas, no rostered days off, no weekends or a decent holiday.

The Wilsons, well into their seventies, would soon head to a small cottage to allow them to be closer to their children, grandchildren and medical help. They had the opportunity to act now they had a buyer, without being distracted by pride or selfishness—to get out now because they could, not because they wanted to.

Jack and his brothers were employed to help with the handover. The new owners intended to do things other than run cattle or sheep.

Back at the loading dock, Ron turned to Jack.

"Thanks, Jack, will do."

Ron strolled back to his new Kenworth cab where his wife, Dianne, was watching their twin girls bounce up and down on the double bed in the sleeping compartment in the back of the prime mover.

Dianne, a confident, eye-catching woman, with long blonde hair that had been tied up for the journey, always gave the impression she hadn't a care in the world, but she was devoted to her eight year old girls and her man. Dianne wore a flowing, light-coloured dress with matching sandals and a wide-brimmed hat with a couple of small feathers attached to its narrow white band.

Ron had some stern words for the twins, while trying very hard to keep a straight face.

"Don't you know this is where Mum and I sleep? I don't think your mother would appreciate all those lumps, and you aren't dirtying the sheets on her side of the bed, are you?"

The twins stopped and dropped their heads, thinking they were in trouble.

"I thought *that's* where you were sleeping," Dianne remarked, pointing at the driver's seat. Ron caught Dianne's look.

"Ha-ha funny, c'mon, got something for you all to see."

Once the twins had put on their footwear, they scrambled out of the prime mover, skipping along the dusty path together and causing the dust to rise up onto Bethany's clean clothes, but not tomboy Bridgette's.

"Oi, Bethany! Stop getting your clothes dirty."

Bethany stopped as Ron walked past, shaking his head. A smirking Bridgette airily continued on her way. They passed Robyn. Ron heard Robyn going on with her interview with the stockmen as he took his family to the viewing area next to a large shed.

"Do you have many problems getting the bulls into the trailer with their wider horns?" Robyn asked.

"Well, they pretty much have that figured out for themselves. Most go in without any help from us," Jack answered. "Mind you, those three over there could be trouble." He pointed to the offending trio, then to another bull on its own. "But that big one, we'll have to leave till last. He'll need a little bit more persuading than the rest of the herd."

He raised his voice in the bull's direction so the bull could hear him. " Especially him!" he shouted sarcastically, smiling.

The bull snorted, completely ignoring Jack.

"Some of these yearling Longhorn bulls still have their horns. Is there a reason for that?" Robyn asked.

"The owners can't always afford to have them removed. Plus, there's money to be made for a complete set of horns."

"Surely most farmers through recent generations have experienced hardships on a similar scale, at one point in their lives?"

Jack nodded. "Sure, but nothing could have prepared even the real smart ones for this drought. I've seen the insecurity throughout the whole country. Even ends in suicide sometimes. There are quite a lot of other farmers in the same boat who are grappling with selling and moving on to somewhere else."

"He's not wrong!" Sean put in.

"The prized yearling weighs in at around one tonne, and, as you can see, he continues to eye off the rest of the herd. He has been separated from this group since birth to protect them from his volatile nature. Longhorns are regarded as docile, especially during their quiet periods and in between mating season. But there's always that one farmer intent on breeding feisty cattle."

Robyn nodded, aroused and distracted by his husky tone. She listened and looked closely as Sean continued.

"For the most part, they're incredibly unassuming animals. They're even calm enough to make great pet cows sometimes."

This brought a surprised expression to Robyn's face.

"Seriously, they can be trained like dogs. But you'd never put 'em in an environment they aren't familiar with, as they can't cope with too many distractions."

"What do you mean? Even in a controlled environment with crowds standing around?" Robyn asked.

"Yes, like a cattle sale or the local showgrounds, anything can spook them, even a balloon," Jack explained.

Suddenly, nervously, Robyn pointed at the pen nearby. "But these ones have been penned overnight, haven't they? Most of them look quite placid from here."

Jack smiled. "Sure, but someone like you looking at them for the first time can get the wrong impression. They're not always what they seem. Also, their horns can grow in different shapes. Some curl up and back or even forward, while some are straight as can be, making them seemingly hostile to the untrained eye, like yours, Robyn."

Sean added, "It's often the prized Longhorn that will cause trouble. It's a bit like when the monsoon season comes. Their whole mood can suddenly change from quite placid to uncontrollable."

Jim removed his hat to have a short scratch of his head and then turned back to Robyn with a more serious look on his face.

"There is now proof it's not the colour red that attracts the bull; it's more the sight of the moving cape and maybe even the challenge of the matador himself.

"I've watched the running of the bulls in Spain on TV. It shows how scary they can be, with hundreds of blokes and the occasional woman all trying to come on all macho-like to achieve bulletproof status."

"Most years it's a lottery for death. So, if your number's up, it's a terrible way to go." Jim grimaced at the thought.

Jack interrupted to explain how this one particular award-winning Longhorn became so nasty.

"That Longhorn's mother died soon after giving birth. He was thrashing about when his legs began to appear. Nobody realised the damage he was causing his mother."

Robyn felt sad for the bull's mother. She couldn't imagine having to give birth to a beast like that.

"A few days later, even the vet found it hard to hold him still. He kicked the poor vet in the groin, and he dropped like a sack of potatoes onto the hard ground. Nearly knocked himself out! The newborn landed squarely on its feet and took off as fast as he could. Nothing was going to hold him back." He chuckled. Jim joined in the laughter and took up the story.

"Being a newborn and not being able to see well enough, he stumbled through the grass and tripped on some rough ground, finally collapsing outside the barn where he was born. But he was smart, and his owners found him hard to pin down. He grew into a tough, fierce beast. One flick from his horns could make a mess of anything—or anyone—that got in his way."

Sean smiled at Robyn. "Rage is in us all, animals and humans alike. All it takes are the right circumstances mixed with an overwhelming impulse to do harm, to whomever or whatever. And then it can be quite unexpected if the right situation presents itself. So, you have to have your wits about you when you're around any animal—not just bulls."

Robyn tried to act professionally by looking at her notes instead of at the stockmen, especially Sean. Then, she raised her head slightly, without making eye contact with him, and continued her questions.

"With rage, do you believe there's a distinction between both animal species and humans that can be attributed to genes, hormones, testosterone or even DNA? Or are there more environmental factors like heat or surroundings? Can we learn to understand how to live together?"

Robyn looked up into Sean's distracting blue eyes as he listened to her. She would have loved to have said, "Yes, we can live together", but squashed the confusing thought.

Jim broke the spell and explained to Robyn, "Yes, there are many ways animals and humans can live together. But it all comes down to understanding, acceptance, patience, love and respect for animals, regardless of what type they are."

Sean added in a more serious tone,

"Yes, there are also many ways that humans can live together, regardless of what colour they are."

A few moments later, back at the loading dock, Jack calmly guided the bulls up the ramp and into the trailer, while Jim and Sean used plastic ribbons to direct the animals.

Robyn continued her questions. "What are the ribbons for?"

"Working cattle this way is the preferred method nowadays. It's taken over. most of the time. from electric prods. Look at this." Sean waved the ribbon. "See how just a small deliberate movement of the ribbon alongside an animal's head will turn and guide it?"

"Yes! Much better," Robyn said.

"Wildly waving a stick is not a good idea, and children are taught very early how to work all animals, especially bulls."

Robyn's interest was obvious. "I read somewhere that most pens or stockades go in a circular, clockwise direction. Why's that?"

Jack answered this time. "Holding the bulls closer together keeps 'em calm with less chance of them piercing one another. Calm animals are easier to guide than agitated ones, and it helps us move 'em without causing stress or pain."

"How do you know which animal to put in first, then next?"

"When a particular animal is selected, we open a side gate to allow the animal to head straight up the ramp and into the trailer. Most can go in at any time, but some are left till last, depending on their character. Like that one over there." Sean explained.

"Yes," Jim added, "that big young Longhorn had a nose-ring put in at birth. After his behaviour on that day, it was crucial to do that. He was much too wound up for a newborn. Maybe he has ADHD?"

It was now time to put the Longhorn bull in. The other bulls, already loaded, were kept in separate holding sections away from the other Longhorn bulls, some of which had their horns caught on wire or in gaps in the timbers. The boys had to make sure none of the other bulls received any accidental damage, especially to their hides, or cut themselves and perhaps became infected.

Jim and Sean used prodders with a low electrical charge in them to coerce the more resistant ones, if needed. That day, most went in without any trouble.

Jack intended to lead the prized Longhorn towards the back of the trailer with a nose-ring connected to a rope to temper any aggression.

The trailer had been backed up to a run extending out into a paddock, where the prized Longhorn had recently roamed and enjoyed himself with the last group of fertile Longhorns from a neighbouring property.

"By this time tomorrow, Robyn," Jack said, "that bull will most likely be in pieces of steak. But I hope for his sake someone might take him off the abattoir's hands and use him for stud."

"Why is this breed of bull so different from others?" Robyn asked.

"These days, Texas Longhorns are a registered breed. They're good cattle for many reasons, their meat is good and lean for eating, and they don't need to have antibiotics or hormones added. Then, there are their beautiful colours and unique horns. Farmers like Mr and Mrs Wilson often appreciate the history and qualities of the breed, too." Jack said.

"Do they breed like other bulls?" She asked with a hint of suggestion in her voice, wondering if Sean would react.

But Sean ignored this. "They're often used as service sires for other breeds of cattle, because they tend to have fewer birthing difficulties. Their quick-growing calves have fewer

23

health problems, and that's partly due to their fitness. Also, they live longer and they're disease resistant. All this helps them survive harsh conditions."

"Cattle that rarely see humans can grow wild and wary, is that right?" Robyn asked.

Jack nodded. "Yes, absolutely, and Texas Longhorn bulls reach about twenty-five percent of their eventual tip-to-tip horn measurement at about one year of age, on average. After four years, they'd have reached approximately ninety-five percent of their maximum length. That's why that big one is standing there motionless. He's ready for *anything*. He has slightly longer horns than bulls of the same age, partly due to his unique nature. Plus, you'd have to be a bloody idiot, not respecting something as cunning as that one."

Robyn smiled. "I'll hang around and watch you and your brothers do your stuff, if that's okay? And thanks for talking with me today."

"Not a prob, Rob. Just in case something goes wrong, I'll get you to head over there with Ron and the rest of the onlookers."

Robyn thanked them all but had a special kiss on the cheek for Sean, who covered his embarrassment by hurrying off with Jim and Jack to load the bulls.

Closing in on the trailer, the prize bull showed the brothers he was more than a match for them. They soon understood they could be in for a bit more than trouble.

Struggling with the rope, Jack slipped on a mound of bullshit while leading the huge beast into the back of the trailer. Immediately, the rope slackened enough for the nose-ring to loosen.

Taking his chance as he walked casually up the metre-and-a-half-wide ramp, the bull abruptly reared up, using his weight and strength to halt his progress.

Jack, on the trailer floor in front of the bull, deliberately lay quiet and motionless, acutely aware of those horns waving dangerously close to his head.

Then, the beast was briefly distracted by Dianne's flapping red dress, billowing around her in the breeze. Jack had just enough time to regain his footing and strengthen his hold on the rope that was loosely connected to the bull's nose-ring.

Dianne had seen it all before and felt bored by the show and the intense heat as she headed back to Ron's truck, oblivious to the drama so close to her.

Robyn, also not conscious of what was happening, continued talking into her microphone, commenting on what was happening in front of her. No one noticed Dianne moving away from behind her children and Mrs Wilson.

Mrs Wilson was also more interested in how the children were reacting while watching the bull than she was about the show. She too had seen it all before.

The bull's eyes showed a familiar steely gaze that signalled trouble.

Jim and Sean forced the creature back up the ramp, ramming him repeatedly on his rump with the electric prodders. Without warning, the bull surged backwards, catching the brothers off guard. And, for a split second, it seemed as if Jack would be trampled to death, but at the last second, the bull switched his attention to Jim and Sean.

Simultaneously, they leapt clear over opposite sides of the ramp, falling hard on the ground, yelling curses at the beast to disguise their dented pride.

The bull stormed back down the already unstable ramp into the holding area where he broke through a weakened part of the fence, as if it were made of cardboard, and turned back around in the direction of Dianne.

Terrified by what she saw in front of her, she scrambled behind a sturdy-looking part of the fence. But her billowing dress further enraged the bull. Dianne froze on the spot as the bull built up speed and continued to charge towards her.

Hearing the commotion, Mrs Wilson and the children looked and saw the large bull heading towards their mother. Frantically, they screamed at her to get out of the way or run as fast as she could.

But Dianne couldn't even hear them as the bull closed in on her.

# 5

# The Brothers

One early evening in a distant part outside the town of Steering, five young men prepared to leave home for a night at the local pub.

Luke, the youngest, wasn't a big drinker like his brothers. About to celebrate his eighteenth birthday, he had no idea of what his siblings had in store for him.

Luke was still scrawny but, at 180cm, was growing fast. His life had changed recently since starting full-time work, adding maturity to his mind and body.

A few years before, he'd almost given up all hope for a normal future. He was prone to various ailments, like a heart murmur and epilepsy. But now, thanks to good medication, he seemed no different from anyone else his age. He'd also discovered his metabolism was excellent, and his energy to carry out physical tasks was gradually improving.

At twenty-eight, Nick was the oldest and hardest of the brothers. He'd assumed seniority over the family after the death of their father. None of them knew where their mother had disappeared to.

But Nick's short stature, non-stop drinking and undiagnosed bipolar condition left him permanently enraged, which he expressed by regular outbursts of foul temper.

Now, his shabby T-shirt and shorts revealed various tatts on the upper and lower parts of his body. Lying on the dilapidated old sofa in the living room, he thought about grabbing another beer. He stood up and went into the kitchen, then flung open the fridge door violently, taking the last can off a shelf. His brothers knew not to touch anything on that particular shelf, or they risked a flogging.

He flicked open the can and downed it in one long gulp. He turned around, belched loudly so everyone could hear him, then addressed the second-eldest brother, Paul, who'd just come in.

Paul, twenty-four, looked very different from his older brother. He wore an ironed white shirt, neat blue shorts and black shoes.

Nick belched again. "Go and get that little shit from his room and let's get this party farted." He hooted, realising what he'd just said.

"Shit, I mean started… no… I like farted." This made him laugh again.

Nick had started drinking a few hours ago, as was his habit. Over the years, his body has come to accept copious amounts of alcohol. Even when consumed over a short period, it seemed to have little effect on him, or so he thought.

The twenty two year old twins, Ryan and Bill, dressed scruffily like Nick, joined him in the lounge room. They'd do anything for Nick, but not out of sibling affection. Both were well aware of his temper and would go to great lengths to avoid ending up on the wrong side of it.

Nick flung his empty beer can into the rubbish bin with a resounding crash, receiving a high-five from Paul for landing it without touching the sides.

Paul, a few years younger and slightly taller than Nick, was every bit as habitually foul-tempered, but something reserved in his nature kept Nick off balance.

Despite the brothers' drinking culture, Paul was an accomplished athlete, a long-distance runner with a good chance of representing Australia in next year's 2012 Olympics in London.

Young Luke, dressed almost as smartly as Paul, was escorted out of the house, into the claustrophobic, humid atmosphere of the early evening. Apart from bossy Nick, nobody said much. Really, they'd all just as soon be back in the air-conditioned house.

But Nick just wanted to get legless—that and take out his frustrations on Luke. Nick had long believed that Luke had got off easy. Why shouldn't Luke have got the same treatment from their abusive, alcoholic father as they'd had meted out to them on a daily basis?

The old man had been dead now for a little over a year, and he'd mellowed before he died, thus sparing Luke the worst of his drunken rages.

The other four never quite understood this and felt like they owed Luke something for what he was lucky enough to have missed.

Nick opened the garage door to reveal his new metallic black SUV with dazzling red and orange flames along each side. He climbed in behind the stainless-steel steering wheel with a small silver skull glowing in its centre he'd recently made. Paul climbed in next to him, while Ryan and Bill sandwiched Luke between them in the back.

Nick, Paul and Ryan worked at the abattoir, with Nick in the killing room, and Paul and Ryan in the boning room. Nick got top whack and had been employed there for close to a decade.

Management had long turned a blind eye to his vicious treatment of the animals, partly because he was productive and partly because no one else wanted his job.

Nick liked to indulge the dark side of his nature by tormenting animals as they attempted to flee back down the ramp that led to the gun he was holding.

He knew how to take full advantage of Australia's typically complex rules and regulations covering the treatment of animals in abattoirs. Those suspected of having diseases or being injured were screened out for isolation slaughter, providing Nick with ample opportunities to indulge his sadistic leanings.

This particular meat was separated for pet food. Standing at the top of the ramp, he placed the device just above and in between the eyes, enjoying the power as he watched the lifeless animal drop. This was done at the end of the current stock, so as not to contaminate the good meat.

Earlier that day, Rex, new in town, spent his first day on the job under Nick's supervision. Dressed in protective clothing, he'd watched an animal drop down a chute, where he shackled the beast by its left hind leg, making sure it didn't flinch while being stunned with the special gun wielded by Nick.

Rex pulled a lever, hoisting the dead animal onto an overhead conveyor railing where a cut in the neck split a group of blood vessels, including the jugular veins. It bled profusely as it passed slowly over a drainage trough. Then, the head, legs and tail were removed from the carcass.

He then placed the tail and legs into a plastic bag to prevent contamination of the carcass. The head was hung up for inspection, while Nick congratulated Rex on his handiwork.

The hide had been chained and pulled off at the flank by a quiet Swedish hide-puller.

The brisket was cut with an electric saw from the breast, and the offal was then taken out and dropped onto a large moving table, before the carcass was split down the middle.

Nick had shown Rex how to use an electric saw to cut the carcass into two precise halves. At this stage, inspectors had checked the carcass and offal.

"They'll officially stamp the inspected carcass and offal as fit for human consumption," Nick explained.

"What's offal?"

"It's the internal organs and entrails of a butchered animal. They can be used for many dishes in the same way as intestines, which are traditionally used for sausages. Makes you wonder what you're eating at a barbecue, doesn't it?"

Both chuckled, but the inspectors didn't join in. Nick clearly held these men in contempt and, Rex soon realised, intimidated them.

"When I first got this job, years ago, someone read out an article in the abattoir newsletter. It said that, in earlier times, mobs of people sometimes threw offal and other rubbish at condemned criminals as a show of public disapproval," Nick told him. Rex cringed at the thought of having that sticky stuff all over him.

"Some even tried to pretend it didn't affect them, and they were soon shown to be the prime undesirables they were," Nick added, cackling, ignoring Rex's response.

"Come with me and I'll introduce you to my brothers," Nick said. "They'll show you the rest of the caper and, when we're through, you can join us at the pub for dinner tonight and a few beers."

After Nick had made the introductions, he left Rex alone with Paul and Ryan.

"Nick showed me some interesting ways for killing animals," Rex casually remarked.

He missed the glance that passed between the two brothers. Paul motioned Rex over to explain to Rex how the basic cutting was done.

"Each side of the beef carcass is cut into two quarters, between the fifth and sixth ribs, by mechanical scissors in the quartering area. Feel down here to get the right spot and make sure you count correctly, as the inspectors go ape-shit when someone stuffs up. You've got to be quick. Roughly one thousand head of cattle, sheep or other animals are slaughtered here in a day. It all depends on what's waiting in the holding yards or if the semi-trailers arrive."

Bill then appeared and was introduced to Rex. Bill, a final-year apprentice electrician, was a regular at the abattoir with his boss, repairing broken machinery and performing maintenance checks.

"So, when you come to the pub tonight, there'll be a bit of 'you-know-what' as the main attraction," Paul said.

Rex, mystified, didn't say anything for fear of poking his nose into what seemed to be personal family business.

Luke was the only one of the five brothers intent on using his head, rather than his hands, to earn a crust. He also didn't share his older brothers' suicidal or bulletproof tendencies. During his final year at high school, he kept his ambition to work in law a secret.

He'd been dreading this night out for months, knowing Nick had carefully planned some form of humiliation, without letting anyone else in on the details.

That evening, Nick drove the SUV out of the garage and onto a dirt road, arriving at the local pub a few minutes later. The first item on his agenda was to get Luke drunk as quickly as possible. Then, the plan was to get him laid for the first time, as part of some misguided initiation ceremony.

This would have been the last thing Luke wanted, had he known about this. He'd have preferred to fall in love with someone of his own choosing in his own time and marry. Then, when he was ready for the responsibility, a son would be good to continue the family line.

Luke thought back to when he was sixteen and had gone off to get some work experience on his own. He certainly didn't want any help from his brothers. He'd gone to a few places during his school holidays and met up with an old school friend.

"Hey, Tony! I remember you from primary school. Think you were a few classes ahead of me, weren't you? What are you doing now?"

"Well, the first job I had, they targeted me. Didn't like my red hair or my face, or something. They made my life hell. Got bullied all the time. I could never relax my guard."

"Didn't the team leader or someone step in?"

"Nah! It was done to all new young employees as a form of initiation back then. It had been done to them, so they did it to me. Everyone just accepted it."

"So what did you do?"

"One day, just before I went on holiday, I'd had enough. I struck down the leader of the group and then stared down the other four. One of the group said, 'He's crazy! Let's get out of here!' I strung up the bastard to the railings of the town bridge. I left him there, naked, to suffer in full view.

"They never touched me again after that."

After hearing Tony's story, Luke often had visions of payback. He sometimes felt he could do so if he had the chance, but then thought he wouldn't have the strength or the guts to do anything like that. It just wasn't in his nature.

But, for a moment, the thought made him feel strong. He wondered if an opportunity for retribution would ever arise.

The recent incessant rain had cancelled the torment of the recent long, hot drought. As they drove through the humid night air, Nick was thinking about the night ahead. He wanted his plans to go smoothly and had high expectations of having great fun at Luke's expense. Given the amount of time he'd spent organising the entire business, he would be less than happy if it went wide of the mark.

At the pub, Nick saw that the car park was nearly full but refused to park a hundred metres from the building, so he parked in the disabled spot. After all, he was more important than any cripple. Nobody inside would give a shit, either. And he couldn't remember anyone ever parking in that disabled spot.

They climbed out of his SUV. Nick glanced skyward, and rain hit his face. He felt annoyed that his precious vehicle would get wet and dirty. Seeing his brother's concern, Ryan said, "Forget the rain, all you need to worry about is lightning."

But Nick was running for the door trying to keep himself dry, and he missed Ryan's comment, or so Ryan thought. Luckily, Ryan was far enough behind Nick to avoid any possible belting for referring to Nick's fear of thunderstorms.

He continued on towards the doors with a slight grin on his face, thinking Nick hadn't heard what he said. He was aware he could get double that if he stepped out of line again.

The brothers entered the main bar, and their entrance brought its normal reaction: a combination of anxiety and contempt from those already there. Conversation died. Braver patrons expressed their disgust with a stream of obscene abuse, not quite loud enough for its source to be readily identified. Nick and his brothers searched for the culprits but couldn't pinpoint them in the general hubbub.

The brothers elbowed their way across the room to their favourite corner, where Rex waited. On his way to the corner, Paul had already ordered a jug and five pots.

"I'll start a tab," he told the barman, handing over a hundred-dollar note. "Stick the grog up the end of the bar," he demanded, as if he owned the place.

"First shout's on me, mate," Rex interrupted, "so keep your money for the next round."

Nick would have handled it differently. He'd probably spend more than that before the night was over. But when the beer arrived, he thanked Rex, grabbed the closest pot and sculled it down, then immediately poured himself another from the jug. He leaned on Luke's shoulder and dropped a crude hint about what was in store, then sculled his third pot.

Luke struggled to turn away, not only because of Nick's bad breath, but also his contempt for his brother.

Luke eyed the crowded room. Fear of whatever was coming filled his mind, but Nick was leaving him alone for now.

# 6

# A Dysfunctional Family

Each member of the Lockwood family looked out of their car window as they drove across their district's drought-stricken hills.

They were heading to a beautiful timber house set on twenty acres, home to Pearl Lockwood's father, Harry, now in his late eighties.

After a two-week holiday in Melbourne, their car was jam-packed, so much so that the driver could hardly see out the back window. They'd decided to visit Harry as a welcome break on their long journey back home.

Pearl's husband, David, had just turned thirty-eight, and was a transport manager for an interstate trucking company. He worked both at home and on the road throughout the year and was looking forward to a break from his dysfunctional family. It had really been a miserable holiday. He wouldn't be doing it again in a hurry.

He loved his wife dearly, but his two elder kids had been intolerable during their time away.

The newborn, Stephen, was the only one who behaved, only because he was too young to behave like his siblings.

Trying to give the impression that he was fit, not fat, David wore a tight-fitting, short-sleeved shirt, dark blue shorts and ancient runners. He suddenly burst into song to break the monotony of the journey.

"Alone on a hill, da-da-da-da," he sang, pretending to remember the words.

Pearl turned to him angrily.

"Why are you singing that?"

"Oh, it just came into my head when I looked up at where your father is right now."

Tiffany piped up from the back seat, "Dad, that's not a very nice thing to say about Grandfather."

Rhys, her brother, was in rare agreement with his sister. "Yeah, Dad, that's not called for."

Pearl chimed in, "What on earth possessed you to come up with that? You know he's up there all alone."

"I didn't say it to be cruel. It just popped into my head, you know, like stuff does from time to time. I'm sorry, okay? You know I sometimes just say stuff without thinking. Jeez, I know he's all alone on that hill."

And then, as an afterthought, "It's such a fine-looking house with fantastic views and all that. Building it with those windows going all the way around, gives the place... you know, something special."

Inside the car, it had gone unusually quiet as David turned into the tree-lined driveway. The sun was just setting on the property, throwing shadows in front of them. He parked the car in front of the weatherboard house, glancing up at the wrap-around veranda.

Intent on being the first to find her grandfather, Tiffany bolted up to the veranda ahead of Rhys. She was disappointed Harry wasn't there with his normal, welcoming hug.

Meanwhile, Pearl took baby Stephen out of the child restraint and carried him inside.

On and off for the past year, Pearl had worn the same one-piece floral dress that went down to her ankles, as though she thought it was the early nineteen hundreds. It was comfortable and that was all that counted for her. She, too, was trying to hide being overweight.

Pearl, a year older than David, had been quite anxious about her most recent pregnancy. She'd begun putting on weight, especially in the later months before Stephen's birth.

Despite Pearl's two previous pregnancies, David had not realised most women could put on between ten to twenty kilograms. He believed she was letting herself go, both mentally and physically.

They found Harry in the kitchen preparing their dinner. Pearl had rung him earlier to let him know they were coming and to tell him not to fuss about dinner. Annoyed, now, she told him to go away and sit down and that she would take care of the meal.

Pearl greeted Harry with a kiss on the cheek and a hug. David shook his hand but sensed some reserve from Harry, who excused himself, leaving Pearl to get on with preparing the evening meal.

Harry gave her a loving smile as he left and then retreated to the living room for some peace and quiet, so that he could continue listening to a program on poetry that was entertaining him before the family's arrival.

He was happy to be away from his visitors. He didn't really have much time for them, apart from Pearl.

Tiffany was running outside on the verandah, her feet making a racket, when she heard the radio coming from the lounge. She came in through the back door wanting to change the station to something she could dance to.

Tiffany enjoyed the freedom to go anywhere she liked in this big house, because it gave her the opportunity to completely shut off from anything that was troubling her.

Sounds of spoken verse could be heard around the house.

*I love a sunburnt country,*
*A land of sweeping plains,*
*Of ragged mountain ranges,*
*Of droughts and flooding rains.*
*I love her far horizons,*
*I love her jewelled sea,*
*Her beauty and her terror...*

Tiffany, not noticing her grandfather spreadeagled across the couch with his eyes closed, turned the dial to look for a music station.

The raucous notes of a pop song interrupted Harry's daydream of visions of this breathtaking land of Australia. It took him a few seconds to come back to earth and realise he wasn't where he thought he was, but at home on the couch.

He was surprised to see Tiffany dancing around the lounge. Then, she noticed her grandfather creakily trying to get up from the settee.

"Oh," he said, feeling foolish. "I was listening to that poem you..." But before he finished talking, Tiffany quickly left the room, embarrassed at disturbing her grandfather, whom she adored.

Harry moved to the radio, but before he had time to switch back to the program of verse, another program came on, presented by Michael Scanlon, a twenty-five year old local radio personality.

Michael Scanlon had recently returned to his hometown after twelve months in the city, where he'd joined the dual cultures of tradespeople and surf nuts. He'd also grown dreadlocks down to the middle of his back.

It had started as a $50 bet between eight friends a couple of years ago, to see not only who could grow the longest dreadlocks, but who could outlast the others to win the bet. Even though he'd collected his winnings long ago, he'd grown to love his dreadlocks and had no plans to remove them.

As Michael prepared his program, his attractive producer Robyn glanced across at him, admiring his height and good looks. Not even his ratty T-shirt featuring Mother Goose on the front, teamed with a wrinkled denim jacket above ripped jeans and bare feet, could detract from her appreciation.

Like many women in the district, she knew what a good catch he would make, completely forgetting how she'd felt at the cattle property the previous morning with Sean the stockman.

Robyn had dressed comfortably for the humidity in a light blue, short-sleeved, floral skirt just above her knees, with comfortable slip-ons that she only wore at the station.

"G'day, Michael Scanlon here on Crazy FM, and it's ten past six on this wet, balmy Friday evening. It's currently thirty-two degrees, with humidity at 100%. I can't stand this humid stuff, it makes you drip all over! Do you know someone who doesn't use deodorant because they haven't been told about personal hygiene? Phew!"

Back at the house, Harry sat on the couch and lifted up his right arm, wrinkling his nose at the pong wafting from his armpit. Even in this heat and without the air conditioning on, he still chose to wear long pants and an ironed, long-sleeved shirt, complete with armpit stains—something his generation has done all their lives. Regardless of what others said, it was all they knew and were comfortable with.

At Crazy FM, Michael said, "Looks like a very uncomfortable evening both inside and out. Hope you're lucky enough to have that magical air conditioning! Imagine being one of those who suffered without it over a hundred years ago."

Harry mumbled to himself, "We just got on with it, not like these wimps today."

"Some of you could have missed the warnings from the weather services about impending doom."

"Fool!" Harry said.

"Now, those weather service people need to understand how the general public misinterprets their warnings, as most people don't have a clue what they're on about. I sure as hell don't. They need to use simple language."

"Right, they've got no idea," Harry agreed.

"The weather needs to be presented in layman's terms, and yes, I'm one of them, like most people who have difficulty making any sense of their riddles."

"Riddles? More like a bloody jigsaw puzzle, and they never get it right," Harry chimed in. "I've actually done some research. I could explain it better."

"Like most things, nature feeds off something. Cyclones are just one of nature's bad moods, feeding off warm water, bringing sudden flows to rivers and creeks that have been dry for over a decade."

"A decade?" Harry shouted. "Bloody hell, mate! Where've you been living?"

"If the weather services don't warn us that something's about to happen, people can be very down on them."

"Bloody oath, we are," Harry said.

"Beware of animals at times like this. They're out there sheltering or looking for food. Their eyes are on you."

"Ya stupid man, what're you on about?" Harry muttered as Tiffany and Rhys entered the room. He wriggled in his seat, taking up as much of the settee as he could so they didn't come and sit next to him. Tiffany hoped he didn't get upset at her changing the station.

"What are you listening to, Grandad?"

"It's something to do with the weather. You wouldn't understand. Leave me be. Go and play outside with the trucks."

"You always say that, Grandad. It's not very nice."

"You wouldn't want us to get run over, would you?" Rhys felt hurt that his grandfather apparently didn't want them around. Tiffany pulled Rhys's loose-fitting shorts down, something she knew he hated, and something she'd done to him for as long as she could remember. Like Harry, she was shocked to find he wasn't wearing any underwear. Rhys immediately grabbed his shorts and pulled them back up to cover his embarrassment.

"Hey, quit that, Tiffany!"

She merely laughed her head off.

"It's too hot to wear clammy, tight jocks!" They went away through the side door, still bickering.

"Little shits," Harry muttered.

The radio claimed his attention again, because of the eerie, ghostly music that was coming from the speakers.

"David, can you come in here, please?" Harry yelled.

David sighed but got up from the kitchen table.

Pearl smiled and said, "Just humour him, please; you know what he's like."

"Yes, *dear*," he said, mocking but smiling.

"Don't you 'Yes, *dear*' me."

David walked into the lounge room, and Harry gestured for him to sit.

"Ssshhh, be quiet. Listen to the radio for a minute."

"Roads are being closed unexpectedly, causing people and livestock to be trapped for days or potentially weeks, leaving them to survive without the most basic of supplies, often with no power or phone coverage."

"Is this a radio story, like you used to listen to when you were younger, Harry?" David asked.

Harry frowned and said, "Listen to the bloody message on the radio."

"Will you be rescued alive or found dead? No matter how long it takes, it's waiting for you."

On the radio, the presenter Michael gave a spooky laugh.

David perked up. "This is good stuff, Harry. Why didn't you call me earlier?"

"Be quiet. It's for real, you clown. It's not something from the past."

"As it diminishes from a Category 5 Cyclone, it's now weakening into a tropical storm. It was heading inland towards Mt Isa, but, over the last hour, it turned south and it's heading along the New South Wales, Northern Territory and South Australian borders. And tonight, it will be in north-western Victoria, leaving in its wake untold devastation from the flooding rains. We've seen nothing like this locally for years. Is it too late to find shelter? Has your luck run out tonight?"

David realised he wasn't joking.

"Okay, we'll pack up and leave straight after dinner, so we can be home before the storm hits." He now listened intently, hoping to find out if and when it would arrive locally.

Back at Crazy FM, Michael continued. "Humans can have a rush of blood. Animals can have a rush of blood. Mother Nature, on the other hand, mixes blood with adrenalin. Suddenly, it brings our unsuspecting minds together in the same place and time, forcing us to panic in an unfamiliar situation. Can you guarantee your own safety between now and the morning light? We'll be back after this break to talk with listeners who have called in about their near-death experiences."

"Bloody hell, is he for real, Harry? Or is the cheeky bastard having a lend of us?"

"Let's go and have a look at the Bureau of Meteorology radar to see where it is. That should give you an idea how much time you have after dinner," Harry said.

Pearl asked David to go and find the kids so they could all eat.

Harry sullenly hoped they were both under a truck. Finishing dinner couldn't come quickly enough for him, even though he loved his only daughter. As for the rest of them, the sooner they left, the better.

After dinner, Harry and David checked the BOM radar again to see where the storm was currently located.

"Get a move on, you lot. We're leaving right now. I don't want to get stuck in this storm," David yelled. They piled into the car.

David planted his foot on the accelerator, to Pearl's annoyance. She grabbed onto the door trying to restrain her sudden sideways movement.

Tiffany and Rhys unusually and simultaneously yelled, "Go Dad!"

The car disappeared down into a valley on the other side of the river, through the town of Steering, towards McKenzie's Bridge, and then finally towards home, a nice comfortable bed and a decent night's sleep.

# 7

# No Bull

2 February 2011

Around 4pm the day before, everyone watching the terrifying events unfold heard a shot that brought down the Longhorn just after it smashed through the sturdy wooden fence.

Paralysed with fear, Dianne couldn't respond to her family's cries to run for her life and was standing stock-still as the lumbering Longhorn crashed to the ground in a cloud of dust, just inches away from her.

As the dust cleared, a stunned form emerged. Then, Dianne's knees buckled, and she, too, slowly crumpled in a dead faint.

Ron rushed to her side and cradled her head in his arms when she started to come around.

"Dianne! Honey! Are you okay?"

"Mmmm…"

"God, I hate to think what might have happened if Mr Wilson had missed his shot. Hey, good job, Mr Wilson!" Jack said. "Damn fine bit of sharp-shooting!"

"Yeah, I learned that skill in the army. But that fast-acting tranquiliser dart in the neck did the trick, all right," Wilson said. Embarrassed by all the fuss, he changed the subject and pointed to the bull's large form, spreadeagled on the dusty ground.

"By the time he wakes up, he'll be as mad as hell and with a sore head to match. We need to get him safely in the back of the trailer before then."

Everyone gathered around the beast to take advantage of the unique opportunity to have a close-up look without feeling threatened.

"I'll have to get the tractor. There's no way in hell we can move this big lump without it," Wilson said.

Robyn asked him how he dropped the bull so quickly.

Wilson explained the different methods of bringing down a very large, charging animal. "This is the most effective area to drop a bull." He pointed to the beast's neck. "You have to know how long the drug takes to cause anaesthesia."

"What's 'ana'-'sthesa'?" Bridgette asked.

Wilson looked at the eight year old and smiled, as did everyone else, at her attempt to say an uncommon word.

"It means putting something to sleep, in this case the bull. Now, where was I? Some drugs increase body temperature more than others, and this can cause an excitable phase before the animal falls over. Over the years, I've learned there are several drugs you can use for very large animals, like Bob here. It's a bit of an art, as different people use different drug combinations in similar situations."

"Why did it work quicker?" Bethany asked. Everyone else nodded as if they were thinking the same thing.

"Good question. It was because it went in closer to the brain and that was helped by the rush of blood the bull had at the time he was heading for your mum. One to two seconds is all it took for me to paralyse the bull and watch it collapse to the ground," he said, scratching his chin. "I must say, though, you are a very inquisitive young lady to be asking a question like that."

Everyone laughed, especially the children.

Jack asked Wilson why he called the Longhorn Bob.

"Ah yes! I named him after Robert DeNiro, the actor. He played a boxer named Jake La Motta in a movie called *Raging Bull.*"

"Never heard of Jake La Motta. Probably before my time," Sean shrugged.

"He was a famous boxer in the United States, unbelievably aggressive in the ring. He boxed during and after the Second World War."

As Wilson described La Motta, he danced around, throwing jabs here and there at Jack, much to everyone's amusement. He looked like a scarecrow in his old work clothes. He and his wife had long since given up worrying about their personal appearance.

He went on, "He used to have his opponents thinking he was losing steam before launching an attack. No matter how many times you hit him, he kept standing. He eventually lost to another champion, Sugar Ray Robinson, the first time they met, and then beat him in '43." He punctuated his words with a few more right feints to Jack's stomach.

"He fought for the middleweight championship and won and then defended it in 1951, I think. He fought Sugar Ray again in a title fight. Robinson hit him hard, but La Motta refused to go down. Gee, I remember it like it was yesterday! The commentator made me feel like I was in the ring with them. The referee stepped in to end the fight during the thirteenth round. I saw pictures later that week." Wilson's bloodshot eyes glistened.

"La Motta looked like a puffer-fish, and he couldn't see. Wow, he was a mess all right, and he only fought a few more times after that before he retired in the late 1950s. He was knocked out only once in over a hundred fights."

"You seem to know an awful lot about this bloke, Mr Wilson. How come?" Jack asked, amused.

"After the Second World War, a lot of things changed, Jack, but a lot of things stayed the same. Boxing was well supported here in Australia, especially in the large Festival Hall stadium in Melbourne, as well as in the States. This was before television. We didn't have that till the Melbourne Olympics in '56. The missus and I would spend time in the evenings with the family, sitting around the wireless. We would hear stuff from overseas via our short-wave wireless. Out here, if you needed help for anything, you could get it by using the radio for help. Get it? Radio for help."

Wilson laughed and shrugged at their vacant expressions.

"Well, it was funny when we said it to those older than you young 'uns, anyway. So that's how I got to hear about La Motta and how he fought. DeNiro showed me what he was like, and my son has shown me a couple of La Motta's fights on YouTube."

Mrs Wilson piped up with, "Plus, he did a bit of boxing in the army, but he doesn't like to talk about it much these days though."

Wilson looked uncomfortable. "Come on, let's get back to Bob before the bloody thing wakes up! I'll go and get the tractor."

As he walked away, Wilson turned and said, "Respect— that's what it's all about. When you get in the ring, or play any sport, you have to respect your opponent. Otherwise, you're not for real. Get it? Okay, good."

He turned again to Jack with a wink. "I call him Bob, because it's short for beast of burden. La Motta was a dangerous fighter, just like our unpredictable friend here."

Everyone stood around Bob, discussing everything from the size of his horns to his enormous testicles. Country people generally felt easier than their city counterparts when discussing such matters, but Dianne and the girls felt uncomfortable with some of the coarser comments.

Minutes later, Wilson returned with the tractor, cutting short the crude comments about Bob's balls. The tractor moved into position, and slings were placed under the limp bull to slowly raise him off the ground. Wilson straightened him up and moved him carefully towards the rear of the trailer. He made sure Bob was above the level of the floor of the trailer then expertly turned him to face the right side of the cage until he was inside.

Jim and Sean, recovered from their recent near miss, climbed into the back section of the trailer to release the slings as Wilson reversed the tractor out of the way.

A sudden nervous twitch from Bob caught the brothers off guard, and they both jumped clear of the trailer in panic. Again. Everyone laughed. Red-faced, they climbed back up and released the slings, and then climbed out again, acknowledging the applause of their audience and grumbling, "Yeah! Ha-ha. Very funny. Not."

Jim and Sean dusted their clothes off and walked to their side of the trailer, locking the pins into place on the doors. They stood back, breathing a sigh of relief when the worst was over.

Wilson was saying his farewells to Ron when they heard a loud female voice from afar. They saw Mrs Wilson waving and calling out "good riddance" to the prized bull. She had good reason, Bob had nearly killed her a couple of times in recent weeks.

The first occasion she'd been leaning on a fence, talking with a neighbour and not really aware of her dress, billowing in the light breeze, might be stirring the animal up. Bob the bull had charged her from the other side of the fence.

She could have been badly hurt or even killed if it weren't for James, the fast-thinking young son of a neighbour, who was there. He grabbed Mrs Wilson around her waist and swept her to safety, and she yelled "What the... put me down!" in sudden fright at being lifted away from danger.

Bob had abruptly stopped in his tracks just short of the fence as the neighbour's son, being over 6 foot 5 inches tall, big and broad-shouldered, stood before him.

Mrs Wilson attempted to compose herself after her shock. Bob snorted at the tall young man standing in front of him just behind the tree. Mrs Wilson couldn't thank him enough, turning to give her rescuer a big hug. James took a nervous step backwards, embarrassed by what had just occurred, and politely apologised to her.

"Sorry, ma'am, I just acted on impulse. Wasn't sure what could have happened to you."

"Oh, don't be sorry! I'm not! Gee, if only I was fifty years younger…"

Shock briefly gave way to fantasy. *Fancy being in a loving embrace with this handsome young man!* Then, a passing car's horn made her realising what she'd just said. She retreated, flustered, to continue chatting with her neighbour. She cursed herself inwardly for saying it aloud, while not really regretting a word of it.

The second time had been only the day before, when Wilson was putting Bob into the holding area. Mrs Wilson had been watching when Bob had heard the creak of a shed door she was peering out of. Bob turned his head and saw Mrs Wilson, wearing the same billowing red dress, then he suddenly took off, heading for the door.

"Oh shit," she swore and, without hesitating, shut the large wooden door and put the crossbar in place just as Bob reached it.

Backing up hurriedly, she landed on a stack of hay bales, narrowly missing the tines of a large pitchfork lying close by on the ground.

With his back turned away from Bob, Wilson was unaware of all this and closed the gate that was keeping Bob in the holding area, then rode his quad bike around to the front of the shed.

He continued on, only to find his wife sobbing on the hay bale. He went to console her, but she dismissed him with a wave of her hand. Her tears were partly caused by yet another near miss, and because she wanted her husband to know she'd had enough of life on the land and wanted to be off the farm.

He tried hard not to laugh at her woeful expression, but she never missed much and caught him with a backhander to his stomach.

The sound of the phone ringing broke the circuit. Ron Williams was calling to confirm he was coming to collect the bulls the following day.

Mrs Wilson struggled to lift herself off the hay and walked stiffly past her husband on the phone, head turned away. She went straight to the house for a cup of tea, which she'd planned to only make for herself.

She also decided that she alone deserved the last bit of cake.

Back at the loading area, everybody laughed when they heard about Mrs Wilson's experiences but quickly stopped when she gave them the stink-eye. Everyone dropped their heads.

"I should think so," she said.

"Where are you boys heading to, next?" Ron asked the three brothers.

"We're off to Margaret River in Western Australia. There's a property that we're going to be working on over the next few months before winter. The owners were in a car accident. Oh yeah and get this! Sean met this girl, Sarina, back in Melbourne and persuaded her to meet him there," Jim told him.

Robyn overheard what happened in Melbourne and decided to quickly take her leave.

"Sarina says she's a registered nurse, so she can nurse the owners back to health, as well as helping us on the station. And, would you believe, she can also handle large machinery like bulldozers, excavators and such like."

"How did you meet Sarina, Sean? And how did you talk her into coming right across the country to meet you again?"

"Well, it's a long, complicated story involving a chance encounter in a cafe in Melbourne a few days earlier," Sean began.

Jim and Sean noticed Sarina as soon as she came into the cafe. The front door was shoved open so strongly that it caused a metal doorstop on the floor to break. The door crashed into a bench next to a row of chairs, smashing glass over the bench and across the floor. Luckily, no one was sitting there at the time.

Everyone in the cafe immediately stopped whatever they were doing and looked towards the loud noise. Sarina cursed under her breath, hoping no one had heard or seen her entrance, but they did. She didn't flinch at the attention but offered to pay for any damage.

"No, love, she's apples. You go and sit down at your usual spot in the corner. Guess your friends will be here soon."

Sean immediately focused on the stunning young Italian-looking woman, taking in her dark, curly hair, hazel eyes and perfect teeth. He felt that her smile could light up a dark room and knew she was used to turning heads. Her eyes somehow met Sean's.

"Hi there! Wonder if I could join you for lunch?" Sean asked her.

"Sure! Why not?"

Jim retreated, joining Jack. They both felt annoyed that Sean had got her attention.

A few minutes later, a group of admirers from her work arrived at the cafe and voiced their disapproval at the attention Sarina was receiving from Sean.

She responded to their taunts by kissing Sean squarely on the mouth.

Not surprisingly, this cemented the instant attraction they both felt, and Sean soon asked her to meet him in WA. Amazingly, she agreed immediately.

"I'll have to go now, but I'm looking forward to seeing you in WA," he said. They kissed again, provoking Bronx cheers from the patrons. The manager shed a silent tear.

Wilson turned to farewell Ron and his family, who were about to enjoy time away together after the final trip on Ron's schedule. They were staying at a beach somewhere along the east coast of Australia.

Ron wouldn't say where it was, much to the annoyance of the family, especially Dianne, who didn't like surprises.

He climbed into the cab of the semi as Dianne and Bethany clambered into the large sleeping compartment behind him.

The vehicle was air-conditioned or heated throughout and could sleep four people in comfort. It also had most of the mod cons available in a medium-sized caravan.

It was Bridgette's turn to ride in the front passenger seat, and she fastened her seatbelt as Ron started the engine, pulled out of the loading area and waved goodbye to the Wilsons.

A five-minute drive took them from the loading area to the main road along a dirt track with numerous potholes and ripples. It hadn't been graded for a while.

Every time the family tried to discuss their impressions of Bob, their voices vibrated with the continued swaying and jolting as the prime mover lurched from side to side between the potholes.

The children started laughing over their vibrating voices, and Bethany got a bad attack of hiccups. They all gave up trying to talk until they reached the main road.

All was quiet in the prime mover. Then, Bethany hiccupped again, and they all laughed as the truck headed towards Steering overnight, before taking Bob and the other bulls to the abattoir the next morning.

# 8

# Cop That

Somewhere in Melbourne's city centre, Senior Constable Scott Taylor and a colleague walked up to the front of an ageing government building.

"Makes me wonder sometimes. Why didn't the architects back then realise how the population would not only grow, but also grow old?'"

"Yeah. Makes you wonder."

"And why would they put in so many bloody steps? Really."

At thirty-eight, Taylor was a likeable, knockabout bloke, popular with his fellow officers and members of the public whom he'd had regular dealings with.

Handsome despite his receding hair, still single and very tall, he'd entered the force later in life than most of his fellow officers. This made his judgment a little more tempered than his younger fellow officers'.

He was dressed in his neatly pressed uniform as he climbed the thirty-five steps at the front of the building, grimacing from the pain in his right knee—a legacy of too many hard knocks during his sporting career.

He struggled to open a large, heavy oak door with carved panels on either side that opened onto a hallway.

Three floors above, a meeting about his future was about to get underway. Scotty checked the letter in his hand and then located the room where the inquiry was being held.

Going up more stairs, he mumbled to himself, "That'd be right, punished even before I get to the bloody room. Bloody architects."

At the designated room 153, more heavy oak doors again confronted him, but this time they featured a long vertical handle that was pushed by a well-dressed attendant outside the room.

Inside, he wasn't surprised to see five people sitting behind a large mahogany desk, waiting for his arrival.

The hearing concerned a high-profile journalist, Jo-Anne McGrath, sitting to one side with her lawyer.

She'd been investigating various underworld figures when she crossed paths with Scotty. Strangely for her, she fell in love with him. Scotty, because he could, went along for the ride.

Everything went pear-shaped one evening when Jo-Anne and Scotty were in bed together in her flat. The bedroom door flew open unexpectedly to reveal a bald, stocky man in a tight shirt and black pants, sporting a spectacularly broken nose.

This was Con, a stand-over man employed by his uncle, known as the Boss. Jo-Anne had been steadily compiling a dossier of highly incriminating details about the Boss's operations.

Con hadn't expected to find a burly cop in bed with his intended victim, let alone a naked one. Introductions were minimal and ended in Con lunging at Scotty, who wasn't exactly dressed for the occasion.

Scotty blocked the first few wild haymakers thrown by Con, but eventually copped one on the nose. He recoiled backwards onto the bed, blood coming from his nose, then crashed into Jo-Anne, cowering behind the sheets.

Jo-Anne fell onto the floor beside the bed with a cut lip as the fight continued.

Scotty glared at Con standing before him. He clenched his fists, intent on defeating this person for interrupting his pleasure.

He was back up instantly and jumped onto the bed, using it as a trampoline to project himself feet first, kicking Con's substantial stomach.

The attack sent Con stumbling backwards, causing his head to crash into a coffee table near the corner of the room.

He lay motionless, seemingly unconscious, while slumped on the floor, blood trickling from the back of his head.

Scotty leant forward awkwardly, grimacing with the pain in his right knee and going down on his good knee to get a better look at the damage he'd done. His body was aching and stiff from the unexpected hard workout.

Abruptly, Con's right leg shot out, connecting with Scotty's bad knee. Excruciating pain shot up through his leg; more grief followed when he lost his balance and fell backwards onto the hard wooden floor. Con followed up with a crunching uppercut to the jaw, flinging Scotty backwards onto the bed.

Con launched himself towards Scotty, with his weight breaking the bed's mattress supports in the middle. However, Scotty had expected this, and when he saw what Con was about to do, he rolled to his left before Con landed on him, and he fell off the bed.

Landing on Jo-Anne, Scotty inadvertently squashed her against the wall. She screamed in pain.

Con scrambled up from the wreckage of the bed and sat on its edge, getting his breath back. A wry smile crossed his face as he relaxed, looking down on Scotty and Jo-Anne.

He made the mistake of thinking that if he grabbed Jo-Anne, he'd have the upper hand. Jo-Anne groggily stood up to shield Scotty and swiped a hairbrush from the bedside table, just as Con was about to grab her, thinking to himself *Why would you want to brush your bloody hair? That's typical of a woman.*

Swiftly, Jo-Anne spun the brush around and rammed the handle into Con's eye-socket, blood squirting out and over her. She found out later that the hairbrush handle had penetrated his brain, killing him instantly.

Collapsing backwards into Scotty on the floor, she sobbed with relief. Then, shock set in.

"What have I done? What have I done?" Scotty could only hold her tight.

She lay in his arms, and, to their mutual astonishment, a flicker of lust passed between them.

"No," Jo-Anne murmured.

They both laughed nervously, expelling the tension. Scotty wiped blood from her face.

"You okay?" he asked, knowing it was a stupid question.

"Never better!" she said. "Not!"

The policeman in Scotty kicked in, and he went to where Con lay spreadeagled across their bed. Even before he checked for a pulse, something told him there wouldn't be one.

Scotty slumped down next to the limp body—hairbrush still stuck in Con's eye. He put his hands to his face and roared his frustration. He knew immediately they were in trouble.

Still stark naked, Jo-Anne went over to hug him, but he pushed her away.

"Just let me be for a second. I've got to think rationally about how I'm going to deal with this."

"But it wasn't your fault, so why would you blame yourself? It was just one of those wrong-place, wrong-time moments. It was purely self-defence, besides…" Her tone and demeanour changed. "I have CCTV throughout the house. That will show that it was me who did the killing, and it wasn't for any other reason."

Scotty knew his big challenge was still to convince Force Command that self-defence was the only motive behind Con's death. He thought about the media furore that was sure to erupt and how this would drive Force Command into a corner.

Some of the more senior police had become corrupt over the past few years, thanks to a lack of direction from the top. Scathing reports from the tabloids and questions in parliament all made it impossible to sweep things under the carpet.

The police minister had made it abundantly clear in closeted meetings with Scotty's superiors: it was not the done thing for a policeman to draw attention to corruption within his own police force. Scotty would have to go, as that was the only way to defuse the ongoing media criticism.

"But sacking me will turn me into a martyr! And don't worry—I'll play that role to the hilt!"

"Look, son," a superior said. "Would you be prepared to accept a transfer to a country town? You could make a fresh start there. That would be good for all of us."

That's how Scotty ended up being sent to Steering.

A few hours later, Scotty left the disciplinary hearing by a side door and walked to his car, parked down a side street.

He was surprised to see Jo-Anne walking alongside the police minister towards the waiting media, all intent on grilling them both.

As he opened the car door, he felt a hand on his shoulder. He spun around to find a young woman clutching what looked like a reporter's notebook.

"I have nothing to say to you."

But she persisted. "Is it true there was a CCTV camera in the bedroom, and you were in the middle of making a pornographic film and were both naked?" she blurted.

Scotty, about to voice his anger, noticed a photographer over the girl's shoulder. This was not the time for further awkward publicity. He jumped in the car, fired the ignition, rammed it into gear and sped away.

Pulling up at home, he took a call on his mobile from Force Command. The officer on the end of the line was clearly enjoying himself.

"I'm letting you know your future. You start at your new posting next Monday. Understand?"

This would give him just a couple of days to get his stuff together.

He sighed. "Okay, where am I going?"

"Look at your computer when you get home."

The call ended. The word "prick" came to Scotty's mind. He pressed the OFF button.

Immediately, his phone started ringing again. This time it was Billy, always a bit slow on the uptake. Scotty had been looking after this youth for longer than he cared to remember.

"What's happened to you? Heard you went in with your balls intact but came out with 'em a bit bruised," Billy said.

Scotty laughed and explained the morning's events, then said he was on his way home to discover his immediate future.

"How far away are you? I'll meet you there in thirty minutes, and we'll have a few beers to cheer you up."

"Sorry, Billy, I finished them all off last night to help me sleep. I've got to call someone else on the way home."

"Oh! Okay, I'll see you later, then."

Scotty thought long and hard before he redialled.

"Hello, this is Emma. That you, Scotty?"

"You know damn well it is, sis. How are you?"

"Was it you I saw on the news before, you naughty boy? What were you playing at with a floozy like that?"

"You know what it's like, Em. Before I knew it, we were… you know, we were up to our armpits in each other, and then, well, *bang*! There's all this mess! Well, guess I had it sort of coming."

"Why do you think that? What'll happen now?"

"I'm being transferred to a station in the bush, probably somewhere remote."

"Oh, no!"

"I'll ring you as soon as I know where, okay? I'll call soon."

A frustrated Emma decided to stay clear of the news for the next few days.

Scotty pulled up into the driveway of the room he was renting from Mrs Emerson, an elderly lady he'd known for years.

Billy arrived at the same time on his electric bike. He wore his helmet over a peaked cap, teamed with daggy fluorescent shorts, a yellow T-shirt and slippers—because he could.

"Hey Knackers, how's ya testicles going, you poor old bugger?" Billy greeted him,

"Get stuffed, Billy, or I'll send you home, you peanut."

"Does the old girl have any pancakes or chocolate cake?"

"I don't know if the 'old girl,' as you call her, is home, but make sure you don't eat them all, you pig, or I'll…"

"You'll what? You're the one who's been a bad boy. I'll have what I like."

"You're just jealous because my legs are all tanned and hairless, better-looking than yours." Back in Scotty's cycling days, shaved legs were essential. But he'd also acquired scars on both legs from a tragic car accident that killed everyone in his family, except him and his sister.

"Oh, you will, will you, Billy?" growled Mrs Emerson, who'd been standing unnoticed in the driveway of the house.

She wore a floral summer dress, a wide-brimmed hat and sneakers, her normal attire while pottering in her well-kept garden.

"Hello, Mrs Em, didn't know if you were home or not," Scotty said.

She knew the hardships Billy endured over the years, so she said, "Oh, go on, help yourself to the cake. Or anything else you can find!"

Mrs Emerson admired Scotty for taking Billy under his wing, mentoring him over the years, but she was as curious as everyone else.

"What's this I hear about you, you sly fox, having an affair with that floozy?"

"That's the second time I've heard the term 'floozy' today, Mrs Em," Scotty frowned.

Billy dropped his bike and headed straight for the kitchen in her impressive home. Mrs Emerson had owned it since 1985, the year both her parents passed away.

A tiny figure, now eighty-three, she never married after her husband-to-be hadn't come back from the Second World War, dying of pneumonia in the final days of the war in Germany.

While Billy helped himself to food, Scotty went to his room and opened his computer. After ploughing through endless pages about the results of the hearing, he discovered that Steering would be his next posting. He retrieved a map from a desk drawer and quickly located the town.

Billy barged into the room and asked, "So where you off to, Knackers?"

Then his face changed, his head dropped, and Billy flopped dejectedly onto the floor.

"Shit, Scotty, what am I going to do without you around?"

Scotty now felt bereft too. He took a deep breath, swallowed hard and wondered how he could break the news. His throat felt dry.

"Listen, I'm sorry, Billy, I'm off to Steering. I hadn't even given it a thought until you mentioned it, so here's what we'll do. When I get settled, you can come up on the weekends, just to see how things work, okay? Depending on my workload we'll have a look at it then. But first I'll have to figure out the logistics. I've looked it up, and it's about five or six hours' drive from here, up near Mildura."

Billy nodded, but Scotty could tell by the look on his face that he wouldn't enjoy the next few months.

"Besides, Billy, you'll like coming up there every weekend on the train. I know how much you love trains. Now, stop being a sook, and go and get me a slice of that chocolate cake, you pig."

Billy's gloomy demeanour changed instantly.

"You're the best-est friend ever." As he left the room, he nearly bowled Mrs Emerson over. "Whoops, sorry Mrs Em, got to feed the womaniser."

Mrs Em chimed in, "I hope for the both of you that things work out. If they don't, Scotty, you can send me a regular payment for all the chocolate cake he'll be eating."

"Sure, Mrs Emerson."

"Mmm... wonder if I should sell the house now that Scotty's leaving. The place is too big for me to be on my own now.

"There's a new retirement village that's just opened up around the corner. They haven't been able to find a cook, and I've told them I'd be happy to do it for a couple of years."

"When will the village open up?" Scotty asked.

"They're hoping before Easter, so if you're really going, I'll put this house on the market now. Then I'll let them know I'll be there when the residents have moved in, including me."

"Sounds like a plan, Mrs Em."

"But I hope it works out for the both of you. I can't imagine what Billy would be like if his two favourite people move out. And he doesn't understand the ramifications like we do."

"No. Probably take him some time..."

"Billy's mother should leave that alcoholic, wife-beating mongrel and take Billy with her. Maybe after you've settled in you could put them both up at your new digs, depending on how big they are."

"I'd have to look into that to see if it would work. I'm concerned for him too. But it's a big ask. You know what a handful he can be," Scotty said.

"Yes, I know he is, but I'm sure you'll make the right decision. You might even settle down there... What's the town called again?"

"Steering. Look, I'm sure we'll work it out, but first I want to enjoy some of your cake with my mate." He smiled as he took his first bite into the moist triple-chocolate mud cake. Scotty wondered how long it would be before he sampled Mrs Emerson's cooking again.

"Yeah, funny name, Steering. Maybe someone drove through the town and then settled there and named it after the way they came steering through?"

"Don't laugh, Mrs Em," Billy told her. "His Dad jokes aren't that funny."

They shared a laugh anyway, possibly for the last time.

# 9

## You're on the Radio

Dianne leaned forward and tapped Ron on the shoulder.

"Could you turn the sound up, please?"

"Okay. Why?"

"The announcer wants listeners to call in and describe incidents in their lives when the Grim Reaper's come too close for comfort."

"Yeah! Sounds like something you should ring up about," Ron said. "After that bloody Longhorn got pulled up only a few feet away from turning you into hamburger meat, you'd have a great story to tell."

The song on the radio ended, and Michael Scanlon's unmistakable voice filled the cab of the prime mover.

"That was *Fanfare for the Common Man* by Emerson, Lake & Palmer, one of the most commercially successful progressive bands in the history of rock music, playing one of their more exaggerated works.

"Looks like we're in for a bit of a storm overnight, and, looking at the radar, there's plenty to be worried about, what with the lightning and all.

"Michael Scanlon here, on Crazy FM, with you until dawn. Our usual night-time host, Maurice Conway, has come down with the dreaded lurgy.

"It's ten past the hour of seven on this Friday evening, so there's a looooooooong way to go. Now, we're asking if anyone would like to call in and talk to us about any near-death experiences they may have faced recently. What determines the outcome of these situations? Who knows? Sometimes it's pure luck, sometimes quick thinking. Okay, the lines are open. Seems we've got our first caller. Hello, this is Michael. Go ahead please, you're on the air."

"My name's Patrick, and I'm from Redcliffe."

"Hello Patrick! How are you feeling today?"

"I'm a bit under the weather, Michael, and I'm just coming to terms with what could have happened today."

"Rather ironic you should mention the weather, Patrick. Sorry, please continue."

Patrick sighed. "I was riding my motorbike along the main drag on my way home, when this bloody car went through a stop sign and nearly took me out. I thought I'd had it! Didn't stop at the sign or even look my way."

"Do you feel you should've died? Or was this a cat-has-nine-lives moment in your life, Patrick?"

"I've recently broken up with my girlfriend of eight years. Found out she's been playing up behind my back. When I confronted her, she was moaning about me not being up to it in the cot over the last few months. So I went to the quack, and he told me I've got cancer." He paused for a few seconds.

"To answer your question, that bloke today in the car might as well have finished me off."

"That's not good to hear, Patrick, can we go on, or would you rather leave it there?"

At the radio station, Michael and Robyn were crossing all their fingers, hoping that Patrick would continue. He did, after another heavy sigh.

"Yep, sure, why not, okay, whatever. It's not as if I have anything else to do tonight."

"Can I ask how long you have to live, Patrick?" Michael's voice was now gentle, sympathising with Patrick's plight.

"The doc told me it looks like we caught it early. He said to think positive and not dwell on the negative. So, I'm hoping for a good outcome. Then there's the chemo..."

"Well, we can only hope for a positive outcome. Did you have any visions of dying in the moment before the near miss, Patrick?"

"I definitely wasn't thinking about me dying. I'd just come from a mate's funeral, and I guess *his* death was playing on my mind. But not mine. Maybe I wasn't paying as much attention to the road as I should've been."

"Well, Patrick, I think I can speak for all of us at Crazy FM in wishing you all the best."

Michael gazed out through one of the large windows at the radio station, unsure as to how the listeners would react to this interview.

Robyn motioned to Michael to look at his monitor. She'd sent him some responses encouraging him for the way he'd handled the interview and to keep up the good work.

Michael now felt a little more confident that this interview would go its course, and he took on a more serious tone with his questions.

"When you saw the car coming towards you, through the stop sign, did you have any flashbacks of your life or of someone or something special?"

In the short pause that followed, Patrick's heavy breathing could be heard on the phone. Robyn and Michael knew this would have a dramatic effect. Then, Patrick began to speak again.

"Mmm. My ex-girlfriend, but that only lasted for a split second before the car." This time there was a longer pause.

"Are you still there, Patrick?"

"Yeah, it's weird and puts things into perspective… kind of hits the spot."

Michael ignored this cryptic thought, and said, "How old are you, Patrick, and what happened after the car nearly hit you?"

"I'm thirty-five, Michael, and yeah, it shook me up pretty badly. I got home about ten minutes later, then I had a beer

69

to calm myself down. Next thing, I'm throwing the bottle through the window, only I didn't realise it was closed, Mum cleans them so good. So, yeah, I guess I was a bit pissed about what nearly happened. I reckon talking it over with you has helped. Like you say, I'm like a cat with eight lives left."

"That's good to hear. Has this ever happened before, something so confronting that you had to question your existence, perhaps with your ex-girlfriend or something else?"

"I dunno, really. Anyway, thanks for the help, man. I still feel a bit numb, but I guess I'm coping. Good luck with the program."

"Thanks Patrick, time will tell. We'll take a… hang on, you still there, Patrick?"

Robyn, frantically waving her arms around, finally succeeded in getting Michael's attention to take this next caller.

"Yeah, ya just caught me, I'm here."

"Patrick, you won't believe this, but we've got the woman who nearly killed you on the other line, and she wants to apologise, if that's okay?"

"A woman, shit! I thought it was a bloke. That's typical! Can't wait to give this bitch some grief. Sure, let's hear her."

Patrick's tone changed, revealing his uncomplimentary thoughts of women in general. Michael frowned, not happy with Patrick's rude comments.

"I suggest we hear what she has to say before you abuse her, Patrick. Hello Emily, are you there? You're on the air."

"Hello Michael, I'm a bit nervous now. I heard… is it Patrick?… talking with you, and I felt a bit guilty about what happened. Now I don't know if I should've called in or not."

"We're glad you did, Emily, and, just to let you know, Patrick is on the other line listening. First of all, if at any time you wish to stop, we'll take a break, okay? Is that okay with you, Emily?"

"Yes, I'm fine with that, Michael."

"How about you, Patrick? Let's see what Emily has to say."

"What on earth were you thinking, woman? You nearly killed me today!" Patrick's angry, strained voice showed he was clearly still affected by what had happened earlier that day.

Michael quickly cut in. "Let Emily have her say, Patrick, and explain why she didn't stop." The last thing he wanted was to have Emily scared off the line.

"Okay, okay, sorry, Michael, I lost it there for a minute. Tell her to go ahead."

Emily began again. "Yes, thank you. I'd just received a phone call from a friend. Her daughter had fallen off some gym equipment in their backyard, monkey bars, I think. Sorry, I'm a bit flustered at the moment. Um, where was I? Oh, that's right, um, her daughter broke both her arms, and my friend needed me to look after her other kids while she took her injured daughter to the hospital."

Michael responded, "That's terrible, Emily, I'm a bit taken aback, um… I hope no one looks at her twice. These days, the mother might have a bit of explaining to do. So, is that why you went through the stop sign? I realise you were in a bit of a panic."

"I didn't see him, and I know it was wrong, but I was thinking more about my friend. I had to get to her as quickly as possible. I realise now I should have been a bit more responsible, and I kind of over-reacted and nearly killed Patrick, but it wasn't entirely my fault." Emily's voice shook.

Patrick's angry voice cut through. "Oh yes it was, you stupid fucking bitch."

"Patrick, cut that out. We don't need that. Let Emily finish or I'll cut you off. Is that clear?" Michael warned. As much as this made for compelling radio, he also had to show a duty of care about sensitive matters.

A sniffle was heard, then Emily interrupted, "I'm not going to do this if he's going to… oh well… There was a huge cattle truck on my right blocking my view. I couldn't see the sign properly, and I thought I could get through okay, but that's no excuse, really. Anyway, you see, my dad was a racing driver and stuntman. When I was growing up, he would take me out on our property and show me what he had to do in stunts, and I always tried to remember some of the things he showed me."

Emily took a shaky breath, "He was killed after he returned from an overseas tour. He missed a sign and crashed on a corner. Anyway, I wasn't expecting this motorbike as the truck had just passed me, and I couldn't see anything else behind it. So, I continued on through the stop sign and suddenly there's this motorbike sort of tailgating the semi. I wasn't travelling very fast. I just didn't expect to see anything behind the trailer, let alone a motorbike. Oh yeah, and one other thing, Michael, now I remember it. It was nearly dark and he... Patrick... was wearing dark leathers. I didn't see him until it was too late, and I swerved to avoid hitting him. But that's not all, Michael."

"What else could there be, Emily?"

"He didn't have his headlights on, and he wasn't wearing a helmet."

"Fucking bitch!" Patrick shouted. A click told listeners he'd hung up.

Ron, Dianne and the children were locked into the drama unfolding before their ears. Dianne could only manage to cover Bethany's ears in case Patrick swore again.

Bridgette just sat there with her mouth wide open, looking at her father who was grinning from ear to ear. She screwed her face up and folded her arms in disgust at the swear word, then smirked at her father.

After a pause, Michael's level voice returned.

"Seems to me you were both at fault to some extent, and you both should learn from this. It's everyone's responsibility to pay attention on the road, whatever else may be going on in your head. It's no good thinking you're more important than the next person, that you need to get where you're going and stuff the rest of the traffic, because it's all about me.

"We still have Emily on the line. Thanks for staying with us, Emily. Unfortunately, Patrick's hung up. We've tried to get him back, but he's not answering. So, I'll just ask you a couple more questions before I take more calls. How did the little girl go at the hospital? Is she back home now?"

"Yeah, she's fine and asleep."

"Have you thought about what happened today?"

"I'm getting a bit tired, but yes, I'm thinking about it now. I realise I shouldn't have driven like that when I was tired and distracted by emotion. I didn't want to let my friend down, so I just acted on instinct. Shows what a dill I was. I was so worried, and I guess it was the adrenalin that made me careless."

"Thanks, Emily, I hope you've learned something about yourself today."

"Yes. Thanks, Michael." Emily's phone was cut off.

Ron nodded his head in agreement, remembering how Crazy FM's Michael had spent time with him on a couple of long trips to get a feel of what really goes on, out on the roads.

Heavy rain continued to fall, making it harder for Ron to see the road in front of him. Lightning flashed violently across the sky.

He saw Dianne and Bethany looking rather tired in the sleeping compartment of the prime mover. Bethany had finally recovered from her hiccups and was sitting quietly.

Bridgette, however, was wide-awake, showing no signs of wanting to sleep anytime soon.

# 10

# Life on the Road

The long journey along a straight, narrow road made the Longhorns restless as they struggled to stay upright in the trailer.

Ron eyed the blackening skies ahead. This was Bridgette and Bethany's first time in the truck with their parents.

"Girls, you can see how wet and dangerous the roads are. So, I really need to focus on my driving to make sure I get the Longhorns safely to the abattoir by tomorrow morning."

"What if there are no white lines or cat's eyes on the road, what do you do then, Dad?" Bethany asked.

"Well, Beth, there are also little white posts on both sides of the road with red and white reflectors on them, see? But you've always got white lines in the middle of the road. The red reflectors tell you the road goes around a sweeping bend to the right, while the white reflectors tell you the road takes you along another, different, sweeping bend to the left."

"Oh, so that's what they're for!"

"So, when you're driving at night, the reflectors show you the way the road is going, or if there are corners ahead. The section we're on now is like that. It's a more winding one, so you can see which way the road turns up ahead. A long time ago, some roads never had white lines, cat's eyes or even little posts."

"What did the drivers do then, Dad?"

"Good question! Most of us truckies travelled these roads regularly, and we just had to remember where all the hills, intersections and other hazards were. When driving in the day, we memorised the roads for the night-time. It was like that not too long ago, when we had to drive blind without any white lines or cat's eyes. It was especially hard when we had to face driving rain as well."

Bridgette asked, "How can the rain drive, Dad?"

"Ha! Asked for that one, didn't I?"

Dianne laughed, "Can't wait to hear you get out of that!"

"Me, too," Ron said. "Well, let's see, driving rain is something we say when the rain is carried fast by the wind and pushed into a building or into our truck. Driving rain is so hard that when it hits you, it's like having little pins going into you."

Dianne nodded her approval. "I think the jury's convinced."

Bridgette and Bethany look anxious at the prospect of being hurt by the driving rain.

"Now, on to the other question you asked. When it rains, my view of what's outside the cab is affected, just as if I close my eyes like this."

"Dad, don't do that, you can't see!" Beth and Bridgette screamed.

His eyes snapped open. "Sorry, I didn't mean to scare you. Why don't you both close your eyes, and see how long you can last without being scared?"

Beth and Bridge looked at one another and then their mother, shaking their heads. "No."

"Now, see how you are already scared?" Ron decided now was a good time to teach his daughters about a few road dangers.

"That's a good thing. You should never close your eyes when you're driving. And another thing happening a lot now is with drivers that look down and text or talk on the phone. Just because you're driving doesn't mean you can turn your head away from looking at the road, or look at the person you're talking to in the vehicle with you. Drivers are using mobile phones when they should be watching the road. They don't understand the distance their vehicle can travel while their attention is diverted. Every second their eyes are off the road, they're moving closer to disaster, like running off the road or hitting and killing someone."

Bethany and Bridgette look at each other, appalled.

"Distances travelled at any speed are easily calculated at twenty-five percent of the speed you're travelling. For example, at one hundred kilometres per hour, you can travel as much as twenty-five metres in one second. That's the length of a B-double semi-trailer! And it takes over one hundred metres to stop safely at that speed. At a slower speed of sixty kilometres per hour, you will travel fifteen metres, that's the length of a normal semi-trailer. So, if you feel it's okay to look away for what you think is only a second, in reality, someone could be dead by the time you listen to me finishing this sentence now."

He didn't like scaring his children, but Ron knew the more they understood, the more careful they'd be when they started to drive. He could only hope they didn't become like some of the dangerous drivers he saw every day.

"Most of the larger connecting roads these days have more than one lane in each direction and are separated by a concrete wall, or what they call a median strip. Some have a grassed area down the middle or wire- rope barriers. So, if any type of vehicle runs off the road, or if someone loses control to avoid an unexpected object or falls asleep, then they won't crash into any oncoming vehicle going the other way. You can see which way the road is going on clear nights and even more so during the day."

Ron noticed the conditions in front of him worsening but put a cheeky smirk on his face. Bridgette, unimpressed, folded her arms and scrunched up her face.

"When your mum and I teach you to drive, you'll have better skills than most other people on the road. You'll be learning what to look out for and what other drivers are doing. Because it's only going to get harder in the future."

"What Dad means, girls," Dianne said, "is it's better to learn as much as you can, as early as you can, even at your age. Most teenagers think they know it all. Never do that! Your father can tell you he still sees new things every day while he's driving. Even with the advantage of technology these days, some people still take things for granted. GPS maps showing you the way to your destination don't have the height of bridges, so if the driver is not paying attention, they will get stuck under a low bridge, or worse, get killed.

The driving rain was now smashing more heavily onto the windscreen, making it harder for Ron to see the road ahead, even with the wipers working overtime.

Most of the continent of Australia had not seen any good annual rainfall over the past decade, and the land had simply dried out. Rivers, dams and creek beds were empty, and animals in the wild, like kangaroos and koalas—even venomous snakes and spiders—were out hunting for water.

Across dried-out rivers and creeks were many old wooden bridges, which were badly in need of repair. Many of them no longer had foundations stable enough to withstand unusually heavy traffic.

A large kangaroo hopped in front of their truck—*Thump!*—hitting the bull-bar on the front of the prime mover. It was instantly bowled over, much to the dismay of Dianne, Bridgette and Bethany.

Some people think that bull-bars are unnecessary on roads where animals and vehicles can meet, but it's more of a safety issue because of the amount of damage a large animal can do.

A kangaroo, say, could cause the vehicle to leave the road and kill the occupants. Or it could come through the windscreen, continuing to fall and thrash about inside the vehicle, injuring, distracting or killing those in the front seat.

Ron had often spoken of the priorities in these situations. "First and foremost, it's better to hit the animal rather than swerving or braking hard to avoid it."

Dianne soothed her upset daughters. "Most people have no wish to kill a living animal, but a human life is always more valuable. Missing a human and killing an animal is socially acceptable, but killing a human just to miss killing an animal is not."

The skies were even blacker now. The storm had obviously been heavy ahead of them and for some considerable time.

They'd already crossed a number of rivers and creeks now full of swirling brown water, flowing at a dangerous rate. Visibility has become terrifyingly low, like a snow whiteout.

"Don't worry! This is something your father is used to," Dianne told the girls.

"For many years, his industry, road haulage, has prided itself that, whatever the conditions are, the load must be delivered, just like the mail. As Dad said before, truckies become familiar with the roads they travel on regularly, and they can continue on at a normal speed even with the changing conditions outside. But it's terrifying not seeing clearly in front of you, though."

"A bit like jumping out of a perfectly good aeroplane without a parachute," Ron explained. "But I've got to drop these bulls off at the abattoir in Steering tomorrow, or I won't get paid, and there'll be no birthday presents for you two on the twenty-fifth."

Hearing that gave the girls a better picture of what their dad did for them.

As they headed down the side of a mountain, lightning forked through the sky and briefly lit up the road ahead, showing the land levelling out more and becoming a bit less hairy. Ron was already looking forward to getting to where they'd spend the night before dropping the bulls off in the morning.

# 11

## Everyone Has Difficulties

The Lockwood family were heading home from Harry's house, a journey that normally took about twenty minutes. Six month old baby Stephen was in the middle of the back seat.

There were no grandparents on David's side of the family, and Pearl wished her own mother could have seen this newborn. Outwardly, she gave the impression of a carefree wife and mother, but, like many women, Pearl had experienced post-natal depression after Stephen's birth. She couldn't help thinking her mum's compassion would have nullified much of this.

She'd felt a bit overwhelmed and tired from the long journey that day and had shed a few tears earlier that night while alone cooking dinner—and not from cutting onions. She'd enjoyed preparing their dinner of roast lamb, potatoes and vegetables, followed by chocolate mousse and ice- cream.

She always liked visiting her father's place, as it helped her cope with the loss of her mother, but being there reminded her she should also be helping Harry more than she did.

The constant bickering between teenagers Rhys and Tiffany didn't help her mood either. Away from their parents' gaze and hearing, they were at it again at Harry's place.

At fifteen, Rhys was showing promise with the local football team and was expected to graduate into the under-seventeens the following year. He was well liked at school, especially by the girls.

But not by his seventeen year old sister, Tiffany, who was too busy to waste time on her brother, instead glorying in the attention she received from many of the more eligible boys at the school.

Adding to her unhappiness, Pearl had seen some of the more unpleasant references to Tiffany on Facebook, where the word " slutty " cropped up far too often.

In most country towns, everyone pretty much knows everyone else, but it wasn't generally known around town that Tiffany had been raped a couple of years earlier by a local hoon. Still acutely ashamed and traumatised by the ordeal, she frequently became emotionally overwhelmed by the memory.

She'd retreated into herself for a time and found solace in being the opposite of what she was, but without the slightest thought for how she was viewed by anyone, let alone her mother.

Pearl struggled with her daughter's mood changes. Tiffany had gone from having a sunny outlook and being popular, both in and out of school, to being a confused teenager.

But Tiffany could put aside those negative memories when she was with those who didn't judge her by her looks or her anger.

The Lockwoods had barely left Harry's house when the two were at one another's throats again, despite Stephen being fast asleep in his capsule between them.

They taunted at each other over some comment Rhys had made to Tiffany in their grandfather's hallway earlier that evening.

One of the older teenagers, regularly seen playing in most of the sporting codes, had visited Tiffany, much to her pleasure. The nineteen year old had arrived at their house on horseback one day, all rugged and tanned, just as they were leaving for their holidays.

As the bickering continued after dinner, David's patience wore thin, and he decided he'd send the pair to their rooms as soon as they got home.

Inevitably, the verbal battle in the back seat woke Stephen, who screamed his outrage. His parents were unimpressed with their children's lack of consideration.

Barely a night went by without Pearl having to get up, either to feed Stephen or try to put him back to sleep. Both she and David were aware that Rhys and Tiffany felt life would be sweeter without child number three.

Then, everyone was yelling at once.

They'd travelled just one kilometre down the road when the storm closed in on them. David glanced across at Pearl, but she was preoccupied with the warfare in the back seat.

David tried to block out the noise, but one of his eyes troubled him. The optometrist had told him he had a problem with how the eye focused when light entered from different angles.

"What you've got is hyperopic astigmatism. That's what's causing your blurred and distorted vision. This gives the front surface of the eye a football shape."

He explained that the hereditary condition could be corrected with glasses or contact lenses. But David's new prescription glasses were performing less than successfully that night.

The road ahead became progressively more difficult to navigate, and, although David knew it well, he became uncharacteristically anxious.

He passed the sign warning of curves ahead, so he knew he'd almost reached the larger of the two old wooden bridges on their route.

Entering the 40-metre-long bridge, David half-turned around to boost Pearl's attempts to quieten the disturbance in the back seat.

Rhys and Tiffany's bickering had escalated to physical jostling. Without realising it, Tiffany fell against the seatbelt restraining Stephen's capsule, releasing the latch.

On a remote stretch of road at night in the Australian bush, they were about to cross McKenzie's Bridge, constructed during the town's boom period in the late sixties to handle the volume of trucks and cars heading to the industrial area, a kilometre down-river.

Everything was shrouded in thick rain and the subsequent spray from the side-wind.

Pearl shrieked as lightning flashed across the sky, illuminating the surrounding area through the driving rain. She saw a jumble of trees and rocks being carried along by the fast-flowing torrent below them. But that wasn't what made her shriek.

David, too, saw the blur of oncoming headlights through the rain. They were on a bridge in a torrential downpour with only inches between his vehicle and the edge of the very old sleepers, which created a fence-like structure along McKenzie's Bridge.

With no time to think, he swerved hard left to avoid a head-on collision. He'd rarely seen another vehicle on this bridge at the same time as him.

Above the escalating discord of chaotic noise, he struggled to hear what sounded like the deep blast of a horn followed by the screech and hiss of air brakes, then the impact of metal exploding on metal.

The two vehicles crashed through the weakened railings at the eastern end of McKenzie's Bridge. David's car plummeted ten metres into the murky depths of the roiling, gurgling torrent. The other vehicle, because of its size and weight, fell more slowly. David's blurred vision and the constant, even heavier rain were not helping him cope. Neither was the screaming coming from the back seat.

But there was another noise, inexplicable and terrifying: the panic-stricken bellowing and thrashing of what sounded like several large beasts.

Both vehicles fell on the eastern side of the river and landed on the sloping embankment but were still threatened by the rushing river torrent just a couple of metres below them.

Blackness cloaked David as he descended into the realms of a nightmare. His mind took him back to where he was sitting in the optometrist's waiting room, flicking through a magazine story about how the mind seemed to slow down in a crisis, taking note of every tiny detail of what was happening.

He read that when a person was falling, they didn't actually observe the fall in slow motion; it was memory at work, not a fast-paced perception. The brain is still recording until the individual emerges from their crisis. This enhanced what they saw; so, when they recalled that experience, it felt like it must have taken place over a long period.

At McKenzie's Bridge, the bellowing of the animals mingled with the sound of human moans as the cold and claustrophobic darkness intensified.

David slipped into unconsciousness.

# 12

## 'Ave a Go, Ya Mug!

Thursday was payday for Steering's drinking class, many of whom were gathered as usual at the local pub.

Storms brought much-needed rain, and the steady downpour had soaked the area over the past few hours. The conditions outside were humid and wet, in stark contrast to the overwhelming heat of the past few months.

Most of the older residents, sitting around their usual table in a corner next to the main bar, were quite content to listen to Michael Scanlon on the radio.

In the opposite corner sat the five brothers, known throughout the town as troublemakers. Other young males were chatting up the local girls with only one thing in mind. As the drinks took effect, the more suggestive their chat-up lines became.

One young man, Jack, had succeeded in attracting the interest of the girl Nick had his eye on.

As usual, the brothers were becoming troublesome and rowdy, although Luke was the most placid. Realising what could be in store, Paul turned to his older brother.

"Watch yourself, Nick! You know Jack's a bit testy."

Nick slammed down his glass, ignored the spilt liquid and Paul's advice and headed straight over to his intended victim.

Aware of what could develop, Ian Milton, the publican, decided, with the help of a few staff, to evict all five brothers. Ian told his helpers to go easy on Luke.

Ian's impressive 135 kg belied his easy nature, but that night he was determined to show he was no pussycat. He suggested to the brothers it was time to go. Nick sneered.

"Ah, get stuffed, ya mongrel!" He reinforced this suggestion with a wild haymaker of a right hook, missing Ian but connecting flush with a woman's shoulder.

Katrina was in a group of women passing the action on their way back from powdering their noses.

Katrina copped the punch; it bounced off her shoulder and smashed into the right side of her jaw. She was a local councillor's daughter, so when she hit the floor, a tense silence descended over the crowded bar. One of Ian's mates, known for his first aid skills, pushed through the crowd and knelt down beside Katrina's prone form.

This was the signal for most of the patrons to erupt into a melee of flying fists. More than one of the antagonists were female, giving as good as they got. It was almost as if the falling rain outside, which had ended the long drought, sparked a similar relief in the pub's patrons, who were now raining blows to ease the tension.

Someone behind the pump called the cops just before one patron was thrown over the bar and landed on Mick the barman, knocking him to the ground.

Paul motioned urgently at his brothers, especially Nick, that it was time to leave for Luke's initiation. They headed for the back door, leaving Rex wondering what had just happened.

Smoke from the pub's fireplace wafted up and out the top of the chimney and hovered above the car park. Five figures could just be seen running for Nick's SUV.

Nick and Ryan climbed in the front, and the other three scrambled into the back, Luke sandwiched once more in the middle. He was used to being the target for his brothers' taunts and beatings. Just because it was his eighteenth birthday didn't mean anything was about to change.

One of Luke's earliest memories was as a toddler, when his brothers surrounded his cot. Their mother, climbing a ladder outside Luke's window while cleaning it, caught the boys in the act.

She'd noticed Nick taking something out of his pocket, something that glistened in the sunlight shining through Luke's bedroom window.

Then, a scream came from Luke, suddenly awoken from his deep sleep. She'd thought Nick held a knife, but, to her relief, it was a metal water pistol.

An outraged shriek from their mother let them know their silent cruelty had been discovered. This made their punishments more severe than usual, leading the boys to carry out further reprisals on the defenceless Luke.

Over time, Luke worked out that they were repeating the same torment meted out to them one by one by their brutal father.

Now, heading away from the pub, Luke wondered what was in store for him. The twins, Ryan and Bill, had ended up in the local hospital on the night of their twenty-first birthdays. Luke knew he wouldn't get off lightly.

Nick took after their father, Tom, whose heavy drinking and random brutality may have stemmed from seeing action in Vietnam and from the post-traumatic stress disorder that followed.

When the boys' mother, Edith, had learned of Tom's condition, the couple underwent counselling to save their marriage. In the end, it was their mother who raised the children, but the damage had already been done to all of them, except Luke. The price he paid for his comparatively pain-free childhood was the jealous hostility of his brothers.

When Edith finally fled the marital home, Tom was free to raise the brothers as violently as he pleased. Once, they stole lollies from the local store and were brought home by the police to face their father.

As soon as the custodians of the law had departed, Tom set about the four older brothers with his belt, inflicting a savage flogging on each of them. Luke only copped a slap on the backside, something his siblings deeply resented.

The brothers now climbed into the SUV, discussing the planned surprise for Luke. Nick gave Ryan a reassuring slap on the thigh as he turned the engine over, and the vehicle growled to life. The SUV took off flat-out across the packed car park, weaving in and out of the other vehicles and narrowly missing a dog.

"Maybe next time, dog!" Nick shouted, letting the animal know how lucky it was.

Nick turned sharply onto the main road heading west, as police cars raced up to the pub with their sirens wailing.

"Yee har! How's that for good timing?"

A few kilometres west of town, he swerved into a side street leading to an industrial area, tyres squealing. Through the heavy rain, a vivid flash of lightning seared the sky, and Nick was momentarily blinded, just long enough to miss seeing the bridge straight ahead and the unfamiliar dark shape looming out of the gloom, blocking the bridge entry.

"Hey! Either I've got blurred vision, or maybe I've been drinking too fast..." Ryan said. "What about you, Nick?"

"Yeah, same here!"

That was all the warning Nick got before the SUV crashed into a semi-trailer, partly submerged in the river, its trailer wedged at an angle into the wooden bridge. The SUV bounced off the protruding trailer and hurtled over the side of the bridge, as if someone had turned on a slow-motion switch.

Inside the SUV, Luke had been nursing an open carton of beer cans on his knees. One flew off, striking Nick on the back of the head then smashing into the front windscreen. Nick turned to see where the can had come from, just as another can sped towards him from the same source, causing a nasty gash on his forehead.

After spinning through three hundred and sixty degrees, with debris cascading around the brothers inside the plummeting and tumbling SUV, the vehicle came to an abrupt stop. The sudden impact forced Nick's head back into the head rest as blood began to flow from the wound.

The vehicle came to rest with its rear end on top of the sleeping section of the prime mover, its bonnet pointing almost vertically skywards. Only the wedged trailer section of the semi stopped the SUV from toppling over backwards into the raging river.

Inside the SUV, surrounded by various loose items, the boys groggily realised the sky was directly above them. Outside, the heavy rain continued.

"Gimme a beer. Quick!"

Even wounded and bleeding, Nick's priorities hadn't changed. Luke grabbed a can off the floor and opened it. But he didn't realise the cans, shaken up in the collision, would spurt everywhere when opened.

Nick and Ryan both copped a spray in the face, complete with foam.

"Aaagh! Lucky I can't see you to punch you, you little shit," Nick screamed at Luke.

"That makes two of us," Ryan said. Everyone laughed except the injured Nick, but Luke had a smirk on his face. Although he wouldn't hurt a fly, Luke felt he'd finally outsmarted them all, especially Nick, and wondered if there could be another opportunity soon.

He remained silent, not wanting to invite further punishment and felt thankful for the darkness shrouding his triumphant demeanour.

Only their seatbelts stopped Nick and Ryan in the front seats from falling back down onto the other three.

The airbags had deployed, and, as the brothers' general panic subsided, they came to the stunning conclusion that they'd all survived, for now.

# 13

## Square Peg, Round Hole

Slowly, carefully, Ron turned the semi left onto a dirt road, travelling another two hundred metres before easing onto the larger of two wooden bridges. He'd be relieved to get his family to their hotel for the night in Steering.

He leant over to speed-dial the radio station on his phone. The truck had nearly reached the far end of the forty-metre-long wooden bridge when Ron heard an ominous creaking noise through the heavy rain. He knew he should've stopped and checked the bridge before crossing. But playing with the phone distracted him. He knew very well how dangerous this could be.

"Hello, Crazy FM. Robyn speaking."

It was Michael Scanlon's producer, and, when he didn't reply, she hung up.

He didn't answer because Ron was suddenly tossed about in the cabin of the prime mover like a rag doll, his body smashing into a series of hard-edged sections of the vehicle, bruising his ribs. Flying debris—sunglasses, kids' books, pens and various other items—was scattered and flung around him. Then, his head violently collided with the gear stick, rendering him unconscious with a deep cut over his left eye.

Ron's heavy logbook had fallen straight onto the seat belt latch, releasing it and him to the changing centre of gravity inside the cab. The prime mover slowly descended towards the waiting torrent, becoming wedged against a light pole that still flickered.

Without his seatbelt, Ron was finally hurled through the already-smashed front windscreen of the truck and into the raging river. His limp body, along with tree branches, stumps, boulders, and even animal bones scoured from the depths of the once-dry riverbed, was swept up instantly by the fierce current and carried downstream by the force of the water.

His body became entangled in the branches of a tree careering along with the current.

Dianne and Bethany were trapped inside the sleeping compartment, now resting against the splintered timbers of the broken roadway timber beams under the eastern side of the collapsed bridge.

Bridgette was unconscious in the front seat with a slight cut on her forehead, blood trickling down her face, now slumped against the side window.

Then, through the pall of rain came another set of headlights and the sound of loud rock music, instantly drowned out by another racket: the screeching of brakes and the horrific sound of metal scraping against metal.

Morning revealed the results of the perfect storm.

A trailer carrying pedigree bulls, leaning precariously on the bridge.

The trailer's cab, half immersed on the eastern side of the torrent.

An SUV with five occupants trapped and concussed.

A new family car, with a Perspex sunroof and sliding wooden section beneath, pinned beneath the semi, which was half-submerged in the river, chunks of shattered bodywork floating around it.

As the prime mover came down on top of the Lockwoods' car, stopped only by its connection to the trailer, it shattered the Perspex, showering sharp shards onto the family inside. The force allowed various objects to be tossed around in the rear of the vehicle, blending in with the various pieces of camping gear and packages packed tightly for the journey home. Other items found their way out through the open sunroof and into the tangle outside.

The vehicle was facing forward, its front resting slightly upwards against a timber beam of the bridge. The oncoming river flowed over the part of the bonnet not covered by the prime mover.

The edge of the fast-flowing river gushed in through the front window and out the back window.

One of the panic-stricken bulls struggled to free itself but succeeded only in knocking itself out, blocking any escape for the remainder of the terrified animals—except for Bob, the pride of the herd.

A slight toss of his massive head was enough to free him. The other trapped bulls became more enraged and frightened, bucking against the confines of their stalls inside the now slightly vertical trailer.

Since the accident, five bulls had escaped from the wreckage and plunged down into the river. But even their huge bulk was insufficient to stop them from being washed along in the current. They finished up in an area where three were able to scramble up the banks and onto solid ground.

And still audible above the thundering rain was the mingled bellowing of large beasts and the moaning of human voices, all trapped and seriously injured.

Underneath this jangled cacophony came the thunderous roar of the river, which had flooded parts of its banks as they narrowed at McKenzie's Bridge and had spread out across the countryside. Daylight, when it came, would reveal only the tops of the tallest trees.

The bulls remained where they washed ashore for a few hours before heading aimlessly back towards the crash site. Two others drowned and were washed away downstream.

The trailer now sat precariously on a slight angle, shaking with the force of the bulls' desperate struggle to break free. Bob had reached the top of the trailer, thrashing in agony from a piece of thick wire that had been forced into his left eye during the crash. He finally freed himself from the trailer and stumbled out, catching his left hind leg on its railing.

The leg snapped and was partly torn away from his body, causing him to fall and smash his head against the side of the trailer. Blood poured from his broken leg down onto the car below. He thundered his fury and pain as he hung helplessly from the tangled wreckage of the trailer.

Bethany and Dianne, trapped inside the sleeping compartment of the cabin, could only gaze in terror at the bizarre sight of an animal's face, eyes wide with fear, dangling outside their window. Then, they saw an animal's severed leg carried downstream below them. Something—or somebody—was hanging by its clothing on a nail on the bridge, suspended over the raging river.

After some hours came signs the swollen river was beginning to subside.

Ron had vanished somewhere down the flooded river, a remnant of a long-ago simple creek before it became the river, after landing on a partly submerged tree-trunk.

Part of the tree had jammed his left arm, breaking the skin but not his arm. He'd lost a little blood but, more importantly, lost his fight to stay awake.

On a remote stretch of road, somewhere inland from the east coast of Australia, night fell, and the storm passed. The wind had died, and the land was quite still. Slowly, the valley was enveloped again in thick fog.

Inside the darkened bedroom of a nearby farmhouse, John Meadows sat up and nudged his sleeping wife.

"Hey, did you hear a strange noise? Like a loud bang?"

"Just go back to sleep, John. It's bloody raining, you idiot," she murmured.

Reluctantly, he said, "I'm sure I heard something."

Over the next ten hours, a gruesome fight for survival would take place. Surviving a calamity is one thing. Fourteen human beings and a herd of Longhorn bulls forced together under chaotic circumstances, trying to survive a perfect storm, is beyond terrifying.

# 14

# An Aside from the Author

Coming home from holidays, my family and I were swept up in the aftermath of Cyclone Yasi, which had reached as far south as Victoria.

Mere minutes away from Charlton, we were redirected to the township of Donald, where we were forced to endure the flood. On the second morning, we heard all the roads had closed, but truckies don't give up so easily.

"How can I get out of here?" I asked a fellow truckie, who got out his map.

"So, if you detour here, then take this dirt road, see, just off the main road, you'll soon be on your way home." My family was even able to take photos of our detour.

But, not having had any experience of how much damage a cyclone could cause, I couldn't understand what people had to go through after a cyclone made landfall.

The following photos were taken in Donald in February 2011. I started writing the novel in May 2015. I published it in October 2019.

The Donald football oval. The top of the coaches' box is just visible.

The road out of Donald.

The entrance to the Donald Riverside Motel.

The view from the balcony of the Donald Riverside Motel.

The entrance to the Donald Riverside Motel.

The road into Donald.

# 15

# Wrong Place, Wrong Time

For the five brothers, aged from eighteen to twenty-eight and united by a lethal cocktail of terror, resentment and alcohol, this night would bring them something more powerful, destructive and vindictive than anything their imaginations could ever have conjured. Something that would either end their lives or haunt them relentlessly for the remainder.

All of Nick's current anger stemmed from his drunken impression that someone had lured them into this situation.

In the front seat, Nick and Ryan were the first to try to come to terms with their current predicament. The airbags had saved them from anything worse than painful cuts and bruises. They were slowly appreciating the fact that they were trapped in the now-vertical SUV.

Over the top of the deployed airbags, in the murky blackness outside the spotted windscreen, they saw something improbably large, something that jerked and changed shape, coming in and out of their limited fields of vision. Something whose movements were punctuated by deafening bellows of rage, pain and fear.

"Is it me or is there a big black balloon that seems to be getting bigger in front of us?" Nick asked Ryan, his voice croaky with blood.

Ryan wanted to ask Nick to repeat himself, but feared the inevitable snarled response, so he said nothing.

"No worries, bros! Everything'll be okay," a still-intoxicated Nick called out, seeing the airbags still inflated. Then, their world exploded in their faces.

Their horrified screams stirred the three brothers in the back, dragging them from their semi-concussed state in time for them to witness something unfathomable coming their way. But, thank Christ, it would have to get past Nick and Ryan first.

The weird image in front of the pair burst through the windscreen as if it were paper. Nuggets of fractured glass cascaded over them both. And then came two thin, curved, yellowy-white arms that somehow ended in sharp points. These apparitions stopped abruptly, one buried deep where Ryan's nose was, and the other penetrating Nick's chest.

The three brothers in the back watched helplessly, aghast, as Nick and Ryan were gored and torn, again and again. They realised they were now looking at horns mounted on the woolly head of a massive, slavering, one-eyed monster. The horns slashed through the front seat's upholstery, perilously close to the three men cowering in the back. The minds of all three had snapped in different ways.

Bill and Paul were now delirious, convulsing and vomiting.

Luke was rigid, almost comatose with terror.

The bull's entire form kept coming into view through the shattered windscreen and then disappearing as he thrashed, violently trying to extricate his back end from the wreckage. He swung like a pendulum, and, every time his head bashed back into the interior of the SUV, more flesh was gouged from the ragdoll forms that now lay motionless, slumped on what remained of the front seat.

As the two bodies were repeatedly tossed and thrown into one another, more blood and intestines splashed over the three surviving brothers in the back, gradually making Bill, Paul and Luke unrecognisable.

Bill and Paul had slipped into unconsciousness. Only Luke remained to witness the evolving horror. He wondered whether this would be the end of the lifelong torment he'd endured at the hands of his brothers. This awful sight... would it cut short any attempt he might make in the future to end his siblings' tyranny?

Bob's repeated assaults severed the steering wheel. One of his front legs protruded through it as he convulsed, as if to rid himself of it. He struck Ryan in the middle of what was left of his face with a powerful lunge that snapped Ryan's neck with a sound like a whip crack, so his head dangled, flopping at an unnatural angle.

Nick had a flashback of himself raping a girl in a drunken stupor a few years ago. Before he slipped away into eternal darkness, his final emotion was an all-encompassing fear and, behind it, the knowledge that his lifetime of pretending to be fearless had left him with all the more to fear.

By now, Bob's convulsive thrashing had reached such a peak of violence that he snapped his own neck, mere moments after doing the same to Ryan. The huge bull shuddered to a swaying stillness.

In the back, Luke had reached a state of almost euphoric oblivion. He dreamt of the time in his cot when his brothers sprayed him with the water pistol.

He recalled their spiteful faces leering down at him. In a brief interlude of reality, he understood that it wasn't water he was now covered in, but blood, slime and something that felt squishy and lumpy.

He checked either side of him, and a sudden vivid flash of lightning revealed Bill and Paul covered with the same revolting mess. The lightning also lit up much more, far too much for Luke to take in.

Two tangled masses of broken limbs, faceless skulls and more blood and slime where Nick and Ryan had been sitting seconds before. Something else could be glimpsed through the shattered windscreen, something immense, its gentle swaying at odds with its sheer bulk.

The lightning and the tumbling loudness of the following thunder woke Bill and Paul. As they lurched back into consciousness, both again began vomiting. Luke pointed silently at the front seat, but the flash had gone, and all that was visible in the gloom was that great bulk swaying gently beyond the front windscreen.

Paul and Bill began to laugh hysterically, realising what they'd just gone through,

"You okay? Can you get out safely?" they asked.

"Well, I'm okay except for the blood," Luke said.

But Paul and Bill couldn't have cared less about him.

"You're lucky that's all that's wrong with you!" Paul said nastily. "Oughta be thankful you weren't in the front, instead of Ryan. That's where you were going to be, but because of the hoo-haa back at the pub, we had to keep an eye on you, just in case you decided to skip out and hide on us."

Paul and Bill now wanted retribution and didn't care how they'd get it.

All three young men were in deep shock, covered in the gore of their dead siblings, but were somehow alert enough to know they needed to free themselves from the horror-filled tomb, which the SUV had now become.

# 16

## Stomach's Hungry

Scotty Taylor had almost reached the end of the long drive to the Steering police station when hunger forced him to stop at the last town before his destination. It had looked like a pleasant enough little place as he had thought about calling into the local store, but he knew first impressions could be deceiving.

He climbed out of his fifteen year old station wagon, loaded to the hilt with his gear, and stretched extravagantly to ward off the stiffness from a five-hour drive. Then he found himself stumbling and ended up on his backside on the pavement outside the store. He climbed laboriously to his feet and stumbled towards the wire door.

"Oh crap," he said to himself, wincing in pain, his stomach growling. Something hot and nutritious would help put him back on his feet.

The elderly woman who flung open the door brought him to an abrupt halt. He hoped she'd get out of the way quickly so he could at least sit down somewhere inside. She gave Scotty the once-over, grunted disparagingly and walked off.

Inside the store, he saw an ageing bain-marie containing wilted meat pies, dim-sims and chips. Over in the corner, next to the drinks machine, a large fridge contained a variety of ice-creams. Other stands were scattered around the general store for children and overweight adults looking for any rubbish they could get their hands on.

His eyes landed on the woman behind the counter. Her name badge read "Mavis".

Her side-eye sent him a clear message: if he thought for one second he'd be treated like a local, or at least with a bit of respect, then he could forget it.

She muttered something, none of which he understood, but before he could ask her to repeat herself, she snapped, "Haven't got all day, sonny."

Despite her rudeness, Scotty decided to use his charm to get something to eat that would be a bit more appetising than the contents of the bain-marie. But, before he could speak, she was at him again.

"Can't make up your mind, sonny?"

He realised charm wouldn't work to convince her to slow down. But wasn't that what was supposed to happen in a country town? He'd had enough of these bush manners and barked impatiently but slowly, "Two pies, three dimmies… and some dead horse."

No please or thank you. The woman's face became even more hostile.

"I keep horses out in the backyard, you ignorant bastard, so less of your crap!" Then she added, "Gimme twelve dollars twenty!"

He avoided her hostile stare, thinking *if looks could kill…* Scotty then placed a cold drink on the counter.

"This, and one of those donuts with the coloured sprinkles on top."

"Seventeen-eighty. Suppose ya want a bag with that?"

Scotty handed over a twenty with a contemptuous, "Keep the bloody change for your wonderful service."

But then he saw something move behind the curtain in the back part of the shop. Quickly, his mood and facial expression changed.

Mavis noticed the same thing and went behind the curtain only to re-emerge with a gorgeous young woman in her early twenties, with dark flowing hair above piercing big blue eyes. For the first time in his testosterone-fuelled life, Scotty's response was one of sympathy rather than lust.

Just as Mavis was holding forth about the lack of real men in the town, Scotty interrupted, "I like that beauty spot you have there." He was referring to a tiny birthmark just beside her full lips. He meant nothing malicious by his clumsy attempt at a compliment, but she seemed embarrassed yet quietly flattered by his directness.

Awkwardly, he quickly pushed through the screen door, climbed in the station wagon and parked across the road under a tree. The prospect of eating inside the store while the women watched him was unthinkable.

Back inside the store, the owner and her daughter giggled to themselves about the handsome stranger with the abrupt manner. They began fantasising about him.

Greasy tucker still sitting uneasily in his stomach, Scotty drove on to Steering to find a note on the door of the police station, right in the centre of town, telling him to phone a nearby neighbour for the key.

Once inside the building, he headed for the toilet, then decided to settle down for a quiet night. He wondered how his young friend Billy was faring, and how he'd cope with the long journey to get up here.

The phone rang: Bert Logan, the senior sergeant from the headquarters in the last big town he drove through.

"Hey, Scotty, I know you've just hit the place, but I want you to meet me outside the Steering pub in half an hour. Apparently, there's a bit of a blue getting out of hand."

Scotty climbed quickly into his uniform, then drove the police car the short distance to the pub. There, Logan and several other officers were waiting in the packed car park, outside the bar door.

Bert shook his hand and then pointed at the door.

"Well, get in there, son, and don't hold back."

Opening the door, Scotty inhaled the stench of stale beer and tobacco. The noise of the knockdown brawl going on inside was bloody loud. And it wasn't just the blokes going at it, he spotted a few women in the melee as well.

A woman landed in his arms. She looked up at him, and, as her face lit up, she squealed, "Hello, gorgeous!"

Scotty reeled back from the stench of her breath, grabbed her by the arm and frogmarched her outside to the divvy van.

"Any men you bring out, put them in here, okay?" The senior sergeant instructed him to put the woman with the other females already waiting under a tree outside the pub.

He did that and re-entered the pub, this time confronted by the huge frame of a bloke blocking his way: Ian, the publican, who thrust out a meaty paw and began to introduce himself.

At that moment, someone behind Ian aimed a vicious blow at the publican, but Scotty quickly pulled him sideways by the hand as he shook it. The blow intended for Ian landed squarely on Scotty's shoulder, making him recoil.

He righted himself and grabbed the assailant by his left arm, twisted it up and behind his back, then seized a handful of his hair and dragged him outside to a second van.

Logan threw open the door, and Scotty flung the now-subdued patron into the paddy wagon, where he collided with a couple of blokes already squatting there. Everyone was complaining about their rough treatment, hurling abuse at their captors, who paid no attention to them.

Scotty turned back to return to the fray, but Ian came over to thank him, so he accepted the publican's second offer of a handshake and introduced himself.

"G'day! Name's Ian, I'm the publican and owner of this fine establishment. When you've had time to settle in, and things are a bit less hectic, drop in for a meal and a drink."

Scotty glanced across at Logan.

"You're not in Melbourne now, so take a deep breath and relax. You'll be fine." He broke off and half grinned, looking Scotty hard in the eyes.

"I know how you ended up here. Don't worry about it. I'd probably have done the same myself. Anyway, come and see me in the morning, and I'll give you the lay of the land. Sorry I wasn't there at the station to welcome you, but I'm only just back from leave myself."

As the various officers prepared to leave the now peaceful pub, Emergency Services called, asking for assistance in diverting traffic because of rising floodwaters. Scotty was sent off to a part of town near the river to check that none of the houses there were underwater.

He climbed into his police car and keyed the address of the riverside street into his GPS, glancing behind to make sure he was clear to pull out onto the main road. Heading off into the darkness, he thought *Blimey! What have I got myself into?*

The severity of the storm had convinced Emergency Services to block off all the roads near the bridge around the crash site, yet they were still unaware of the crash itself. Visibility was poor now, certainly worse than it was when Scotty'd arrived at the pub.

# 17

## That's Just Criminal

"Oh, no!" the Boss shouted.

Loud footsteps could be heard coming closer from two floors above. Young Carlo never used the lift. He liked to show the Boss, and anyone else in the group, that he was fit and healthy. If he needed to make a fast getaway, he could. As for the rest, they could look after themselves.

Most of them were larger-than-life Italians. They always had difficulty cramming into the lift with the Boss, who was no lightweight either. This mob prized brawn more highly than brains.

They were in a building above a barber's salon on Lygon Street in the northern part of Melbourne's city centre. A door opened to the expansive loft on the third floor, an old, spacious, dark-timbered room. Carlo entered with a swift spin of his body, allowing the door to close behind him with a gentle click.

His graceful entrance was spoiled by him sniffling before he said, "Yes, Boss, you called for me?"

"Will you knock that off? For fuck's sake, Carlo, would you blow your nose? I hate the sound you're making. One of these days someone's gonna pop you full of holes, and I wouldn't give a sweet goddamn if they did."

Carlo scoured the room, taking in the angry faces. He believed any one of them would take pleasure in doing him bodily harm. His antics *were* a bit over the top at times. He turned to face the Boss and asked nervously, "What you want, Boss?"

"Go and get me the *Book of Fools* in the basement. It's next to the fridge. And while you're at it, get me two bottles of the '85. They're directly opposite the fridge. You got all that, Carlo?"

"Yesssss, Boss."

At the door, he turned to catch the room full of big, hardened men laughing at him. He slammed the door hard to annoy the Boss, whose large frame startled at the racket.

Back in Sicily in the seventies, too many of his Sicilian cronies were being rounded up too quickly for his liking. So, Mario Sculini decided to leave and had arrived in Australia with other immigrants. He had quickly decided to go it alone.

He'd distanced himself from their more conventional drugs and money-laundering, finding his niche instead in the booming construction industry and using his restaurant as a cover for these extracurricular activities.

Jo-Anne McGrath, the journalist, had been investigating those activities when Con had paid her a visit. She had gone into hiding soon afterwards.

Carlo took the stairs three at a time, nearly knocking over Lara, the Boss's niece, at a corner of the stairwell. She gave him a brilliant smile, causing him to miss a step and stumble, falling in a crumpled heap at the bottom of the stairs.

Humiliated, he sprang to his feet again and went down to the basement.

"Shit!" About to open the door, he saw he didn't have the keys, so flew back up the stairs. Just in time, he remembered the protocol, took a breath, and knocked lightly before poking his head around the edge of the door.

"Forget something, Carlo?"

The Boss dangled a bunch of keys, while the other men in the room laughed their heads off. Seething and mortified,

Carlo tiptoed over to the Boss and retrieved the keys. Again, he noticed Lara sitting quietly on the sofa.

She aimed an amused but warm smile in his direction, much to the displeasure of the Boss.

"Don't come to me if you ever get involved with that one! He's a klutz! He's eighteen, and that should be his IQ score. He's more trouble than you need," the Boss told her.

"Oh, he's okay, Uncle, he just needs some TLC," she said.

"Oh, so now you're over twenty-one, you're old enough to know your own mind, eh? Me? I'm just looking out for you, like I promised your dead mother I would."

Carlo dashed back down the stairs, reached the basement cellar and unlocked the door. He entered a room filled with numerous smells, one of which he instantly recognised. Chocolate. He was prepared to risk the Boss's wrath for the supreme joy of sampling some of his personal stash of imported chocolates.

The Boss marked them off every time he had one, two, three—or even the whole box, as he did yesterday in one of his stuff-his-face moments, without even sharing with anyone except his niece.

"Greedy bugger!" Carlo grumbled, then he went over to the wine cellar and picked out two bottles of 1985 chardonnay, then searched through various documents to find the *Book of Fools*, which was bound inside a hard cover and locked. Only the Boss had the key. Carlo examined the book, as he had many times before, curious about the title.

Shrugging his shoulders, he walked out the door, closing and locking it behind him. He stood there motionless for a moment, wondering whether he'd forgotten anything, then bounded back upstairs, taking care not to drop the bottles.

He knocked on the loft door.

"Come in! Nobody's going to shoot you," Lara's gentle voice invited him.

Carlo took the wine and the book over to a large mahogany table, where the Boss was sitting at the head.

"Here you go, Boss," he said in an unusually quiet tone.

The big man leant backwards to get a key out of his vest pocket and unlocked the *Book of Fools*.

"What's in that book, Boss?" Carlo asked.

"None of your fucking business," the Boss snarled, dialling a number listed in the book.

"Hey, Boss, no swearing! There's sensitive blokes around," Carlo dared to say this, intending to protect Lara.

To his surprise, the Boss glanced briefly at both of them.

"Oh! Very sorry, I'm sure."

Then he beckoned Carlo over and whispered in his ear, "Get stuffed."

In a single-bedroomed apartment around the corner, someone was receiving a phone call from the Boss.

The place also contained a kitchen/dining room and a king-sized bed that just fit inside the bedroom, touching the walls. The doorway was at the base of the bed.

A large man with long curly hair in a soiled tracksuit was sprawled across the bed. Milo was watching *Tom and Jerry*, concentrating so hard that he was dribbling slightly. The ringing phone annoyed him. Milo enjoyed cartoons, partly because people got shot, blown up, pushed over cliffs and run over by semi-trailers, but also because they always got up and dusted themselves off as though nothing had happened to them.

Sometimes he wished a few of the people he'd been paid to kill would react the same way. Now that he had to wait to watch another episode, he picked up the phone.

"Hello, Boss."

He listened for a minute.

"On the way, Boss," he said with a guttural, central-European rasp. He'd been a member of the Boss's crew for the past few years since being dishonourably discharged from the army in Ukraine, where he'd grown up with his large family.

A number of kills had been attributed to Milo, the last of which was one of his immediate superiors. He fled to Australia aboard an illegal boat through pre-arranged links and began working for the Boss.

Back in the loft, loud, elephant-like footsteps could be heard leading from the lift to the door, then a loud knock. One of the minders opened the door to admit a man built like the proverbial brick shithouse, who ducked and swayed his huge frame into the room. His sheer bulk seemed to shrink the loft and its occupants. The floor creaked under his weight as he walked towards the Boss.

It made those already in the loft a little uneasy, fearing the floor could open up and they'd all be taken down with him to their deaths. One of the minders closed the door behind him.

"Oy! I want everyone out. Now! Milo, you stay," the Boss ordered. The door opened again immediately to let them out.

The big men trooped through the door one at a time, turning sideways to squeeze through the narrow entrance. Lara took Carlo out into Lygon Street into the restaurant next door for dinner while they waited for the Boss to join them.

"What's up, Boss?" Milo asked when the last footsteps fell silent.

"You remember that fucking woman journalist that killed Con, my nephew?" the Boss said, knowing he could swear as much as he liked now with no one around to offend.

"Yes, that was a bad thing, Boss! What can I do to make things better?"

"I need you to follow her to find out what she's up to and then let me know. Later, I'll tell you when and where you can see her off and that fucking copper she's been seeing. I heard he's gone bush somewhere, but he's got a mate still living here. The journalist might get in touch with him to find out where the pig's gone. Now you got your orders, you know what you need to do. Let me know when you're on to something, okay?"

"Yes, Boss, I'm thinking this means terminating. What's my share?"

"It's twice the normal fee and a bonus as long as there is no comeback on me."

In his unique accent he replied, "Understand. Talk soon, Boss."

# 18

# Warning—Warning—Warning

"It's a quarter to eight here tonight on Crazy FM, and this is Michael Scanlon. We have Wayne from the SES on the line. Got some bad news for us, I hear, Wayne?"

"Yes Michael, the tropical storm has hit with a vengeance, as we expected, with some of the district already under water. So, we're asking residents in the areas not already affected to pack up and leave unless they're on high ground. Even then, you should consider coming to town before this gets out of hand."

"What areas are most at risk, Wayne?"

"Mainly the western and northern regions at the moment, as that's the direction the front's coming from. It's travelling slowly right now, but it's important to understand what's happening here. As you know, we've had over ten years of drought, and the ground's been rock-hard for so long. This will cause flooding to move around the district quicker, making it flow faster than if the soil were soft."

"What are the chances of the entire district being under water come morning?"

"The weather service says the system is slow moving, and some of the district could miss out on the storm's worst effects. It goes without saying that it's better to be safe than sorry, to evacuate sooner rather than later. For some people, it might already be too late. It's hard to know who is still out there."

Michael, anxious about his next question, didn't know whether to stop at just one. His voice peaked.

"Is the tropical storm building or weakening as it enters our district? And do you know where it's heading once it leaves us? How much more rainfall should we expect tonight?"

Wayne chuckled. "According to the weather service, it'll diminish in its size as it moves further south, but it will intensify. Before it leaves this district, they are expecting between three and five hundred millimetres more over the next twenty-four hours. After that, it will head towards the Mildura–Renmark region. And, by all accounts, it'll continue on through some of the western towns in Victoria. Then it'll move on to some of the Melbourne suburbs around the southeast, then towards Phillip Island. It's unlucky it will arrive just in time for the Penguin Parade."

Wayne took a breath before revealing the major news.

"Figures from the weather services say they're expecting the tropical storm to dump between one hundred and one hundred and fifty millimetres down there over the next forty-eight hours. This will cause major flooding in most areas around Melbourne's south-east."

"Thanks, Wayne. We'll talk again in about an hour. Back with more of your calls soon, as I take another break. Phew! All this rain coming, I'm just overwhelmed by it, as I know you all must be too. All this humidity doesn't help either. Everything feels clammy and sticky. It's still early, but I'm stuffed already, oh poor me." He sighed theatrically as he looked at his co-host.

Off-air, he said, "I don't know if I can keep doing this until morning, Robyn."

"I'll take over from you sometime during the night if you need a break."

Michael sighed again, relieved. "Thanks, it'd be great if you could manage that."

# 19

## Where Am I?

Valley fog, which settles into the hollows and basins between hills and mountains, is a type of radiation fog. It occurs when cooler, heavier air, loaded with condensed water droplets, is trapped beneath a layer of lighter, warmer air. Hemmed in by ridges and peaks, it can't escape, often lingering for days.

Radiation fog forms in the evening, when the heat has been absorbed by the earth's surface during the day and is radiated into the air.

As heat is transferred from the ground to the air, water droplets form. Sometimes people call it "ground fog", but true ground fog does not extend as high as any of the clouds overhead. It usually forms at night.

The fog that is said to "burn off" in the morning sun is radiation fog. Freezing fog occurs when liquid fog droplets freeze onto solid surfaces. Mountaintops, seemingly covered by clouds, are often under a freezing fog. As this lifts, the ground, the trees and even objects like spiderwebs are blanketed by a layer of frost.

You could cut the air—or, in this case, the fog—with a knife. Those unlucky enough to be conscious in the aftermath of the disaster at McKenzie's Bridge were overwhelmed, numb and uncertain as to their whereabouts.

The speed at which the floodwaters receded in the river was incomprehensible, as the river emptied as fast as it filled. Only the chirping of unseen crickets and other nocturnal insects disturbed the ominous quiet. Occasionally, creaking sounds came from the trees and the wrecked timbers of the bridge.

Those trapped in the chaos didn't realise they all shared in the terrifying nightmare, their eyes darting vainly from one place to another, unable to see anything. Wanting to say something. Brains a blur. Heads spinning. Mouths dry. Lumps in their throats. Hearts banging away. Unable to feel much beyond what's next to them. Or on them. Passing out was not an option. It was even worse for the children in the claustrophobic, foggy dark.

Dianne and Bethany were still trapped inside the sleeping compartment of the prime mover and knew their situation was rapidly deteriorating.

When the trailer toppled from its upright position to one level with the raging river, it nudged the brothers' SUV into the river. This caused more water to gush into the prime mover's sleeping compartment.

Then, a massive log, carried by the swollen current, crashed into the weakened chassis of the cab. Already violently stressed, the cab then split into two sections.

One part of the prime mover, with Bridgette still inside, fell into the eastern side of the river and was swept downstream, passing what looked like a body hooked onto a branch. But the section containing Dianne and Bethany remained intact as it also sped down the river like a floating bathtub.

With a grinding wrench, the SUV broke free from the wreckage and raced down the river, the body of Bob the Longhorn swirling along beside it.

Paul, Bill and Luke scrambled out into the flowing river, and, as they were swept towards the bank, Luke's two brothers grabbed him and held him fast against a tree root.

From there, they scrambled up the muddy bank, soaked and covered in debris, before they all collapsed on the wet ground.

Luke was relieved to be out of the vehicle that also held so much horror and not just from tonight.

He lay still, wondering how he felt right now, and what the situation might bring next.

As the rain eased and the wind died, a milder, cooling temperature surrounded the valley; the fog increased.

On the bank, exhausted, it was as if the brothers were incapable of speech—or maybe they simply couldn't bring themselves to discuss what they'd just witnessed: the bizarre, violent deaths of their brothers, Nick and Ryan.

Luke, typically, was the first to think of helping others who may have been injured in the accident. But he had no idea of how many humans, animals or vehicles came to grief. They were all dimly aware that more than one bull was involved, and they might still be dangerously close.

The sleeping compartment, still containing Dianne and Bethany, was wedged on the river's eastern bank.

Trembling, choking, Bethany asked, "What's happening, Mummy, where's Daddy and Bridgette? I'm scared! Mummy, are we going to die?"

"I'm not sure what happened to your dad. But you know him. He'll find us, and he'll have Bridgette safe and sound with him." Dianne had no idea where she and Bethany were, nor what they should do next, but she instinctively reassured her daughter that they'd all survive this ordeal.

As if to point out her lie, something bumped roughly into the sleeping cabin, dislodging it from the bank. They both screamed for help.

However, their positioning kept the partially broken cab from turning over and stopped it from falling completely into the river.

Hearing their cries from across the river, Luke sat up and tried to pinpoint where they were coming from.

"Forget those screaming bitches!" Bill said, grabbing him. "We need to get out of here."

Two nearby bulls were startled by the screams and ran headlong into the fog. Then, they heard the sound of someone shrieking in pain and terror where the bulls were stampeding.

Bill leapt to his feet, his hair standing on end, but he couldn't see anything in the gloom. Couldn't see how close he was to danger until the ground abruptly gave way beneath his feet. Paul impulsively grabbed him but was dragged down into the river by his sibling.

Cautiously, Luke approached the crumbling bank where his brothers had vanished. Wondering if this was his chance to finally get away, more earth broke away, sending him into the water too.

When Luke stopped falling, he felt something clutching his left leg. *Bill? Paul?* Terror filled his mind. To his surprise, it was a young girl and an older woman. Together, they all groped and struggled up the embankment.

As the drenched, muddy trio scrambled to the top of the embankment, Luke asked, "How many of you are there?" Then he added, "My name's Luke, by the way."

"I'm Bethany," The girl replied timidly, looking at her mother for reassurance.

The older woman told Luke her name was Dianne. Her soaking red dress clung uncomfortably to her body as mascara ran down either side of her face.

"Luke, have you seen a man and another girl?" she asked urgently.

"No. Who are they?"

"My other daughter and my husband. There are four people in our family, the two of us and them. They were in the front of the truck, and we haven't seen them since the crash. Are you here to rescue us?"

"Sorry, no! Our vehicle was in the crash, too. I think I was the only one to escape."

Dianne gulped, forcing back hysteria. The trio stood motionless in the gloom.

Dianne sensed something uncertain in the young man before her but, strangely, a strong resolve also.

"Did you hear those noises? I heard something very strange just before you rescued us from the river."

"Probably just the bridge timbers shifting. Don't know, really."

The last thing Luke wanted was to encourage her to help his brothers. He tried to get his shocked brain to figure out what to do next to get away from his tormentors.

He didn't know where they might be. He'd have been appalled to know they were semi-conscious at the water's edge and quite near them.

By now, the fog had blanketed the area, making a surreal scene.

For the survivors, it meant they had no way of clearly seeing what was around them, nor where they were along the river. They knew nothing of their whereabouts and, worse, nothing of their chances of survival.

# 20

## Help Us

---

Back at the radio station, Robyn took a frantic call

"Hello? Robyn? It's Margaret calling. My farmhouse is surrounded by water, and my landline is out. I used my mobile to call the local SES and the police."

"What did they say, Margaret?"

"They said it'd be a couple of hours before they could get to me. They've had so many calls. Yeah, and they've told me to keep calm. Ha! As if! Then, they hung up on me, and here we are about five minutes away, and we've had to climb onto the roof of the house."

"Just hang on for a moment," Robyn said, forcing her voice to sound calm. "I'll put Michael on to see if we can get one of our listeners to come and rescue you."

"Hello, this is Michael here. Can you tell me what's happening at the moment, and what can we do to help?"

"Everything around the house is under water. Is there someone with a boat who could rescue us?"

"Can you let us know exactly where you are? I hope there's someone listening with a boat to come and get you. Can I ask what your name is, please, instead of me saying *you* all the time?"

"My name's Margaret. We're on the Lake Road, about a kilometre from the main road, on the northern side of Steering. You can just see the top of the shed to the left of the house. But you'll need to be careful. All the trees on the property are nearly under water at the moment. At this rate, we'll be swimming or drowning in about an hour."

Anyone listening could tell Margaret was trying hard to choke back the fear that she and her family wouldn't survive this ordeal. She went on with her directions.

"The property drops away after you enter from the Lake Road, so it'd be best to head towards the house and shed. Come up the dirt road, though you probably won't see it anymore, but you have to keep to the right of the gate. You should be able to see two large trees on either side, just behind the gate. Bring strong spotlights, otherwise you won't be able to see the house. Then go in a straight line between the shed and the house. The highest point of the house is on the shed side."

Michael interrupted, "I've just had a call from a guy called Frank at the pub, and he wants to know how many of you are stranded on the property?"

"There are five adults and three children, and I'm running low on battery, so I've given my number to Robyn if you want to pass it onto Frank. He can ring us when he's about to come through the front gate. When I see or hear him, I'll turn the phone back on. It's about two hundred metres from the front gate to the house."

Michael could hear the terror in her wobbly voice as she went on.

"It's really frightening! I'm seeing the rising floodwaters around the house, and it doesn't look like we'll survive that long without help." She barely held back her tears, trying not to alarm the other nervous family members with her on the roof.

Frank left the pub to hurry to his car, working out tasks and a route. His house, on the other side of the river, meant he'd have to go the long way round to fetch his boat.

Once at home, he connected the trailer and checked the engine, making sure he had enough fuel.

Soon after he launched, Robyn called him on his mobile. "Where are you now, Frank? And can you tell me when you think you'll reach the farm?"

"Yes, Robyn, I'm now in my boat, about fifteen minutes from Margaret's property."

Floating above the flood, he tried to think about where the Lake Road started; he knew it was somewhere off the main road he was now on. Despite the dramatically undulating topography of this part of town, he eventually picked out certain landmarks he knew, then he saw the front gate with trees on either side.

"Think this must be it!" he said to himself, aiming his boat between the trees.

He flicked on the switch of the six stronger spotlights and started to search for the house. The lights of the northern part of town that normally appeared had disappeared.

"Bloody hell!"

He could barely make out the shed and the house roofs. The house was almost completely submerged. Focusing on the house again, he could only make out a television aerial on his right.

"Blimey! They must all be dead!"

Margaret, hearing the boat, forgot to turn on her phone. She started shouting at the top of her voice as her family joined in.

Frank located the family, who'd moved from the house to the top of the shed with the roof inches away from going under. He turned the boat towards them, completely forgetting about the trees, and got his motor caught on one of them.

He cut the motor and groped below the waterline to find the branch that had snagged around the propeller.

"You'll have to swim to the boat. I'm stuck on a tree and can't move." The water level had not only flooded the property but, because of the topography, had become locked in place. The drought-compacted soil beneath also prevented the water from being absorbed, creating a permanent fixture like a large lake or dam.

Rebekah, one of the children, dived into the water and swam quickly to the boat. The two men, Andrew and Adrian, put Amy and Jake, the two smaller children, on their backs and swam towards the spotlights on the boat. Frank helped them clamber aboard, wondering how he'd get Margaret and her daughter Norma into the boat.

"I can't leave Norma, Frank. She can't swim!" Margaret said.

"Okay. Just sit tight. We'll work something out," he called, then turned to Andrew and Adrian.

"Gotta go overboard. Gotta untangle the propeller so I can take the boat close enough to the shed to let the women climb in."

"Think we'd better stand as close to the edge as we can, Norma," Margaret said. "Good thing this roof is almost flat!"

As the water kept rising, they both feared they'd fall in at any moment. They hugged each other, mumbling confused thoughts about their possible deaths and their love for each other.

The water continued rising and began to cover their knees, pulling more strongly than before. Then, they heard the roar of the outboard engine.

Frank steered the boat over to the shed and steadied it as he watched the men help Margaret and Norma climb aboard.

"I thought you said there were five adults?"

As blankets were draped over their shoulders, a sudden lurch knocked the boat off balance.

# 21

# Pinned!
# Claustrophobia, Who Wants It?

Pearl Lockwood was the first occupant in the car to regain consciousness. As she gazed around briefly, deep in shock, through the remains of the window, she could hardly believe that her family's car was pinned beneath an SUV and a semi-trailer, much less the broken timbers of the bridge and the flowing river. She swiped at her eyes and face to clear the dust and dirt, trying to make sense of what she could barely see in the dark and gloomy environment.

The river had now slowed. Even so, it had filled their car up to her knees and felt strangely warm. Her clothing and upper body were still quite dry. She felt eerily calm.

Despite the chaos, she mused, "What a blessing it was that we recently acquired a decent car! I don't want to even consider what would've happened to us if we were still in that old wreck we had." She turned sideways to look at David, still out of it and looking concussed, half-covered by his airbag.

Pearl leaned as best she could in her confined position to try to unfasten her seatbelt. While doing so, she squirmed around even more to see how the children were in the back. It never occurred to her that they mightn't be safe and sound in their back seats.

Calm changed instantly to hysteria when she saw the capsule had disappeared.

"Stephen! Where's Stephen? Where's my baby? I know I fastened his capsule properly. Where is it? How could it just vanish? Ohhhh!"

The back seat was obscured by various items strewn about when they crashed. In the gloom of the night, she couldn't see where her other two children were either. Her cries roused David from his state of shock.

"Wha—what's going on, love?"

Pearl, almost incoherent, was babbling something about Stephen having vanished. She tried desperately to get out of the vehicle to find him, unaware of the extent to which they were trapped.

David shouted back at her, "All right, woman, stop yelling and give me a moment. I need to see what I'm dealing with."

He was totally confused, until he remembered driving onto the bridge and the crash that came immediately afterwards.

Pearl yelled at him again. "Find my baby! Just find my baby. And where are the kids?"

"Shut up, Pearl, because your bloody screaming isn't helping."

Pearl went quiet, sobbing to herself.

David struggled to come to terms with the situation he now understood. His mind went into overdrive to find an answer, strangely switching back to the problem-solving strategies he used at work.

He looked for his flashlight and then remembered the light on his mobile phone. He reached into his shirt pocket for the phone, then knew something was wrong with his vision. He took a deep breath, wiped his eyes again and squinted at the phone to find the light button. He had to turn the phone around in his hand before he could locate it.

"Bloody hell! I don't need that," he cursed, temporarily blinded by the bright light that now pointed directly at his eyes.

*How did the capsule disappear?* He felt around for his glasses to examine the rear of the car, hearing Pearl's broken sobbing. He knew yelling at her wouldn't help, so he spoke much more calmly than before.

"We need to get out of this wrecked car before we can do anything."

He found his glasses on the rear-vision mirror, put them on, then realised they were filthy. He cleaned them on his shirtsleeve.

"We'll have to swap seats, otherwise you'll have to get out first. For some reason my side's blocked. I can't see why," he said as calmly as he could.

The water in the car sloshed around with his movements as David clambered over Pearl. He tore his tightly fitted shirt and a couple of buttons flew off. With enormous effort, he pushed open the front passenger door then wrenched open the back passenger door.

The open doors allowed the water inside the vehicle to gush out into the river faster than he expected. His contorted position and the release of water also meant David was washed out of the car.

Swept along, bobbing with the turbulent flow while trying to stay upright and move towards the bank, he grabbed hold of a branch in desperation.

But it wasn't a branch, it was a severed leg from one of the Longhorn bulls. Horrified, disgusted, he jerked his hand free then screamed in pain as he twisted his arm badly. He tried to catch hold of the roots on the bank, but the current pulled him back into the river. He had no idea how far downstream he would be carried.

Witnessing the renewed horror threw Pearl into hysteria again. Her precious baby had disappeared, the older kids too, and now David was gone. She turned once again to search the car's back seat for Tiffany and Rhys, praying they were there somewhere in the wreckage and still alive, but Tiffany has gone. Her door was open.

Then, she found Rhys, slumped forward, clearly unconscious. She moaned as she struggled to stroke his face, but there was no response.

Overwhelmed, she passed out.

David had been washed into the eastern side of the river, where the water was less deep. He lay on his back, the lukewarm water gently ebbing and flowing around him. He lay still, exhausted, his hand throbbing. He'd almost enjoyed the sensation of the water washing over him. He saw a blurry object nearby and made out part of a truck.

"What's a truck doing here at the bottom of a river?"

But this lifted him out of his trance, and then he remembered the moment he'd been blinded by the oncoming truck's lights, seconds before the crash. He rolled over and leaned onto the cab. Empty.

*If only I could have my glasses! Then I could see properly, he thought. I need to do something to help my family, or maybe others who survived the accident. Bugger it, where's my damn phone?*
He needed to call for help but couldn't find it there in the mud.

"God! Could things get any worse this ghastly night?" He went limp, defeated.

# 22

# Oh, That's Where They Are

When farmer John Meadows moved onto this property just after the Second World War, he completed fencing his boundaries within a year and then had good grazing areas for his sheep.

Today, the property was bounded by a dirt road (a shortcut into Steering) running along the southern side to a corner, where it turned left along the western edge, parallel to the river. The dirt road was just wide enough for two cars to pass at the same time, something that happened rarely. John had only ever experienced this on one occasion when his wife was returning from town. He'd had to pull over to let her pass or she'd have gone down the ten metres of the embankment and into the river.

At this point, the lower part of the river was fifteen metres across, and its banks were around ten metres high. On its far side, vacant land stretched towards derelict buildings that once serviced a small industrial mine. Reaching the mine involved going over the longer of the two wooden bridges, continuing along a dirt track on the western side of the river for five hundred metres and then over another, smaller wooden bridge, to finally make an eastern turn onto another dirt track for five kilometres.

The larger of the two wooden bridges had a span of around forty metres and the smaller around thirty metres. They were initially designed for larger vehicles to deliver animals and various other goods to the area.

At the time, a width of five metres was considered sufficient for both bridges—enough room for just one large vehicle at a time. Signs showed westbound vehicles heading to the area had right of way. These vehicles needed to go up a slight incline just before the bridge, whereas eastbound ones had a slight downhill run, continuing on to the town of Steering.

Now, on the eastern side of the river embankment, a pile of volcanic rocks had been left by the local council. The road was already on the western side of the river. The council had decided to forgo clearing the rocks in favour of building another, somewhat smaller, bridge. This allowed better entry into the industrial area that was already part of the road, which headed up towards the mountains and a few hours' drive west to the Wilson farm.

The bridges had been built more fifty years before when the town was prospering but were allowed to fall into disrepair during the 1980s and 1990s.

An abattoir owner, Councillor Jeff Steering, maintained the bridges during that time. He owned most of the town and land in the district that had originally been settled by his great-grandfather, who'd migrated from the United Kingdom more than a century ago. The name Steering dated back to pre-seventh century Anglo-Saxon times and denoted someone who tended bullocks and oxen. *Steor,* meaning a steer or bullock, resulted in a medieval- assumed nickname or occupation, was very appropriate for someone with a defiant or aggressive nature—in fact, much like Bob the bull.

When Councillor Jeff Steering's great-grandfather arrived in Australia, he changed the name from Steer to Steering.

Most of the young people in the town were employed part-time. The abattoir offered jobs when it was up and running, and it opened and closed depending on the highs and lows of the industry. It survived by buying stock from farmers when prices were low and selling to buyers worldwide when the prices picked up.

The abattoir was where the brothers had intended to take Luke for his birthday initiation.

# 23

## A Hero is Born

Luke was unwilling to leave Dianne and Bethany on the western side of the embankment, while he went in search of help. He was unaware that Paul and Bill had regained consciousness and they were angry about their predicament. The thick fog also annoyed them. They didn't know where they were.

It wasn't that Luke had forgotten his brothers altogether; he just had so much going on in his head, he wasn't thinking straight. He felt his way cautiously through the fog, then unexpectedly bumped into someone: Tiffany, startled at first.

The instant attraction between them perhaps had something to do with the surreal nature of their misty surroundings but was quickly snuffed out.

Tiffany sensed movement behind Luke and gave a startled cry.

"Well, hello there! What've we got here?" Bill said, grabbing Tiffany by her arm, squeezing tightly.

"Hey, Paul! Grab her and help me hold her down. Let's give her one."

For a few seconds, Bill's memory flicked back a couple of years to something stored in a dark part of his mind, retrieved only in moments of desperate need: the time Nick violated a younger Tiffany. And here she was again.

Bill had watched, fascinated, as Nick had satisfied his animal lust, knowing it was his turn next. But just as Nick had grunted, signalling the end of his episode, and lurched up from Tiffany's struggling form, it was already too late. A man with a dog was approaching.

Luke was appalled that Bill, minutes after watching his two brothers die horrible deaths, was still motivated by lust.

Although the fog affected her vision, Tiffany also had a flashback. Bill resembled someone but she couldn't put her finger on who.

But seeing his brothers die seemed to have stripped Bill of his last layer of civilised behaviour, leaving a vicious animal intent.

"Bill! Don't do this to the poor girl!" Luke pleaded.

But Bill punched Luke in the stomach, winding him. Doubled over in pain and struggling for breath, Luke collapsed to the muddy ground.

Bill started to grab at Tiffany's wet clothing as Paul held her down. Paul's reaction seemed driven more by an instinct to support his violent brother than any great need for carnal gratification.

And then, a streak of lightning ripped across the sky, illuminating Bill removing his clothes, ready to rape Tiffany.

The flash spooked a cluster of Longhorn bulls ambling past. Immediately, they stampeded, heading straight for Tiffany and the three brothers. One of the bulls turned at the last moment, narrowly missing the two forms on the ground but careering into Bill, still on his feet, half-undressed.

A single horn pierced his chest, splitting open his beating heart. Blood spewed from the wound and from Bill's mouth. His eyes were still wide open, now vacant.

He slumped onto the horn as the bull tossed its head, catapulting Bill into the air and then downwards into the river. The Longhorn, also off balance, followed him down the bank into the swirling water. Bill landed heavily on a rock protruding from the bank. The snap of his spine echoed in the night.

Tiffany's fear and revulsion erupted from deep within, and she vomited wildly. Luke was still winded from Bill's blow but tried to comfort her until a sudden movement in the shifting fog distracted him.

Paul, now in pathetic form, stood before him. It was now one on one. Before Paul could attempt to imitate Bill's attack on Tiffany, Luke punched him hard on the temple, knocking him off his feet and away from him and Tiffany.

Luke nursed his painful left fist. "Shit! That hurt."

It was as if this one blow had lifted a weight from Luke's shoulders.

Tiffany and Luke looked at each other.

"That bastard! I remember him now. He was the one who raped me a couple of years ago. You're all the same, you're bloody thugs! Leave me alone!" she sobbed hysterically

"No! I'm not like them! And I just stopped Bill from attacking you..."

But Tiffany's priority was getting out of there as quickly as possible, wherever *there* was.

"Ha! Don't believe you."

Luke tried to calm her with a distraction. "I need to go and help find a young girl who's been separated from her parents. Want me to take you where the girl's mother and sister are? If I can remember where they are."

Luke saw that Tiffany was still in shock and had no idea what to do.

"Look, just follow me back up the embankment. I won't touch you."

At first, Tiffany refused so Luke shrugged and walked away.

"No, wait. I don't want to be alone with *him*!" Sobbing quietly, she followed him cautiously along the bank to where the fog had thinned out.

Dianne and Bethany were huddled together when Tiffany and Luke appeared. Bethany lunged at Luke in sheer relief, giving him a big hug, while Dianne planted a kiss on his cheek.

Tiffany was confused not only about who Luke was, but why these women were so delighted to see him. This was the second time she'd felt a twinge of affection for him, but she fought it off instinctively. It had always ended badly for her in the past.

"This is Tiffany. I found her lost and confused in the river. You can tell her your names. Look, can Tiffany stay with you for a while? I have to go and see who else is alive."

Bethany was happy to see someone else and stood up and welcomed Tiffany with a hug.

Tiffany, being Tiffany, responded gently but was unsure of this attention.

Seeing this, Dianne just said, "Hi. This is my daughter Bethany, and I'm Dianne, pleased to meet you." Tiffany just smiled and nodded.

Watching this exchange, Luke knew the loved ones of these people might well be dead. He didn't relish having to tell them.

"Don't move from here and try not to make any sudden noises. I think there's some sort of wild animal s around. I'm not sure what they are, because of the fog, but they seem to be easily spooked. Just stay together and keep your eyes open."

"They're bulls, and yes, they *are* probably wild, as I found out earlier today," Dianne said. The others were too immersed in their own thoughts to take in what Dianne had just said.

Almost against her better judgement, Tiffany clutched his arm and said, "Be careful and come back safe."

Tiffany went over and stood next to Bethany, who looked nervously at her mum and asked, "Are we going to die?"

Hoping his words would bring some reassurance, Luke said, "No way! We've been through enough tonight, it's not our time." With that, he walked off into the gloomy surrounds.

After a while, he squatted close to the ground, closed his eyes, listened intently to his surroundings, trying to block out the sounds of the river. A frog croaked close by, but nothing else. He glanced up at where the sky should be but saw only thick fog.

"Wish I could see like Superman. Aaagh! What a stupid idea. Superman had X-ray vision, not fog vision."

Luke closed his eyes to try again. More as a result of his intense fatigue than anything else, he fancied he was in a shipwreck. The ship lurched hard to port, throwing a couple of the crew overboard.

Luke was standing on the edge of the ship, watching helplessly as the two crewmen disappeared into the depths.

The dream ended abruptly. He awoke to find an animal urinating on him before moving away. Luke felt sick and crawled towards the river to wash away the smell.

# 24

# Chop-Chop

The main building of the Steering abattoir was on the only level ground in the industrial area, just south of the wooden bridges. The remainder of the property, including the grazing area, sloped downwards, steepest in the area south of the main building, heading down to the creek that flowed into the main river. The rest of the grazing area undulated between ridges and valleys, wedged next to the river between the two bridges.

In the hundred years of the abattoir's existence, it had only experienced one flood, back in 1953. Most of the buildings and some of the surrounding property had to be repaired or replaced.

During the recent storm, the water level around the abattoir rose. When the storm hit a few hours before, the animals on top of the main slope became stranded. Hundreds of sheep and cattle were mixed together. Stock had been brought in from properties all around, ready for slaughter on Monday. This would bring work for many of the townsfolk for a week.

Because sheep were individually smaller than the other livestock, most of the sheep were forced down the slope onto the flooded area where they drowned, carried away downstream. Many of them were caught on the ageing wire fences surrounding the abattoir.

After the storm had passed, the cattle followed the receding water line along the creek and onto the dirt road. Mostly bulls, they led the other animals back towards the town via McKenzie's Bridge.

Councillor Jeff Steering fought tooth and nail to keep the abattoir operating for at least six to nine months of the year. Because he made good annual profits, he paid good casual wages, and that helped many townsfolk and the town itself to survive financially.

A new, long-term deal had been recently signed with two Asian countries, helping to boost production and job security. The few employees who were around the day before to handle the influx of new sheep and cattle were caught by surprise when the storm broke. Weakened fences hadn't been inspected to show they had deteriorated during the drought.

The creek that flowed from the abattoir into the river, formed decades ago, was about three metres wide but less than a metre deep, with volcanic rocks dotting its surface. It reached the river where the small wooden bridge was located.

The banks of the river angled slightly downwards in some sections, steeper in others, especially near both ends of the bridges. Both bridges were badly in need of repair, mainly because they could carry only limited large-traffic volumes. Smaller vehicles could cross without any danger, but semi-trailer drivers coming to the district could find themselves in trouble if they were new to the area.

The animals being led by a couple of the larger bulls had found their way along the creek and into the river without incident. It was easy to head into the nearly empty river and continue on towards McKenzie's Bridge.

The animals comprised about fifty-three sheep, fifteen milking cows, five horses and fifty-three bulls of various shapes, sizes and ages. Some sheep, cattle and one horse had moved away from the main herd, seeking new grazing areas.

Most of the herd had been kept awake during the storm and were now hungry and tired. The remainder were following the bulls upstream and were a few hundred metres from the wooden bridge, and the unknown territory beyond.

# 25

# We're Back on the Air—With Whom?

Back at the radio station, Robyn and Michael were going about their individual tasks.

"Are you feeling okay?" Robyn asked Michael. "We're back on the air in two minutes, and there's just one more ad after the weather report. You've got three callers to choose from, and they're on your screen. It's your call, Michael."

Michael started reading out the call-log on his computer.

"Okay… let's see… Someone called Kevin wanting to comment on Patrick. Another Emily wanting to comment on Patrick, and Jeff Steering, the councillor. I'll go with the councillor first, so what's he calling for?"

"About the floods and wanting to let people know about the abattoir, I guess, and if it's affected by the storm, I guess." Robyn said.

"You do realise, Robyn, you guessed twice, so I guess we'll see, won't we! Let him know he's on first, and I guess I'll see what we can do with whatever he wants to tell us. So, if he's on first, who's on second and third?" Michael grinned to himself.

"What?" Robyn snapped. "What are you on about?"

Michael's attempt at imitating the humour of a 90 year old movie sketch by Abbott and Costello went completely over Robyn's head.

"Never mind, Robyn. Okay, thirty seconds to go. I'll get the radar up so you can see what's going on and how much has fallen and where. Ten seconds."

Michael heard the station's intro and looked at Robyn for the thumbs-up to start talking. He was on air, but tiredness had set in, and he was on autopilot.

"Sorry, folks, just a moment frozen in time. Didn't even know what time it was. Gee, if I'm like this now, I'd hate to think what I'll be like after midnight. Anyway, it's ten past nine here on Crazy FM, and we have Councillor Jeff Steering on the line. Good evening, Councillor. How are you going this evening? I believe you want to alert people about the abattoir?"

"Good evening, Michael, and thanks for taking my call. Yes, I'd like to talk about the abattoir. As you and your listeners are well aware, we're having one helluva storm going through the district."

"Yes, I can see it still passing us on the radar in front of me, Councillor. It looks like nearly all parts of the district have had a lot of rain, about one hundred millimetres so far. Like one of those storms that's here one minute, gone the next."

"Yes, great news for the farmers and their water tanks, but not for their pastures and crops. But it's the abattoir I'm concerned about. Now, tomorrow morning, a few of the locals and I will be going down to check on the animals and the facility itself. Then we can work out if it's viable to operate as normal on Monday. If there's only minor damage, it shouldn't be a problem. Not forgetting the most important part—the animals. I'm not sure how many would have survived the storm. We might not have any left. The buildings should be okay, and I'm hoping the renovations have kept the worst of the weather out. Those people already lined up for work can have at least some idea if we're delayed. That should put minds to rest. Thanks again, Michael, and as soon as I know, I'll give you an update."

"I'm not sure when this storm will finish. I'm looking at the radar again, and it's starting to show another front building. It looks like it could be in the district in a couple of hours, bringing similar amounts of rain to what we've just copped. We need to be prepared for the worst."

"Thanks Michael. I'll be in touch. I'm sure the SES and others involved are on top of it all, anyway."

"Goodnight, Councillor, I hope the news is positive. I'm wondering what it must be like for those animals outside in the storm, getting drenched. I'm just glad I'm here."

Michael switched to the next caller.

"Hello, Kevin? You called in to talk about Patrick."

"Yes, g'day, I'm at the Lakeside Motel on the corner of the intersection, where Patrick and Emily nearly crashed. I reckon Patrick should think himself very lucky. Emily must have missed him by inches. Just because she was taught by her dad, who she says was a professional driver, doesn't necessarily mean she'll be a good driver herself. As I've found in all my years of driving! If you're in the wrong place at the wrong time, then it's in the hands of fate."

"Well, that's your opinion, Kevin, and I'm sure there are others who agree with you. We'll see if another Emily does too, but I'm guessing… there's that guessing word again, see what you've done, Robyn? Emily, you're on the air. What's on your mind?"

"Hi Michael, well, I'm actually agreeing with what you said about both being at fault."

"That's good to hear, Emily. Are you having a good night, whatever it is you're doing?"

"It started out okay, but it's gone a bit pear-shaped. It's gone quiet now, but there was a big brawl at the pub about an hour ago. We are only just cleaning it up now. I'm glad I'm not outside with some of the other women, nursing sore heads. It was something I've never experienced before! Anyway, goodnight and good luck with staying awake all night, Michael."

"Thanks, Emily, I'll try my best, I guess."

Emily hung up, and Michael off-air, said to Robyn, "Guess that went pretty well, I guess."

"Once more, what are you on about?"

"Go onto YouTube and type in Abbott and Costello *Who's on First*, it's a riot. Oh yeah, and then go to Abbott and Costello again, and type in *Seven Times Thirteen Equals Twenty-Eight*. That's also a riot. Ron, the truckie, showed it to me last year."

"Thirteen times seven equals twenty-eight?" Robyn asked.

"Yeah, I know, I guess, right?" Michael said, a big grin on his face.

"Really Michael, sometimes you can be such a baby."

# 26

## The Clean-Up Begins

Back at the pub, most of the patrons had left, many of them taking home sore heads and bruised prides. Some, like Emily, volunteered to stay and help clean up the mess.

Outside the pub, Senior Sergeant Logan climbed into his divvy van to transport the drunken offenders to their overnight accommodation in the lock-up.

Ian the publican went back inside the pub after helping Logan load the divvy van and felt grateful for certain patrons' willingness to return tables and chairs to their normal positions, and help generally with the clean-up.

Mike the barman approached with the night's takings, sporting a cut above his left eye that'd be a shiner by morning.

Mike ambled away to find some ice to put on his sore head, and Ian went to the office to put the takings in the safe. He returned to the bar and heard Michael on the radio talking to Councillor Steering. He signalled to the remaining patrons to be quiet and listen.

After discussion on the probable immediate fate of the abattoir, they heard the interviews with Kevin and Emily about Patrick's near miss. At that moment, Emily walked back into the bar to a round of applause for her part. Then everyone got on with the business of drinking and cleaning up the place.

Senior Sergeant Logan pulled up outside the police station and walked around to open the divvy van's back door. As he swung it open, he reeled from the combined stench of liquor, tobacco, vomit and sundry bodily fluids. He placed his hand theatrically over his nose and grimaced. Five blokes of all shapes and sizes were strewn across the floor, most of them either too drunk to move, sleeping or both. Logan couldn't and wouldn't put them all in the cells at the same time.

To avoid injury to his already bad back, caused by lack of exercise, too many beers and an old sporting injury, he went next door to the hardware store. He removed a bunch of keys from a chain connected to his belt and unlocked the door. He found a four-wheeled trolley and slowly returned with it to the van.

Senior Sergeant Logan had been in the district for more than thirty years and had shrewdly taken the liberty of having a spare key to all the local businesses—useful if he needed something for emergencies, just like this one.

He struggled, dragging the first drunk from the van, and placed him onto the trolley, reeling again from the smell. The trolley was big and sturdy enough for two comatose bodies. Logan held his breath again as he leant forward and grabbed the next limp body's legs, pulling him out and dropping him as gently as possible on top of the first. Not that it would have mattered, anyway.

"Why do they do this to themselves?" he mused.

Grunting and puffing, he wheeled the trolley down to the cells—luckily, the path was straight and level—and then entered through a back door. Once inside the cell, their size, combined with their dead weight, brought on another grunt. Then Logan simply tipped the trolley up and stood back as the two drunks slid onto the cold floor. Both moaned as they reacquainted themselves with their relaxed state.

The next three were big country boys. To protect his back, Logan took them one at a time. Two were half-awake and abused him as he dragged them to a separate cell. Local knowledge had already told him it would be unwise to house all five together—there were hostilities there.

When all were secured, Logan lay down on a bed he'd set up for just such occasions and was asleep before his head hit the pillow. Nobody would drown in his own vomit on this cop's watch.

In another part of town, Scotty found himself ankle-deep in water while patrolling a partially flooded major road. It was still safe for cautious drivers, but nobody was out and about on this foul night, and Scotty was starting to wonder why he was there.

The rain had stopped, but the fog had come back faster than expected, making visibility nigh impossible for more than a few yards. He remembered Billy would arrive the next morning. He knew Billy would regard the train journey as an adventure.

A call from the SES interrupted his thoughts; he'd be required for another hour, even though the water level was receding faster than first thought.

But Scotty had had enough. "Nobody's driven along this road since you got me to come here. I'm going home. I'll leave the warning signs up." He hung up, tired and frustrated at being in this tedious situation that was just part of his job.

Scotty drove home and hit the sack early. Too wound up to sleep yet, he'd showered before going to bed. He had to be up in the morning to meet Billy's train.

Back at the pub, Emily was unsure about the attention coming her way from Gazza, one of the late drinkers. She'd heard his chat-up lines a hundred times before but surprisingly, warmed to him.

Tonight seemed different. Everyone looked relaxed and jovial, even after the brawl earlier. That surprised Emily. So maybe she should enjoy herself and take a chance.

She'd spoken to Gazza a few times, but tonight he'd gone up a notch in the attraction stakes. Maybe because of the amount of drink she'd had.

Gazza, wondering if he was on to a good thing, jumped when another patron banged into him from behind. He turned around, about to fly into a rage, and then Emily flung an arm around his neck and planted one squarely on his mouth. Loud, raunchy cheers echoed around the bar as they held the kiss for what seemed an eternity.

When they finally broke off to get their breath back, Emily grabbed him by the top of his shirt and led him outside to somewhere more private. With all this fog around, nobody saw them tear the clothes off one another.

# 27

# That Was Close

Frank's boat was big enough to hold ten passengers, but even so, the bump from under the water was enough to alarm everyone on board.

Paddling along by the side of the boat was Bert, the family's fat, aging labrador.

"Oh, Bert! Dear old Bert! We're so glad you're okay, you poor old boy!"

After pulling the frightened game dog into the boat, Frank calculated that Bert's weight equalled a fifth adult from the comments the other adults made. Frank continued to navigate his way along the river, watchful for partially submerged trees.

The receding water level meant that, having gone as far as he could, Frank was still fifty metres short of the trailer. Frustrated, he moored the boat against the bank and helped the family clamber out from the rear.

As they climbed the slippery bank, someone said, "Geeze, look how foggy it's become."

Someone else said, "Think I heard noises coming from the river, down near that old wooden bridge. Can you hear that?"

No one responded, so the comment was promptly forgotten as they scrambled to the top of the embankment. Then, guided by Frank, they started walking towards the town.

Volcanic rocks hampered their progress along the embankment path, adding to their sense of disorientation from the fog. They were all talking among themselves about how to get out of their unpredictable situation.

The three girls were scared of the surrounding fog and clung as close to the adults as they could.

Bert the dog was happy to be going for his evening walk, even if it was in a different location. But he had to stop when nature called.

The dilemma made them realise the only safe way through was in twos or threes, keeping close to each other. The children held hands. Frank, as well as guiding them through the maze of volcanic rocks, was looking after Bert, enjoying his new-found companion. It took his mind off the misjudged boat landing too. He could watch Bert lead the way, hopefully, back to the pub for a well-earned beer.

At the entrance to McKenzie's Bridge, they paused, looking down into a damp, dark, foreboding place. They wondered what to do but dared not venture into it. In the claustrophobic fog, it looked worse than where they'd come from. They turned right, towards Steering, not wanting to seek refuge down there.

They plodded on towards the town and the pub, longing for some warmth and rest from their ordeal.

Being above the valley, Frank saw he had one bar on his phone. He rang the radio station and Robyn answered.

"Hi! Frank Saunders here. I thought I'd ring to let you know the family are all safe and well. We're two kilometres from the pub at McKenzie's Bridge. We should be at the pub in about an hour, unless you can call someone at the pub to come and get us. I don't know their number."

Robyn connected Frank to Michael on the air.

"Yes, Frank, would you please repeat that?"

"Yeah, um, if anyone is listening? A few people I have rescued here might struggle with the journey. Could someone come and get us? But we're going to need a couple of cars though if that's okay."

"Okay, thanks, Frank. I'll call the pub now in case they didn't hear the message. Hang on! Just got this message. Two cars, including one being driven by Emily, have already set off to look for you. They're probably about halfway between McKenzie's Bridge and the pub by now."

Michael thought, *I hope they get back to the pub before the next storm comes.*

# 28

## COO-EE

When the river receded, David moved away from the empty cab, now sticking half out of the water. First, he had to work out which way to go, despite being befuddled by the combination of his recent ordeal, his painful, badly twisted hand and the thick fog.

He stood up cautiously in the water, using his good right arm to help, then winced in agony. He put his aching left arm inside his shirt between the two remaining buttons, making a sling out of the sopping garment. He was wary of taking another step forward in case he tripped and fell, further damaging his hand, and in case he ran into whatever animals were around.

*Now what do I do?* he thought. *Which way is which?* Nothing moved in the impenetrable fog.

Nearby, invisible, Luke was also trying to work out where he was in relation to the town. Unlike David, Luke had recovered and stood upright at the same time, unaware of anyone else within a coo-ee of him. He heard someone sneeze and then curse, sounding as if they were only a short distance away.

"Who's that?" Luke called, loud enough for his voice to carry. Luke stood motionless, half in fear, half in hope, as he waited for a reply.

After cursing at the unexpected sneeze and consequent pain shooting through his hand, David answered.

"Hi there! My name's David. I've just been in a terrible road accident. I Have no idea where I am. Please, can you help me? I think I've broken my hand, and I can't see anything without my glasses. Lost them some time ago."

"Sure David, the name's Luke. Just stay where you are. I'll try and come to you. Keep talking so I can work out which direction to go. But keep your voice down because there are some dangerous animals close by."

"Are you alone?" David asked, hoping he wasn't.

"No, I'm not. I found three other people, a woman, her daughter and a teenage girl. They're not far away."

"Oh, really? What's their names? My entire family's missing. I've lost all four of them. I think they're still in my car."

Luke sensed David's urgency and said calmly, "I don't know. We did exchange names, but I'm sorry. In all this confusion, I've forgotten. They're all female, if that helps." He stopped talking as he reached David.

"It doesn't sound like my family, but I guess I'll find out soon enough if this bloody fog clears."

"Which hand did you injure, David?"

"The left one."

"Okay, I'll walk on your right side. Let's just take it slowly. There's bits of debris strewn around everywhere. I'll try and get us back to where the others are."

"How far are we from the accident?" David asked.

"Why?"

"I think my wife and three kids might still be in the car. I'm terrified of what might have happened to them." David's voice was now slurred, and his body ached from the ordeal. He was leaning forward, as though he thought he was going to fall head-first again into the slow-running river, now just above their ankles.

"Let's get you somewhere safe first, and then I'll find the three women again and work out what we should do."

David gathered that Luke had stopped talking, but he began, "But wha—"

"Look, best not to concern ourselves with what-ifs at this stage. I'll try and find your car, okay? We don't have much further to go. Save your strength for the climb up the slope at the edge of the river. Depending on where we are, it could be quite steep."

David's anxiety for his family and his confusion still plagued him, and he began to wobble on his feet. For the first time for as long as he could remember, he felt totally helpless.

They reached the riverbank and worked their way up to the top of the slope, David slipping and cursing quietly in his pain, frustration and worry.

*Strange to think a short while ago I would've been glad to see the back of my kids while they were arguing with each other*, he thought, *at least temporarily*.

At the top of the embankment, the look on David's face was one of triumph. He felt like he'd just climbed Mt Everest. He recklessly threw his arms up, then realised his error when sharp, intense pain shot up his left arm.

"Aaagh! It bloody hurts!"

They walked along the edge of the embankment, David trying to ignore his pain and discomfort, then they saw the three women behind a veil of fog.

"Hey!" Luke called in a low voice. "I found someone in the river."

With the thick fog, the girls couldn't see properly, but without hesitation Dianne and Bethany rushed to him, hoping it was Ron. They tried hard to hide their disappointment.

But Tiffany was ecstatic and went to hug her father. Luke caught her before she did.

"What did you do that for?" she yelled.

"Look Tiffany, he's broken his left hand. He's in agony."

Tiffany, ashamed, started to stomp off but couldn't see where she was going. She turned back.

"Oh sorry! Sorry sorry sorry," she said to Luke.

Tiffany was overwhelmed, wondering why she was in two minds about him, and it made her even more irritated.

"Do you reckon you could look after David? There are obviously more people out there who need help," Luke asked Dianne and Tiffany.

"So, I'm looking for your husband, Ron, and your daughter, Bridgette, right?" Dianne and Bethany both nodded, too choked up for words.

"David, who am I looking for with your family?"

"That would be my wife, Pearl, our teenage son, Rhys, and our six month old baby, Stephen. Rhys and Stephen were in the back seat. The baby was in his capsule between Rhys and Tiffany. We don't know where the capsule's gone. It's just disappeared."

Tiffany started crying and put her hands over her face, fearing she could have been responsible for Stephens's disappearance. She wondered if she and Rhys could have done anything to save Stephen.

Dianne and David moved over to console her. But her guilt about Stephen made her back away from them—just a couple of steps; she didn't wish to be alone in this thick fog.

"Okay, I'll see you all later. Just stay here and stay together," Luke said as he ventured off into the fog once more. When he'd worked his way back to where he thought he'd found David, he turned ninety degrees to his left and hoped he was facing the large wooden bridge.

He wasn't sure how far away it was, nor was he aware of any animals behind him. Stumbling through the fog, he couldn't always see the ground he was walking on. But this only strengthened his resolve, even though a voice in his head was telling him "You're going to die".

He tried to dismiss this by thinking about Tiffany, the girl he'd just met, when he bumped into what looked like a stationary vehicle looming out of the fog. He ran his hand over the cold metal and knew this was the rear of the vehicle. He backtracked, passing the door he'd previously found, but felt no more panel, nothing. Then his hand encountered some form of fabric and what felt like a body. Whatever he'd touched then twitched and moaned.

"Who's that? Who's there? Get ya bloody hands off my tits, ya filthy bastard!"

Luke jumped back. "My name's Luke. Who are you? I'm looking for survivors from an accident. I've found four other people who were also in the accident. They're on top of the riverbank for now while I go and look for others. Like you."

"Oh. That's okay. I guess." The woman pulled herself together.

"My name's Pearl…" she started, then broke off. "What's your name again?"

"Luke."

"So, do you know what happened to my husband, and please," she hesitated again, "please, can you look at my son in the back seat? He's unconscious, I think. I'm not sure how long I've been unconscious. Or asleep… I don't know…"

Luke moved to the back door, opened it, and water spilled out at his feet. He felt around and realised he was running his hands over someone's face. He identified drying blood and then felt a pulse. He thought the boy was unconscious or concussed, but definitely alive.

"He's okay, but we need to decide whether we should move him or leave him here. I can't tell if he has any injuries or how serious they could be. Maybe you should stay here with him until we can get help. I'll see if I can find anyone else," Luke told her.

"That's good. But my other son's a baby, and he's only six months old. He disappeared from the car in the capsule. I'm not sure what I'd do if I lost my precious Stephen. Can you help me? Please!"

Luke, startled by his new predicament, had forgotten what David mentioned earlier in the night. Now he wondered what to say to her.

"Okay," he said, "I'll have a look around, but this fog is making everything hard to see, even right in front of me."

"Oh, thank you. My name's Pearl Lockwood. I'm also missing my husband, David."

Luke was relieved to have some good news. "Oh, I found him before, and do you have a daughter, Tiffany?"

"Yes, I do!"

"They're safe on the riverbank, looking after one another and some other people I've found."

"Thank God. Do you know where they are?"

"Yeah, sort of, I've been counting my steps while groping around and trying to remember the directions I've been going in. Anyway, if it starts to rain again, just close the doors and you should be fairly safe inside here. I'll see you soon."

"Do you know what time it is, so at least I know when the sun's coming up?"

"Sorry, I don't know."

"Oh well, goodbye, Luke. Oh, and thank you for finding my family."

As Luke was leaving, he asked, "When did you see the capsule last?"

"Just before the accident. Why?"

"That means it should be around here somewhere. I'll feel around here, then work my way up to the top of the bridge."

Luke was starting to think all this would be easier if he had another person helping him. He headed back to the others.

"David, good news! I found your wife and son Rhys. Pearl was unconscious, but she's recovered. Rhys is still unconscious. Probably a concussion. But Pearl said she was happy to stay and look after Rhys, not that she had much choice in the matter."

"But what about Stephen, Luke? You haven't mentioned him... Is he dead?"

"Look, I don't know. But I want to get back and see if I can find him. Don't want to waste time just talking. Okay?"

Luke wasn't comfortable with all these things going on at once. He knew he needed time to take all this in, to try to accomplish one thing at a time.

He turned to Tiffany. "Could you come with me to help me find Stephen? Because I could do with another set of eyes in this bloody fog."

Dianne stood up. "I'd rather come and help. It'd be better to leave Tiffany here with her father and Bethany."

Tiffany agreed. "Would it be okay for me to stay here? I can look after Bethany and Dad, without being on my own... with you. Not that I..."

Luke cut her off. "Okay, that's settled then. Let's go, Dianne."

As they walked away, David blurted, "Thank you, Luke." He knew he couldn't help but tearfully expressed his gratitude by slowly holding up his right arm. But no one could see this clearly, either.

As they ventured into the fog, Dianne took hold of Luke's hand. "This is just so we don't get separated while we try to get to the bridge. God, I hope we find them safe."

Holding hands with Dianne reminded Luke of walking along the dirt road to school with his mother when he was little.

"I think we should look for baby Stephen first and then Bridgette, then your husband," Luke told Dianne. She wanted to search for Bridgette first, but she understood the greater vulnerability of a baby in these circumstances.

"Why are you counting your steps, Luke?"

"It was something I taught myself at scout camps, back in the day. It seemed to come naturally to me, and sometimes it helps. Occasionally someone would get lost in the dark, so I'd ask questions of those who saw them last, and the rest took care of itself."

"Sounds like a good idea for now," Dianne said.

"David's wife Pearl said the last time she saw the capsule was moments before the accident, so it can't be that far away, Or..."

"Or what?" She glanced down-river, appreciating the awful possibility that the capsule had washed away downstream, with Stephen inside... or not.

# 29

# Haven't the Foggiest

Bridgette still lay, concussed, in the front seat of the semi-trailer where it rested on the eastern side of the embankment. Most of the bulls had freed themselves and fled or died.

Luke and Dianne separated slightly to widen the area of their search. They nervously felt their way around the crash site for anyone who might still be alive. Progress was necessarily slow.

Dianne found the thick fog very difficult and stumbled into a branch. It pierced her face just below her left eye and blood flowed down her face.

In pain and shock, yet remembering what Luke had said about dangerous animals, Dianne quietly called out for Luke. He spent a couple of seconds trying to locate her.

Once he was close enough to see the damage, he found a deep cut on the cheekbone. He decided they should return to the others, where the fog was less dense. The journey seemed to take forever with Luke now needing to guide Dianne over the rough terrain.

When they got back, they saw the girls had put together a makeshift bed of branches and leaves for David to lie on.

Tiffany was glad to see Luke, as was Bethany. Luke needed to clean the cut on Dianne's face, and David offered his relatively clean handkerchief.

As Tiffany passed it to Luke, their hands touched briefly. Luke looked up at Tiffany and gave her a slight grin.

He held the handkerchief aloft for a few moments in the foggy atmosphere, long enough to dampen it. After cleaning Dianne's wound, he found the blood had stopped flowing. He wiped away the crusted blood and mascara running down her face.

Normally, Dianne would have been annoyed to have seen her messed-up face, but now she chose to be brave, thankful that she'd survived this terror, for now.

"Folks, I'm going back to the SUV to get the first aid kit," Luke said.

"Can I come with you?" Tiffany asked.

After her reservations about going with him earlier, Luke was unsure about this. He was about to refuse when Dianne agreed.

"Let her help. I'll stay here and look after David and Bethany, so off you go, Tiffany, but be careful you don't do something stupid, like I just did. I was trying to watch where we were going."

Luke reluctantly consented, and, as they headed off into the foggy, he turned to Tiffany.

"Hold onto my hand." Luke missed the smile of satisfaction on her face.

"How do you know exactly where to go, Luke?"

"I'll tell you in the morning, if we survive until then," Luke said as they plunged into the foggy darkness.

"Gosh! It's got even worse!" Tiffany said as they went down into the murky depths of the riverbank. She began to imagine shadowy shape-shifting figures in the gloom.

"Please make sure you don't leave me on my own. I'm terrified, this is… wow… this is scary… this fog out here."

Luke was annoyed with himself. *Damn! Why did I think Tiffany could cope with this environment?* He stopped and said, "Okay. I'll take you back to the others."

He headed back up the embankment to the top, dragging Tiffany along. They reached the others, and Tiffany mumbled tearfully, "I didn't realise it would be that bad out there."

Luke was gone in an instant before anyone could speak.

Putting his own feelings aside, he chose to leave Tiffany for her own safety. This was neither the time nor place for any romance.

Adrenalin surged through his system as he continued his search for survivors around McKenzie's Bridge. First, he checked on Mrs Lockwood and saw Rhys still out cold in the back seat. Pearl was half-dozing, gently snoring in the front seat, stretched out as much as she could to make herself more comfortable in the wreckage.

Walking slowly and cautiously to his left, Luke found his way to the edge of the river. He staggered blindly until he found a more accessible section, where he climbed up the bank.

On hands and knees, he reflected on how many hundreds of times he and his family had driven over this bridge without ever giving a thought to how unstable it could be. It had been named after his grandfather Cyrus McKenzie, who built it when he settled here in Steering. There'd never been more than a trickle of water in the river for as long as he could remember.

It took him a couple of minutes to get to the top of the embankment, where he collapsed on the level ground, exhausted from the night's ordeal. Virtually sightless in the thick fog, once he got to his feet, he pulled a branch from a tree to swing from side to side in front of him as he stumbled on.

*Lucky it's not the middle of winter now*, he thought. *But then again, being unable to see anything is almost as bad as freezing half to death.*

Reaching the bridge, he swept the branch along its rickety boards, hoping to snag the capsule, perhaps with Stephen still inside, yet was well aware the capsule may have been carried a considerable distance from the bridge. But he had to start somewhere. Knowing the dimensions of the bridge, he thought it would take between twenty and thirty minutes to search it thoroughly.

Unaware he had passed the bottom part of the capsule twice, he decided to go over the bridge one last time. This time, he bumped into something on the bridge, stumbled forward and knocked whatever it was over the edge. He snatched wildly at it, but it tumbled into the riverbed below. It became stuck, as the water level was now quite low.

"Shit!" he mumbled to himself and turned to head down to the riverbed. He started down the deep embankment on his hands and knees, and then went head-first in his panic to recover the capsule.

As he crawled hastily on, trying to work out where the capsule could have fallen, he bashed his head on one of the bridge's timber uprights. Despite the pain in his forehead, he kept moving, aware of what was at stake.

He then headed across the river. In the back of his mind, he knew it would be at least eight hours before the sun came up.

Mindful of what was at stake, he moved on, continuing to feel around for the capsule, opening his arms as wide as he could to cover as much ground as possible.

*I once caught a fish this big*, he thought before refocusing on the job. *Where did that bloody thought come from? Doesn't matter. The capsule shouldn't be that far from the edge of the bridge…*

Without finding anything resembling a capsule, he started to wonder if it had been the capsule after all.

On the other side of the river, having found nothing, he returned to where he started from, at a loss as to where the bloody capsule had gone. He bumped into what felt like two separate vehicles and piles of debris before he found the capsule, but no Stephen.

*Could the baby have fallen out when I knocked the capsule off the bridge? Or had he already been swept down-river when he fell out of the capsule? But there's hardly any water now,* he thought.

"But, if Stephen fell out anywhere close by, I should be able to hear him crying, unless he's dead or is some distance away, and I can't hear him…" Luke was now talking aloud. "Bloody hell, this is too much to think about! What to do, what to do? Which direction is next? Whichever way is bound to be the wrong way." He continued as though someone was listening to him ramble on, then realised he was talking to himself. "Uh-oh! First sign of madness. Silly me."

Sitting on his wet bottom in the river, frustrated about his next step, he thought, *Do I go this way or that way? Whatever I do, it'll be the wrong bloody decision. Go with your gut. What's your gut telling you?*

Luke eventually climbed the embankment to look over the wooden bridge area again.

At the top, his stomach grumbled, but he dismissed it and continued over the wooden bridge, looking for the baby. Then, he thought he could be spending too much time looking for a body that could be dead, when he should be looking for Bridgette, who might be still alive.

Luke stood upright, stretching his back, and put his arms out and up as if to signal defeat.

"One more sweep for Stephen, and then I'll look for Bridgette," he decided.

He crossed the bridge and the river without finding Stephen or Bridgette, then he remembered the first aid kit in the SUV.

*But where's the vehicle? I don't particularly want to find it, nor see the gruesome remains of my brothers splattered and smeared across the front seat.*

Instead, he returned to Pearl in the Lockwood car, opened her door with a creak that woke her. "I'm sorry, I haven't found the capsule or the baby yet." He hated telling her this.

"Look, I need to get a first aid kit from one of the cars. David or Dianne might need it to help them through the night."

"Look in the back of this car. You might find something next to a big blue bag filled with baby stuff." She started sobbing softly.

"Yeah! Found it!" Luke retrieved the kit, closed the door and said goodbye again to Pearl.

Back with the others, Luke checked Dianne's head wound first, before thinking David's hand should probably be a higher priority. He tried to remove the shirt sleeve, which made David wince in pain.

With Tiffany and Bethany looking on, he removed David's shirt sleeve. They saw bruising and, more significantly, a bone poking through the skin of his wrist. The girls recoiled, shocked.

"Can you hold your father's arm, please?" Luke asked Tiffany. "I'm going to put some antiseptic cream from the first aid kit onto the break, to stop infection."

"Okay."

"Bethany, could you find me a piece of branch or something that could act as a splint," he asked. Bethany, scared to go too far, eventually found something the right size close by. He placed it along the uninjured side of David's arm and wound a bandage around both arm and splint, clipping it in place.

Then, he walked over and put iodine on Dianne's cut, causing her to gasp at the sting. He put a couple of Band-aids over the cut, and, as he moved away, both Bethany and Tiffany gave him a big hug.

Luke took a deep breath. "I'm not having much luck in finding anyone."

No one said anything but he ploughed on. "What happened with the prime mover? How did the sleeper compartment split? Any ideas what might have happened to Bridgette?"

Dianne described the accident in as much detail as she could. "The last thing I remember is Bethany and me in the back. Bridgette was wide awake in the front. My best guess is that she and her father are still in the prime mover, wherever that is."

Luke nodded, wondering if he would ever get any information that would help him deal with this, or any other situation, tonight. He knew he could give up searching and wait here with the others until the sun came up, or go on looking for survivors.

"Oh, bugger it," he said before he stood up and headed off into the fog again without another word.

# 30

## Good on Ya, Frank

Michael Scanlon was on the phone to Frank.

"Well, that's good news to hear, Frank. I hope they're doing okay."

"Yes, they are, except for being a bit wet and tired, especially the old dog, Bert. It helped having Malcolm at the pub."

"Isn't he with the St John Ambulance?" Michael asked.

"Yes, and they'll get a proper examination from him when we arrive in a couple of minutes."

"When you got to the property, Frank, was the family on the roof, where they said they'd be?"

"No, not on the roof of the house, they'd swam a few meters to the shed. It's higher than the house. That was all Margaret and her daughter Norma could manage, and they were bloody glad they didn't have to do it again."

"Yeah! Bet they were."

"When I got to them, they'd managed to get to the top of the shed. That kept them just above the water level, as both the house and shed were down the hill near the river. We were just below and surrounded by the rest of the property. We just managed to get them out safely."

When Margaret and her family arrived at the pub, Malcolm immediately insisted Margaret should lie on a couch so he could examine her.

Frank didn't mention the problem with the propeller when he was on the radio. Now, seeing everyone safe and being looked after, Frank enlisted the help of some locals to go and retrieve his wedged boat.

Brenden and his eight year old son Eric used Frank's GPS to navigate their way through the thick fog but couldn't locate the boat or Frank's car.

Back at the pub, Brenden, Eric and Frank went to the back room to see how the family was recovering.

"Would you three like a beer?" Ian asked.

"Yes, please!" they chorused, then meandered over to another corner in the pub. Eric was excited to think he was getting a beer, but his expression quickly changed when a glass of lemonade was placed in front of him by a smirking Ian. Eric had been happy to be on this adventure, instead of being stuck at home, bored, but still wanted a beer!

Michael Scanlon's unmistakable voice was still blaring from the pub radio.

"It's 10:28pm here on Crazy FM, and, as you heard, all's well with Margaret and her family, who are now safe and sound at the pub. I have Wayne from the SES on the phone. Good evening, Wayne. How's it going out there this evening?"

"Hello Michael, I'm calling about the rescue and what some of the patrons from the pub did this evening. I'd like to pass on my thanks to them. I hope we don't have to call on them again tonight."

"I'm sure they appreciate your thanks, and I hope they're listening to us as they settle in for the night."

"As most people are probably aware, most of the roads around the town are now blocked after the last storm, so please, stay indoors where it's safe. And thanks again, Michael. If I need their help again, I'll surely call you. Goodnight."

"Looking at the radar, we still have a couple of hours to go before the next storm arrives, so if you're in this area, be aware, as we've got more rain to come. Back soon!"

# 31

## What's a Telegram?

After standing ankle-deep in water for the past hour, Scotty was glad to be home in his new digs. He'd showered, put on a T-shirt and shorts and drunk a glass of warm milk to settle his stomach. Then the phone rang: Wayne from the SES.

"Hello Scotty, how's it going? Don't worry! I don't need you out there again. I just want to know what you left on the electronic noticeboard back there."

"Okay. Just three phrases, first SLOW DOWN, then ROAD CLOSED and then finally TURN LEFT HERE."

"Would you mind leaving your phone on, in case it floods again? I'm letting you know this, Scotty, 'cos we're expecting another big storm sometime in the morning."

"Okay, Wayne, sure. Thanks for the heads-up. I'll be ready if it comes to that."

Scotty hung up his phone. He was looking forward to seeing Billy in the morning. He'd missed his little mate.

Back on the embankment, David was resting as comfortably as possible, watched over by Dianne. She interrupted Tiffany and Bethany's quiet conversation to ask, "What are you planning on doing for a job when you leave school, Tiffany?"

Tiffany wasn't really interested in answering; she just wanted to be away from there. But she decided to bite her tongue and suck it up, for not too much longer, hopefully.

"I'm not sure at the moment, but probably something to do with children. Nursing or childcare are high on my list, teaching maybe. Perhaps paediatrics, but that's a lot of study."

"Time will tell. Before you know it, you'll be doing something you love in a couple years."

David butted in, "I don't know what's been in her head for the last few years. She hasn't been herself. Whether that's your normal teenager or something else, I don't know, but something's been wrong. There's been a spark today I haven't seen for a while, so we can only hope."

Tiffany wished he'd shut up. She felt embarrassed, emotional and sad all at the same time. But this was neither the time nor place to bring all this up, so she hid her feelings with a fake smile. Dianne had noticed these signs before, but she didn't know what was troubling Tiffany.

Bethany piped up. "I like what Luke's doing to keep us alive and safe."

"Me, too," Dianne said. "He's doing a great job for such a young man. What was your first job, David?"

He smiled, "Oh! I was a paper boy in the western suburbs of Melbourne. I think I was about ten, twelve. Something like that. I had to get up before most people every morning, I can't remember. I got paid sixpence, if my bike was in good working order, every week. I think when the currency changed in 1966, I got maybe one or five cents per paper."

"What do you mean, the currency changed?" Bethany asked.

"It went from pounds, shillings and pence, like they have in England, to what we have today, Australian dollars and cents, and my pay would have been about $5 per week. It was a lot in those days. I did that job for a couple of years, then when I left school at fifteen, I delivered telegrams for a couple of years on my pushbike."

"What's a telegram?" Bethany asked.

Feeling very old, David explained, "It was like a very short letter. During the Second World War, people were told by telegram when a family member had been killed.

"People complained back then that the government should have been more sympathetic, so eventually someone came with the telegram and offered personal condolences, instead of it being delivered by a taxi," David said.

"Telegrams marked happy moments in our lives, too. They were very special. I know some people still have them in albums from their wedding or other treasured moments."

"Wow, wish I could get a telegram!" Bethany said. "What did they look like?"

Despite their precarious situation, they were all enjoying the conversation—it distracted them.

David said, "Well, it came in an envelope with a clear plastic window at the front. When the telegram was typed up on a machine at the post office and then folded properly, it would show the name and address of the person it was going to in the clear window. Telegrams were always typed all in capital letters. And, as you know, this is taboo today." David laughed.

"We now know upper case, capitals, as *yelling*, except when you want to get your point across. Oh, and there was always the word STOP in capital letters, for the full stop, instead of the dot we use today."

"What sort of people got them?"

"They were usually sent to congratulate someone, or to express sympathy, as well as to deliver money or urgent news. Many people would rush to telegraph offices when someone got married, if they couldn't go to the wedding for any reason. Then, for a bit of fun, you could send a souvenir telegram to families and friends, or even to yourself. At wedding receptions, during the speeches, those telegrams would be read out to everyone, especially the funny or naughty ones."

Bethany giggled a little, much to everyone's amusement, releasing some tension.

David went on, "I went to Beechworth recently, not far from here, and sent a message by Morse code, which first went to someone else, who then sent a telegram to my mother-in-law for her birthday." David described to Bethany what Morse code was and how it worked.

"I believe some companies still have them today, but with emails, Twitter, Instagram and other social media sites, that's probably why they're not heard of much. I reckon there could be a market for some people. Especially some of the older generations that could send one to their children or grandchildren, or even their great-grandchildren. But they were discontinued by the post office sometime in the 1980s or 1990s. Not sure when."

Conversation over, they all wondered what else the long, foggy night would bring.

# 32

## Beware: Animals Ahead

The animals from the abattoir were milling about in an area of about a hundred square metres in the shallow section of the river. All was quiet until the sound of footsteps spooked them. They moved on wherever they could in the fog-dense river, not yet stampeding but very unpredictable.

Luke heard them and stopped dead, trying to work out where the sounds were coming from. He wasn't sure what sort of animals they were, nor how many, so he walked more quietly. Then, a couple of sheep strolled past, almost casually. He fervently hoped it was only sheep he'd heard.

He worked his way along the western side of the river towards McKenzie's Bridge, still keeping a lookout for baby Stephen, Bridgette or Ron.

He found the bridge when he bumped head-first into a timber object, just missing a protruding nail. It seemed like a large wooden fence, so he went on a little further before again walking into something sharp, which hurt his left leg.

"Aaaggghhh! Shit!" he cursed under his breath, aware that a dangerous animal could still be close by.

His hand found what felt like a large tyre. Was this part of the trailer that Dianne had told him was holding the bulls? How many of them were still at large? And where had the prime mover gone?

He wanted to check out the other side of the trailer, but his path was blocked. He walked back, trying to work out how many bulls the trailer could have held but had no idea. Were the animals he'd heard from somewhere else? But

Dianne had said nothing about sheep in the trailer. Then it occurred to him. *Of course, they'd escaped from the abattoir!*

He headed back to the others over the slow-flowing river to the top of the embankment again. He was going to ask them about the abattoir but saw they were all asleep, except Dianne. He was also very tired and sat down to rest, wondering what to do next.

"What's the latest, Luke?" Dianne asked.

"You know I'd have told you straight away if I'd seen any sign of your daughter or husband. I'm sorry, but I haven't. And we're still not out of the woods. I've covered the bridge twice now, with no sign of Stephen, although I did find just the bottom part of the capsule. David's wife Pearl and his son Rhys are still unconscious or asleep in their car. I'm not sure if it's safe to try to move him." He yawned. "I'm stuffed, so I came back here to rest for a while. Don't you go out there. I heard some animals before in the river, and I think I startled them. But here and now, if the weather gets worse again, we'll have to work out where we should go, away from the river."

He paused. "I never thought I'd ever be involved in anything like this."

The consequences of his brutal upbringing—like being constantly told he was useless—had various psychological effects on Luke. However, knowing he was being useful tonight had strengthened his resolve and helped him cope with this horrific night.

Luke had often wondered why he and his brothers had turned out so differently. He'd never know. Perhaps it was his mother's calming influence, compared to his brothers'. They'd all followed in their father's example, making Luke the scapegoat of the family. Being the youngest forced him to learn resilience, yet he was vulnerable at the same time.

"Luke, despite what I know of your family, you've actually had the guts to help us all tonight," Dianne said, "You know, there are those that watch from a distance, while others like you try to work through their difficulties."

"Mmm. Perhaps," Luke said.

"No. Think about it! Our lives are splashed around the world by the media, especially social media, every minute of every hour of every day. Makes you realise that, even though we're all different, we're fundamentally all the same, from our beginning to our end."

"Yeah! I think you're right. I like helping people, and it shouldn't matter if I know them or not, or what colour their skin is either, we're all in this together. We all start out as new human beings. It's the environment and outside influences that shape our lives. In my case, I needed to wake up to the reality that I had to change, like I seem to be doing now, for my own sake." He yawned, tired and overwhelmed.

"It's a bit different from finding someone who's lost on a Cub or Joey Scout camp. This is extreme stuff! Reckon it'd make a great reality TV show."

"Sure would!"

"Look, I've really had it. I don't mean to be rude, but I'm tired, I need to sleep." Luke moved away from Dianne and dropped down on a pile of leaves under a large tree. He closed his eyes and thought, *I must sleep, sleep, sleep and sleep*.

Dianne lay down next to Bethany, worrying where Bridgette and her husband might be. She covered her face so no one would see her cry. Not knowing if her other family members were dead or lost somewhere off the beaten track, she closed her eyes and fell asleep from exhaustion.

Apart from the occasional trickle of water and some nocturnal creatures, all was quiet as the blanket of fog thickened over the river and valley. The temperature, still mild, meant nobody needed a cover over themselves.

With the unrelenting fog, it was a white night in the valley. Everyone knew they should be looking for those who'd disappeared, but in his case, Luke could only do so much in the circumstances.

As the time slowly ticked by around the crash site at McKenzie's Bridge, the survivors' minds were empty.

All the crash victims were confused, injured and mentally drained. Their bodies and minds were screaming for rest, so, eventually, they passed out.

# 33

# Dreamtime

Now that the little darlings, their father and Pearl had gone, Harry wondered why his beloved daughter had been so devoted to David for so long.

He saw his twenty year old cat, Yolly, named after a mate who'd died in the war, sleeping peacefully on a chair facing the window. The cat liked when the afternoon sun appeared. It also let him keep away from the kids' prying eyes. The cat felt more comfortable with old Harry.

Harry had been fifteen when he enlisted in 1943. Like many misguided young Australians seeking the glory of battle, he put his age up when he enlisted.

He always went to bed at around ten p.m. every night, especially since his wife died, allowing him more "me time" than he used to get. He slept well, except for the occasional snort after one too many beers, generally drunk in the company of wartime mates.

He always woke around seven a.m., then pottered around the house or went for long walks, because he still could. Harry hated interruptions to his daily schedule. Life was peaceful and relaxed, like the dream he was having right now about his mates from the war.

Nothing made him suspect that Pearl was now in deep distress.

Pearl had long suffered from insomnia but accepted this as part of her sometimes-jumbled existence. Unlike her father, Pearl welcomed surprises in her life and was always ready to offer a helping hand. The lessons she learned as a Girl

Guide never left her. She was a dedicated mother to her family but equally happy to spread her good nature outside the home.

She often wished that Rhys and Tiffany were involved in Scouts and Guides, but, being in a small community that didn't offer that, their passions leaned more towards sports. She still hoped to involve Stephen in the Scout movement when he grew older. She knew David was not that way inclined but promised herself she would go on camping trips with Stephen as he got older, just the two of them, regardless of what the others thought.

If she ever found him again.

She choked down tears as this hideous thought intruded on her drowsiness.

As for David, sleep had always been good, except for the constant waking brought on by sleep apnoea, a weak bladder and Stephen's frequent crying during the night.

But now, sleep was far from his thoughts. His hand and wrist caused him too much agony for that.

Being in the company of strangers made him determined not to show weakness by whinging about his hand or his missing family. Normally, David couldn't tolerate being disturbed. He had a highly stressful job in transport, after all. He welcomed sleep whenever he could get it.

He'd tried to achieve a reasonable work–life balance, but, after this recent deplorable family holiday, he'd sworn it would never happen again.

His long working hours and lack of good home-cooked meals didn't allow him to socialise with his family and friends as much as he'd have liked. But he got along really well with some of the people at work. He enjoyed meeting other people outside his family and his work.

With an ever-increasing appetite for takeaway, his lifestyle was just as disturbed as his sleep. He could only dream about ever achieving that healthy work–life balance before his bad health habits killed him.

Dianne was holding up well, and so were Luke, Bethany and Tiffany, in spite of what they'd been through. Tiffany was trying not to allow the surrounding gloom to remind her of the night of her rape.

To her surprise, she wasn't feeling the least bit bothered about her current company: Dianne, Bethany and Luke. They didn't look upon her with disdain as her mother did.

In the darkness, nobody could see the restlessness that the awful memory brought on. Here, she had to hold in her emotions. To lose it, to witness the disapproval of the others, was unthinkable. She knew her father was keeping his fears in check too. She had to follow his example.

Eight year old Bethany had never been troubled by peer pressure at school. Now, she was fast asleep, dreaming about her school. Before she fell asleep, she suffered pangs of anxiety about her twin, Bridgette, wondering where she could be. She felt lost and alone without her, even though her mother was next to her.

Bethany excelled in all forms of dance and her favourite instrument was the clarinet. At home, she usually had music to lull her to sleep. Tonight, without this, she played clarinet melodies in her head. Eventually, this helped her fall asleep on the leg of her new friend Tiffany.

Bridgette was still lying semi-conscious in the front section of the prime mover. She drifted in and out of a nightmare. Why was there nobody with her to help her deal with the situation she was in? Where was everyone? To keep panic at bay, she tried to think of her father, his strength and work ethic. She thought about how he always acted as if things would be okay—eventually.

So, she lay back and hoped she'd get through this terrible night. Eventually, sleep claimed her as she thought of playing as many sports as she could. Then, her thoughts settled on her mother, Dianne.

Odd circumstances could unsettle Dianne. Like Bridgette, she'd been a tomboy growing up, yet still retained some feminine charm to use when necessary. Tonight, she was feeling drained by the threatening nature of the weather and her uncertainty about what to do next.

She gazed at the sleeping Luke, who'd heroically set out to help them through the night. Lying there uncomfortably, she wondered what Luke was dreaming about. No one except Luke and his family would know how much he'd been tormented during his childhood, but everyone who'd met the family knew something. To Dianne, he'd been an absolute hero tonight, trying to help as many people as possible.

Still in awe of this 18 year old, at last she drifted off to sleep herself.

Luke had an overwhelming desire to give up his search for Stephen and Bridgette. His failure to find them was preying heavily on his mind, as was the absence of any sign of the truck driver.

Luke normally experienced restless sleep, and there on the embankment he slept with his body contorted, as if preparing for whatever malice Nick might have had in store for him. Some nights were more tranquil than others, but he often stayed half-awake until the early morning, wondering when his siblings would come to torment him.

Maybe everything would look better in the morning, if he survived the night. He'd already witnessed the deaths of three of his brothers, and a part of him was sickened that this had happened, even though he knew it meant the horrors of the past had finished. His light sleep now settled into a deeper slumber.

Near the top of the embankment on the eastern side of the river, Paul still hadn't regained consciousness. Anxiety, shock and the amount of alcohol in his system had caused his collapse. He lay next to a heap of large rocks that he believed would shelter him from whatever might come his way.

Over his life, he'd found a decent night's sleep to be essential for dealing with the rigors of full-time employment. He enjoyed his life, as well as the good money he earned. Having his own room helped him sleep soundly.

Luke's twin brothers had always shared a room with Nick. Born followers, both of them generally enjoyed trouble-free sleep, and the amount of alcohol they regularly consumed helped. Now, though, Paul was lying either asleep or unconscious; it was hard to tell just by looking at him.

Ron, now semi-conscious, lay in river water that was inching up his lower legs. It slowly encroached on his contorted body, still stuck in part of a tree torn asunder by lightning earlier in the night.

With twins and his work life, he hadn't been sure if he wanted to try for a son. Bridgette had seemed more like a boy every day, so he felt he might just not bother.

Unlike most people in the transport game, Ron's waistline and fatigue levels had never caused him concern. He regularly substituted a lunchtime nap for the junk food that most long-distance truck drivers guzzled. Often, Ron would just eat a sandwich he'd prepared earlier in the day.

# 34

## This is Horrible

Blearily, David wondered why he'd only slept for such a short time. But rolling over in his sleep and putting pressure on his broken wrist wasn't helpful for untroubled slumber.

Dianne had too much on her mind to stay asleep for long, and, on finding David was awake too, she decided to keep him company.

They couldn't believe they'd found so many different topics to talk about for so long. "Time flies when you're in good company," she'd remarked to David about two hours before dawn.

Luke was locked in a frighteningly realistic nightmare. Initially, it had just been a sound of something tapping, softly at first, but then with increasing force and volume. Then the sounds were reverberating inside his head. Or were they blows, crashing into his skull from the outside?

Fear pumped adrenalin through his system. He sensed a deep chill, although something else told him the temperature was relatively warm. Someone was smashing a hammer on his head, but there was no pain, just terror.

He raised his hands in his sleep to protect himself, then he screamed, "Please, stop!"

This woke him, and he felt something damp on his face, then the next droplet fell on him from above.

*So that's all it was! Moisture, raindrops or whatever.*

He wondered if the others heard his screams and was ill at ease at the thought.

He felt a slight breeze and saw the fog had lifted a bit. He thought he should wake the others and set some plan of action in place. He saw Dianne and David smiling in his direction. So, they had heard.

"I've just remembered where we were supposed to be staying last night. Do you think the hotel people might be wondering where we got to?" Dianne said.

"My father-in-law's probably snoring his head off right now," David said. "I wouldn't expect him to be worrying about where we are, except maybe about Pearl."

Tiffany and Bethany were woken by the sound of voices and noticed it was starting to rain again. *Not another storm on its way, surely?*

Now that the fog had lifted, the group spotted animals, mainly sheep and horses, wandering through the bush. Someone mentioned the bulls in the truck, but Luke suggested the animals they could see were more likely to have come from the local abattoir.

"What do you reckon we should do now?" Luke asked David and Dianne. "I'm clean out of ideas, but I think we might have another storm on its way, in which case we're going to need to move—and fast."

As if on cue, a flash of lightning illuminated the river and their immediate surroundings, including the animals, startled by the sudden flash.

"Hey! I think I can see a fence over there," Dianne said.

"Nah, sorry. It's the trailer that was transporting the bulls."

"Oh! You could've fooled me."

"I thought the same," he said, "when I banged my head on it last night." Luke pointed towards the bridge and the trailer in the distance, figuring it was about five hundred metres away.

"That's where your wife and Rhys are," he told David.

A crack of thunder and another flash of lightning sent the animals stampeding towards the bridge, frightened and therefore unpredictable, making it all the more difficult for Luke, David and Dianne to decide where to seek refuge from the approaching storm.

"Folks, why don't we climb down the embankment and find David's car? It'd be big enough to be a safe haven for all of us, from both the weather and the animals. And that way we'd all stay together," Luke suggested.

As they gingerly scrambled down, they realised how unsteady they'd become after their long night, hungry, wet, injured and uncertain.

David was so affected he nearly fell head-first but was stopped by Luke both from falling and from further aggravating his broken wrist. They kept a watchful eye on the animals on the other side of the river.

As they reached the bottom of the embankment, the rain bucketed down, accompanied by another flash of lightning and a deafening clap of thunder. The animals underneath and on the other side of the bridge stampeded along the western side of the river.

Luke and the rest of the group decided to go back up the embankment, as another loud peal of thunder scared the animals into a renewed frenzy.

Worse still, the little group recognised a couple of Longhorns in the pack. Horrified, they watched one spear a sheep through its body, lifting the animal off the ground with its left horn. The bull knocked other animals down, adding to the general chaos along the riverbank. Animals were now running in all directions, making it impossible for the group either to reach David's car or to seek refuge elsewhere.

As they attempted to find a safe place away from animals that could kill them, they missed any opportunity to see where Bridgette or Ron might be. Nor could they see the other parts of the river now that torrential rain permanently blocked their view.

Once more, the rain had caused the river to engorge to breaking point. Their visibility was almost zero, as it had been during the fog.

The pounding rain drowned out his voice as Luke tried to scream out to the others. He tried using short phrases, so the others didn't miss out on anything.

"We have to make—a decision. Should we head—for David's car? If this rain continues—it might get washed away—with all of us inside. If we stay here—we've got to keep away—from these bloody animals—particularly the bulls. I still think—the car—is the best option. We can always leave it—if the water gets too high."

"See that?" Bethany pointed to a fallen tree-trunk she'd noticed earlier, lying across the bridge. She yelled into her mothers' ear, "We could climb down—that big branch—and get into the car—through the sunroof."

Nobody stopped to think how impressive a plan this was, especially coming from a frightened eight year old. Dianne gave Bethany a big hug.

"What're we waiting for? Let's go!" Luke shouted.

At the embankment near McKenzie's Bridge, fatigued but excited, they all surged forward without further thought. Slipping and sliding in the mud, the rain intensified as they attempted to clamber further up the embankment. David was trying hard to stay focused to protect his injured hand.

Tiffany had been reflecting on their predicament. She decided she'd be the one to help her injured father into the car, via the large branch. She hoped this might show Luke and the others that she recognised the seriousness of their situation.

The river was rising faster than they'd expected, so when they reached the branch on the bridge, Bethany's brilliant idea seemed fraught with difficulty. Luke still thought it was strong enough to take their weight, one at a time, starting with David.

"Okay, now we're here, I think we ought to shift this branch over here a bit. That'd make it easier to get to the car."

"No, I think it should stay right here, because what if…"

Still arguing, everyone looked like drowned rats; they didn't yet understand the torrential rain made it impossible to manoeuvre the branch anywhere.

As tempers frayed and the debate raged, Bethany shouted, "Stop yelling at each other," and started crying.

"With all this bloody rain and with animals on the loose, we were just blowing off steam." Dianne's explanation didn't work with Bethany.

"What are you talking about, 'blowing off steam'?" she asked.

Again, Luke took control. "Hey, I couldn't shift it before, so I need you guys to help me wrangle this large branch into a better position."

"Yeah, sure."

"Think it might be a good idea to throw something at the car first, to wake Pearl?" Tiffany surprisingly spoke up, yelling, and grabbed the other end of the branch. "We need to let her know what we're planning."

"Hey! Yes! That makes sense. Also," Luke continued, "Tiffany, you can hold the far end of the branch steady."

Luke hurled a small branch down onto the car, where it landed with a thump, but Pearl didn't appear.

They squinted over the railing but saw no movement from below, not that they *could* see much. Luke now wanted a bigger piece to throw. When another flash of lightning lit up the area, he found a thicker piece of branch and could see the car more clearly.

He saw the water had reached the door handles, then Luke was momentarily blinded by another flash of lightning. He tripped and fell heavily.

The same flash struck a tree at the end of the bridge, sending it crashing down towards where Luke still lay. At the last moment, adrenalin kicked in, and he scrambled out of the way, just as the tree slammed onto the bridge with a mighty *whoosh*.

He climbed shakily over the tree, found a suitably thicker branch, and once again flung it down onto the car. This time it made a resounding thud. The large sunroof, cracked and warped, opened, and Pearl's head popped out.

Again, Luke's voice battled the racket of rain and wind. "Hey, Pearl, we're coming to join you. There's a few of us here."

She yelled back, "Okay, fine, but have you found my baby yet?"

Luke and the others looked at each other's perplexed expressions. Nobody knew quite how to answer this, so they pretended they hadn't heard her.

Luke and Dianne lifted up the end of the large branch, attempting to slide it over the edge of the bridge, but it simply wedged in the railings.

They freed it with Tiffany's help and guided the bottom end of the branch into the open sunroof. Pearl peered up at them, rain pelting down on her face, and she gamely tried to grab the branch and pull it down into the car. The heavy rain was making it hard for her to see. When the branch smacked into her shoulder, she fell back into the vehicle as the branch slid across the roof and away towards the side of the car.

On the bridge, everyone held on to the other end as tightly as they could to stop the entire branch plunging off the car into the river. Luke climbed over the edge of the bridge then climbs down its support timbers to the car, grabbing onto the bottom of the branch then straining to lift it.

"Pull! PULL!" he shouted. Eventually, with great difficulty, he succeeded in manoeuvring it in through the sunroof.

"You go first, Bethany. It was your good idea," Dianne told Bethany.

"And when you get there, get into the back seat," Luke told her.

She climbed down gingerly, making sure her feet were in the right place. Her early years spent climbing frames in parks and the playground now came in handy. Eventually she made it into the car, as directed, then climbed, exhausted and shaking, into the back seat.

She looked across and saw a boy lying in the seat next to the other window, and wondered if he was dead, unconscious or asleep.

Luke then climbed back up to the bridge in time to stop Tiffany from helping Dianne onto the branch.

"Hang on. I need you up here, Dianne, to help David get down."

Tiffany went next, scrambling down the branch and in through the sunroof without incident. She hopped into the back with Bethany, glad to be out of the rain, while Pearl remained slumped in the driver's seat.

She turned to the two girls. "Did Luke find my baby?"

Both looked at each other, hesitated, then said, "No." Pearl gave a loud sob and turned her back on them.

Back on the bridge, Dianne helped David climb over and onto the branch, Luke right beside him on the slender length of wood, while Dianne held onto the branch with one hand and David with the other. Together, they guided him down the branch.

David winced and moaned with pain from his wrist and the effort involved. The combined weight of the three of them set the branch creaking and wobbling.

David eventually reached the top of the vehicle and was lowered carefully into the passenger seat by Luke and Dianne. As he dropped down, he knocked his broken wrist, sending pain shooting through his arm, but this didn't stop him from reaching out for Pearl. They embraced awkwardly, with Pearl sobbing while gabbling words that only David could interpret.

Equally concerned at the fate of his infant son, David tried hard to comfort her, without admitting he had no idea where Stephen could be.

The river's raging torrent had now reached the top of the car.

"Quick! Get in, Dianne!" Luke urged. "Close the sunroof!"

"You follow me!" Dianne screeched over the rain at Luke.

As she placed her feet inside the sunroof, she accidentally stood on David's thigh, pushing his broken wrist against Pearl's body. David screamed in agony but moved out of the way to give Dianne enough room to get inside the car.

Luke, however, scrambled back up the branch. He knew there'd be no room for all of them in the vehicle. He pulled the bottom of the branch free of the sunroof, but a sudden gust of wind caught the branch, sending it spinning down onto the embankment. Luke, thrown clear, landed heavily on the same embankment.

The car's distraught occupants could all see this but were unsure whether he'd been knocked unconscious. Dianne and David struggled to close the sunroof, but it had been warped in the accident and now had a gap of a couple of inches. Water was gushing into the vehicle and was now above their ankles, working its way up their legs towards their hips. If they couldn't stem the flow, water would eventually fill the car.

Dianne turned in the cramped space to ask Tiffany, "Is there anything in the back of the car we can use as a hammer?" While Tiffany searched the back of the car, David groped for the steering-wheel lock and handed it to Dianne.

She started hitting it against one end of the sunroof, but David stopped her.

"Sorry, I don't think that's helping. Maybe we should try and remove the bottom part of the sunroof, and then hopefully we can see the other side of it and force it forward enough to close it."

"David, where's Stephen?" Pearl asked, oblivious to all else around her.

"I don't know, darling. Luke told us about finding you alive and how worried you were about Stephen. He looked for him for nearly two hours in the fog but couldn't really see or feel his way around."

"There was fog? Oh yeah, that's right, sorry. I've been asleep—or out of it. I forgot how thick it was."

"I'm sorry, Pearl, but right now we need to get this roof closed before we all drown. Stephen's life is in the hands of the gods right now."

Pearl reacted violently and unpredictably. "You never wanted Stephen in the first place, did you? You're to blame if he dies, you prick." She began whacking his broken wrist. David cried out in distress, then Pearl slumped forward, passing out once more. Anguish, fear and sorrow all at once became too much for her.

Everyone else in the car remained quiet, unsure how to react. David cleared his throat, took a deep breath then broke the silence.

"Dianne, could you find something to rip open the material on the inside of the roof?"

Focused only on the water pouring in uninterrupted, no one noticed something moving towards them.

Whatever it was, it slithered down one of the bridge supports, plummeted into the river, found its way through the roof of the car, then fell onto someone's shoulder.

# 35

## We Can Help

Steering's population of five hundred and fifty-three residents had remained stable until twenty years before, when the town's economy began to decline. In the boom years after the Second World War, Jeff Steering, his father and grandfather had worked hard to maintain a healthy and motivated community.

The family name still commanded respect for its integrity, but people had noticed an element of arrogance as well, perhaps stemming from the strong ties the family enjoyed with those in high places.

Now, with the town facing the aftermath of the recent floods, the Steerings sought information from the SES about families still needing help or rescue. The senior management team consulted a list of likely properties and rang them.

Jeff Steering had suggested going to the Miller property first and then working back towards the town. Proximity to the river could mean problems for the Millers, particularly if the renewed rainfall persisted. In fact, the entire town could be under water within a couple of hours. The current radar described the storm as slow-moving but with the possibility of dumping more than another one hundred millimetres in the next two hours.

Jeff and his helpers headed off through the steadily increasing rainfall towards the Millers' property, directly in the path of the oncoming front as it moved slowly southeast.

# 36

# Weather Update

At Crazy FM, Michael and Robyn were intent on providing the vast area they covered with regular updates from the SES and weather services. Michael was hoping to hear from any residents who needed help with specific problems.

"Maybe they're ringing in just to help you stay awake," Robyn joked. She answered a call from Wayne at the command centre in town and put him through to Michael.

"Hello Wayne, what can you tell us about this latest storm-front? It came through here about fifteen minutes ago. Jeff Steering and I were talking about it just before midnight. I saw it on the radar back then, and I had some sort of idea how long it was going to take to get here. For some reason, it hasn't done what I thought. So, can you explain to me what's happening with it now, and what you expect it to do over the next few hours?"

"Hello, Michael. Okay, what it's doing is quite simple. It's slowing down. The gap between this system and the one we had late last night is part of a high-pressure system forcing its way in between them, and this is causing the second front to stagnate." Wayne paused.

"As you can probably see on the radar, the more colourful parts are around the district and the town of Steering. This is worrying the SES, as it's uncertain how much time they have to get people off their properties and who they should prioritise. This all depends on a number of variables, which the SES has under control. But, because of the first storm, there are places where the water hasn't receded as quickly as it has in other areas. Anyway, we'll push on through the night and hopefully save those who are stranded and get them to higher ground as quickly and safely as possible. And, as you can understand, people take priority over livestock."

"Thanks Wayne. This Saturday morning here on Crazy FM, I'm talking with Wayne from the SES here in Steering. Can you tell us how long you're expecting this current low-pressure system to last? And what parts of the district are you focusing on presently?"

"We've got most of our volunteers out on the eastern side of the town, where it's been raining the longest. We're moving residents from there onto higher ground. Most of those on the western side of town are well above the current river level. It's estimated to flood sooner rather than later. But that doesn't mean the rest of the district won't receive its fair share of rain.

"Then, there are the valleys near the abattoir that are prone to flooding. But the only part likely to be affected is the river between the two wooden bridges. Nobody in their right mind would be out there at the moment. It would be suicidal. Other than that, most of the roads around Steering are flooded and cut off. Most of the shops, especially the pub, petrol station and the police station, are above the flood levels."

"That's good to hear, Wayne. I know there's a few people at the pub who'll probably be relieved to hear that news. Ian, Emily and a couple of others are looking after those folks who've just been rescued. Thanks again for that, Wayne, we'll talk later to get another update."

"Bye, Michael. It certainly helps having your station keeping residents updated. And I know you had to do a double shift tonight, so hope that's going okay?"

"Yeah, it's been tough, but Robyn has helped me out, and I grabbed a couple of hours sleep when she took over. Robyn's younger than I am, and she's used to staying out late partying, as you can imagine."

"I can indeed! On that note, see ya, Michael."

The interview ended and Michael moved on to his next caller for an update. "I have Ian from the pub on the phone. Hi Ian, what's happening at your end, mate?"

"Yeah, it's all quiet here, most of 'em are asleep, and it's only me, Emily, Tommy and Frank still awake. I don't think Frank's all there. He's forgotten he doesn't know where his boat is any more, and I don't want to spoil the party. He's in the other room so he can't hear what I'm saying. We'll keep listening to the goings on for the rest of the morning, till sun-up, about seven."

"That's still another couple of hours away, Ian, and anything could happen before then. We won't even know till the morning what the full extent of the damage is. Thanks, Ian, we'll talk again soon."

Michael wound up his session and disconnected the call.

"Meanwhile, if anyone wants to give us a call, if there's anyone out there still awake, please do. I was going to talk about other things, but I'll cop some zeds instead and let Robyn tell you what the rest of the morning brings." Michael yawned theatrically. "G'night—oh, hang on, I mean good morning."

# 37

# Amusement Ride... Not

Fifteen centimetres of water in the bottom of most family cars will make them either stall or lose control. Twice that amount would float many vehicles. Sixty centimetres or more of rushing water will move most vehicles along with the current, even heavier ones like SUVs, station wagons and utes.

Being unconscious for more than thirty minutes can cause brain damage, sometimes irreparably. But it's not always possible to determine how long someone has been unconscious or whether they're asleep or suffering severe concussion. An unconscious individual on their own in this state is obviously at greater risk.

Ron and Rhys were both in this condition off and on since the accident. After being thrown from the prime mover, Ron now faced the threat of drowning. The water had reached his waist and was rising. The force of the river was beginning to loosen the large branch wedging his arm against the bank. Eventually, he fell free and was washed down the river towards the entrance to the creek.

Here, the flow from the creek entered the river and diverted Ron over to the western bank, out of immediate danger.

Luke, meanwhile, was climbing up the embankment moments after being thrown off the bridge. The car carrying his companions was lifted from its temporarily secure spot on the eastern embankment and now hurtled down the river towards the smaller wooden bridge.

After scrambling to his feet, Luke ran desperately along the top of the bank, keeping pace with the car's progress along the fast-flowing river. He had difficulty keeping the car in view through the driving rain, but he recognised the second bridge looming ahead.

*Will the low-level bridge stop the car? Or will it become jammed or continue speeding under the bridge and on down the river?* he wondered.

Then, he glimpsed what looked like someone floating in the river.

*God, was someone washed from the car because they couldn't close the roof in time?*

Luke crawled down the bank again, leaned out over the water and snagged the body, dragging it out of the way of the car just in time. Despite the fast-flowing current, he hauled the body above the river level and onto the lower part of the embankment.

The car floated past, rising up and down with the undulating flow as if in slow motion. He could see Dianne doing something inside, to the car's roof. Luke could see it wouldn't make it under the bridge and winced when it hit the ancient timbers with a cracking sound.

His worst fears were realised when the car stopped, jammed in the limited space between the bottom of the river and the bridge and facing into the raging torrent. Water flowed over the bonnet, up the windscreen, over the top of the car, and in through the still slightly partially open sunroof.

Helpless, desperate and frustrated, Luke dragged the heavy, wet body along the slight slope of the embankment, away from the river until he reached the dirt road. He turned the body on its side, then again onto its back. He checked for a pulse but couldn't find one. Thinking this unknown person had died, he returned to the embankment.

Back at the river's edge, a flash of lightning showed him the fully submerged car stuck under the bridge. Luke could see that if the river was a foot lower, the car would have gone under the smaller wooden bridge. Mindful of the unstable terrain, he hurried towards the rickety, creaking bridge, climbed up on it and over the lower railing, then scrambled carefully down to the car.

With his feet on the cross-members of the bridge, he reached the roof of the car, ignoring the floodwaters furiously rushing past him. He thumped downwards with his boot, hoping he wasn't not too late, and they weren't all dead.


Inside the car, Dianne squinted against the driving rain through the sunroof, praying it was Luke making that noise on the roof.

"Open the roof, and I'll drag you all out onto the bridge!" he yelled. But the sunroof was stuck fast.

"David's been bitten by a snake! It got in through this fucking sunroof." She cursed, and, at the same time, he heard muffled cries for help coming from the two girls in the back seat. Kneeling on the roof, he asked, "Where's the snake now?"

"It's curled up at David's feet. It's either asleep or protecting... I don't know... guarding its prey, do they do that? It hasn't moved since it bit David. Don't know what it's doing! Don't know anything about snakes."

"Okay. Got that. But if it's not moving, maybe you're all okay for now. Just hang in there, okay? I'm going to get something to cover this opening to stop you all from drowning."

He was torn between wondering what he could use as a cover, and how he'd tell Dianne he thought he'd found her dead husband. That was if the body was her husband's.

He went back to where the body lay. Despite the ceaseless rain, it was still quite mild.

He started removing the heavy, soaked clothing from the body, thinking it could be jammed into the sunroof. The body moved, and a voice demanded, "What the bloody hell's going on?"

Luke recoiled. "I thought you were dead!"

"Well, it's bloody obvious I'm not. Who the hell are you, and why are you trying to undress me, ya filthy pig? Ya think I'm dead, so what did ya want me clothes for, ya mongrel?"

Luke stood there dumbfounded until the man kicked him on his leg, snapping him out of his stunned state.

"Well, answer me, for god's sake… shit."

Overwhelmed, Luke burst out, "Are you Ron? Your wife's trapped in the car down there in the river, and I was gonna take your clothes to stop the water from getting in through the sunroof. It's stuck open."

"Shit, why didn't ya say so, son, we could have been there by now. C'mon! Let's go then."

As Ron stood up quickly, dizziness made him nearly tumble head-first down the embankment. Luke rushed to him and turned him over. "Are you all right?"

"Just get me pants off and get over to the car, quick smart."

Luke did as he was told, and, by the time he reached the car, struggling to keep standing on the slushy, muddy road, the water had almost reached the bottom of the windscreen.

He clambered once more onto the roof and jammed the pants into the open section. "Does that help?"

"Yes, it does." Dianne scrambled around in the front of the vehicle, looking for some reassurance, but they were all preoccupied with how they felt.

She frowned as she stared at the pants, now shoved into the gap.

"Where'd you get these pants? They look familiar."

"I got them from your husband. I thought he was dead, but he's not, he's alive. He's up there by the bridge. He'll be here as soon as he can. He's just recovering."

"Oh my God, how is he? Where is he? Is he okay? Give him my love," then, as an afterthought, "The pants seem to work, at least they're keeping the worst of it out. It should be okay till it stops raining and the water goes down. Now, all we've got to worry about is that bloody snake."

"Okay, I'm going back to where Ron is now."

But then, as he headed back to the bridge, he turned, hearing the sickening sound of heavy timber creaking, just in time to see the bridge break slowly into two halves, its bottom timbers heaving out of the water. This freed the car, but Luke could only watch in helpless horror as it was carried away down the river and out of sight.

"Go and follow the car and see where it goes," Ron hollered. "Don't worry about me!"

Luke sprinted off down the track, trying to catch up to the car.

At the northern end of the river, past the larger wooden bridge, some of the bigger animals had gathered. They'd felt safe, as there hadn't been any lightning or rain for a while, but had now become trapped in the river with this latest burst of flooding.

Some of the smaller sheep were tossed about along the now raging river. Luke heard another crash and saw the animals that were trapped in the other end of the river had begun scrambling over and bouncing off some of the fast-flowing tree-branches. Sheep were being flung about in the current, but, more alarmingly, a couple of the larger bulls had crashed into the remains of the smaller bridge, breaking it into still smaller sections.

The rain had eased, but Luke's vision was limited to around ten metres. He saw no sign of the car, so he continued on, watching as waves of water surged down-river carrying a large dead horse. Then, during another flash of lightning, he spotted the car, lying on its side on the far side of the river, its roof clear of the flowing water.

Urgently, Luke searched for something big enough to hold onto while he manoeuvred in the torrent and saw an old car tyre on the bank. He checked the tyre for snakes, then the river, and, taking a deep breath, waded in carefully, clutching the tyre. Seconds later, his feet were swept from under him by the current that forced him under water.

When he resurfaced, he'd been taken past the car and was still moving away from it, so he tried desperately to grab onto something. He missed a branch and went under again, working his legs and arms to get himself to the eastern side. One last shove, and Luke grabbed onto another branch.

A few hundred metres down the river, he saw the river was widening and slowing down. The tyre had long gone, so he made several futile attempts to clutch at another branch before swimming back to the bank he started from, but some distance downstream.

Gasping, he struggled onto the muddy embankment and collapsed. He rolled over to see how far he was from the car but found no sign of it.

"God, I hope this is a dream," he thought aloud. "I'm getting tired of this brave-man shit." He got to his feet and started back upstream towards the car, stumbling on the uneven ground, noticing the odd animal corpse floating past him in the river, hoping to see no human ones.

When he reached the car, he knelt down, out of breath and panting loudly, not realising those noises could alert those inside that someone was outside to help them. He had to stand up to take a few deep breaths, then knelt down again to look at the occupants through the front window. They all seem senseless or maybe dead. Frantically, he tapped on the window, and, to his relief, both Dianne and Tiffany stirred.

The car was sufficiently far enough out of the water for Tiffany to open the door. Luke grabbed the open door and forced it backwards as far as he could until the hinges snapped. Then, he dragged Tiffany, then Dianne, out of the car and onto the embankment.

Rhys, who'd come around at last, was checked by Luke to see if it was safe to move him. Satisfied, his injuries were not serious, at least not visibly so, Luke pulled Rhys clear and then Bethany. Luke wrenched the front door open to find David and Pearl slumped together. More alarmingly, he saw the snake stirring in the muddy water at their feet.

He spoke as calmly as he could. "Are you okay, Pearl?"

"Yes. Who's that?"

"It's me, Luke. Is David okay?"

"No, I'm not sure."

"Okay, I'll be back in a second."

"Have you found Stephen yet?"

"No, I bloody haven't," Luke replied with more venom than he meant to. Then his face changed to regret and shock. He couldn't believe he'd just said that in that way. All these experiences tonight must be getting to him; he'd never reacted like this before.

Tiffany yelled at her mother. She'd wanted to do that for such a long time. But Luke pulled her away without realising her built-up anger was ready to explode. Now, she could only grind her teeth in frustration.

# 38

## She Listens to the Radio

Enthusiasts have a habit of improving their toys. Just like Ron did, when he bought his new prime mover. Adding another set of 24-volt batteries under the bonnet improved the function of the mobile phone, and also meant the radio could function in all kinds of situations, like the one now faced by Bridgette.

Bridgette lay semi-conscious in the front of the prime mover that was still resting on the town side of the embankment. After the trailer fell into the river, most of the bulls had struggled free.

Now, consciousness was returning, and Bridgette slowly moved her head away from the side window, opened her eyes and sat up. Her eyes flickered as she tried to focus on her surroundings. The darkness didn't help.

She expected to see her father but found only an empty seat. She twisted around to her right, looking for her mother and sister. To her horror, she found the compartment empty. It hit her like a blow to the stomach: she was all alone.

She screamed out for anyone who might hear her, but, after a while she collapsed, hoarse and exhausted. She began to sob hopelessly. The heavy rain was still hitting the outside of the prime mover, and she knew nobody could hear her over the heavy backdrop of falling water.

She could see the front of the prime mover lying almost at the top of the eastern side of the embankment, with the noisy river surging past.

Where was her family? What if the river came into the cab? Aware now of the absolute vulnerability of her situation, her sobs and screams merged into a desperate wail.

After a while, she stopped, slumping back into her seat. No sound was coming out of her mouth. Looking around the inside of the cab, she spied the radio and phone on the dash. Bridgette unbuckled her seatbelt and turned on the radio, amazed that it hadn't been affected by the crash and still had plenty of current from the batteries. She heard a voice, Michael Scanlon. She listened, hoping she might learn what had happened to her family.

"Michael Scanlon here on Crazy FM on this wet and eventful Saturday morning. We have Wayne on the line from the SES."

Bridgette stopped crying, astonished at how much time had passed since... what?

"How's it going out there, Wayne?"

"It's still raining in most parts of the district, Michael, but nearly all the heavy stuff's passed, and it's headed towards the western part of the state before turning towards Melbourne. They won't get as much as we got here, as it's breaking up now. The worst is over. I'm even expecting sunny skies for the rest of the day."

Bridgette liked the sound of that. She yelled at the radio, her muddled brain thinking someone might hear her.

"That's when the sun finally comes up, in about two hours from now. We'll get to see what and where real damage has been done to the district."

Bridgette shouted again at the radio. "I'll drown if someone doesn't come and rescue me soon!"

"At the moment, there are a few annoying showers around, but I'm only expecting them to last for about another half an hour at the most. As for the flooding, the worst part has been in the river on the western side of town. To our knowledge most of the town of Steering's population has been accounted for, except for a couple of families. They could be out of town for whatever reason, and we won't know until about midday. Luckily, no lives have been lost so far, and we hope there won't be any, but it's too early to tell. As for injuries, well that's something else we're not fully aware of, either. The number of people rescued by the SES, including that family at the pub we discussed earlier, won't be known until later in the day. The only concern we have here at the command centre is another possible storm later in the week. Hopefully, we can clean up as much as we can from this one and be ready for the next one, if and when it comes."

"Thanks, Wayne, for your time and the updated information. I'll call you again in about an hour to see if you've got anything further to report. Bye for now."

"Thanks again for your support, Michael. I hope things can calm down a bit now."

Bridgette thought, *Nobody knows about what happened to us! I have to tell them*. Her eyes fell on the phone. She picked it up and could hear a woman talking. She tried to get her attention by yelling into the mouthpiece, but quickly became frustrated when there was no response.

Somehow, the phone line was still connected to the radio station from earlier in the night when Ron called Michael. But the light above the switch at the station was not working, and the switch was in the up position, so Robyn was unaware Bridgette wanted to speak to her. Some of the equipment at the station hadn't been fixed for a few weeks.

Although the station had had a number of callers from around the district over the past few hours, most said they were okay. Calls had come either from those still at their properties or from truckies on the roads in between towns on the outskirts of the district.

# 39

## Let's Party

Bridgette, frustratingly, could still hear voices on the other end of the phone, but no one was listening to her yelling and screaming. She fervently wished Michael would stop discussing the weather and do something about coordinating her rescue. She cheered up a bit when she noticed the sound of the rushing water seemed to be lessening. Sitting uncomfortably in soaking wet clothes, all she could do now was wait.

"Is there anyone out there in radioland wanting to call in at this godforsaken hour?" Michael Scanlon asked. "Robyn, what's it like being awake at this time? I'm usually off with the fairies."

"You don't really think about the time if you're having a lot of fun dancing or making out with someone on the dance floor. Then, before you know it, three or four hours have passed, it's time to go home, and you hit the pillow and fall asleep. The next thing you know it's Sunday afternoon and, depending on how much you've had to drink, you could have one hell of a hangover that won't go away till the next day. But I know what I'll be doing tonight, if I can get out of here with all of this bloody flooding! Each one of us girls will be texting each other about six p.m. to decide where to go."

"How many girls are there?" Michael asked.

Robyn replied, "Oh, about thirty-five of us, and sometimes some of the girls bring their partners along, but it's better with just us girls. If they have partners, hopefully they won't find out if we let our hair down. As they say, what they don't know won't hurt 'em."

Michael was amazed. "Thirty-five! Bloody hell, I might even have a chance with one of them. And who knows, I might just be ready to settle down with someone on a more permanent basis, so look out. I think we'll leave it there, Robyn, just in case someone underage is listening to this."

"Come on, Michael, it's five in the morning, so not even the farmers are up for their morning milking. The only others listening are the folks at the command centre, a few truckies and whoever's listening at the pub."

Bridgette couldn't believe what she'd just heard and started to giggle at what Michael said about underage kids listening in at five a.m. Well, she was underage, and she was listening, even if she *was* in the middle of nowhere.

She tried again to get someone's attention on the phone but, after a few minutes, put it on top of the casing, disappointed. The water outside had almost dwindled to a trickle, and Bridgette leaned against the back of the seat and wondered where her family was. As the river continued slowing, she watched a vast amount of debris being carried along with it, wondering where it had all come from.

A song came on the radio that she recognised, and she sang along with it. With no one else around, she let her voice carry through the early morning. Above her, on the top of the bank, were a few of the animals from the abattoir. They turned their heads in the direction of Bridgette's voice, but then went back to what they were doing: nothing much.

# 40

## Follow the Leader

Back in Melbourne, journalist Jo-Anne, Scotty's lover, had worked hard to discover his whereabouts. She was now waiting at the railway station for Billy, because she knew he was going somewhere to meet Scotty. Billy was due to catch a train to a strange-sounding country town in north-western Victoria, Steering.

Unbeknownst to her, Jo-Anne had been followed to the station by hitman Milo, under instructions from the Boss to eliminate both her and Scotty.

The Boss had told Milo in a recent meeting that Jo-Anne's snooping was starting to have an unhealthy effect on his business interests. Milo was to contact him when he'd taken care of both his targets.

A message came over the loudspeaker at the station: "All passengers on the train to Steering and all stops before are advised that the train has been cancelled and replaced by two coaches. All passengers should proceed to the rear of the station, where you will find the two coaches. Please show your tickets to the stationmaster. One coach stops at all stations until it reaches Bendigo. The other will travel express to the end of the line, from stations between Bendigo, Steering and Mildura."

Since Milo had no idea where Steering was, he struck up a conversation with Billy, who, in his naïve way, looked up at this big man standing on his right and wondered if he was also confused about which coach to catch.

"Where do you go?" Milo asked,

"Steering," Billy told him.

"Me too," Milo said.

They approached the stationmaster to ask him which bus they were on when the stationmaster turned to a colleague. "We can get moving once we get these knuckleheads on their right coach."

Deeply insulted, Milo grabbed the back of the stationmaster's collar, lifted him off the ground and asked him to repeat what he just said.

"Now you can give apology to me and my short friend here," he growled in his Ukrainian accent.

The stationmaster could hardly get the words out, terrified by the sheer size of Milo and having difficulty breathing.

"Gosh, mate, sorry! Didn't mean to cause any trouble," he sheepishly apologised to them both. Milo put him down gently, and the stationmaster pointed nervously to the second of two coaches.

Jo-Anne, patiently watching the proceedings nearby, climbed aboard the relevant coach, leaned her seat back and prepared for a nap. Milo did the same, also looking forward to some much-needed rest. He set the alarm on his watch so he wouldn't miss the stop and lose his targets. But the lump on his right side was making him uncomfortable.

"I hope you don't mind, because of large size, I'm going to sit on own, so I can spread out bit more. One small seat not comfortable for big Milo." He knew immediately he shouldn't have spoken his name aloud, but nobody seemed to have noticed.

Billy nodded and replied, "You stay here, and I'll go over there. There's plenty of other empty seats available. I think I understand why they cancelled the train."

Jo-Anne observed all this, thinking that where they sat was unimportant as long as she could keep an eye on Billy. She wasn't sure whether or not Billy has seen or recognised her. Milo lifted the centre armrest and found a more comfortable position to rest in the twin seats.

Billy was also comfortable and ready for the long journey ahead.

# 41

## Please Hold My Hand

The wind had died down and the rain had stopped, but the fog quickly replaced it as a barrier to good visibility. Tiffany and Bethany were looking after Rhys, who was still a bit drowsy.

"Hey, Dianne," Luke whispered, "can you find me a long stick? I still need to deal with this damn snake near David's feet."

Luke, about to plan his attack on the snake, heard Pearl ask him yet again about baby Stephen. Then Dianne returned with a branch, giving him an excuse to ignore Pearl's question. Instead, he asked, "Do you know where the snake bit David?"

"Somewhere on his neck, and I think it was only once, but I can't be sure. I saw it slither down to where it is now. It's been there ever since."

Luke guessed it had probably been a couple of hours since they all went down the tree into the car, and, because neither he nor Pearl had been able to find a pulse, he wondered if David was dead. He knew he'd have to deal with the snake before he could get David out of the car.

Imagining how difficult that would be, he decided to tell Pearl what he planned to do and get Ron to help him.

Earlier, when Luke had told Dianne and Bethany the good news about finding Ron alive, they'd both wept with relief.

"I hope I can fetch Ron to help get David out of the car," he told them. Then he stopped. "Oh shit, that's right."

"What?" Dianne asked anxiously.

"The bridge is broken in two so there's no way I can get to Ron, and he can't get to us unless we wait for the river to go down, and that could be another hour. And we can't forget about Bridgette and the baby. Bloody hell, where on earth can they be? This is ridiculous. It's about five in the morning, there's another two hours to go before sunrise just before seven a.m., we can't see anything. And I'm stuffed again."

Dianne could see Luke was running on empty. "Look, just sit down for a few minutes and get your breath. Now, how do you know when the sun comes up?"

"Oh, I just know shit. Shit! Sorry, I didn't mean to say that."

Tiffany came over to console him, but he moved away from her.

"Just leave me alone to think!"

Dianne could see Tiffany was in a huff. "Let's go over here with Bethany and Rhys. Let's see if *we* can think of what to do."

Because of what he'd done for them all, Tiffany's feelings for Luke had increased, and although he'd rebuffed her she knew how shattered he must feel.

"Do we wait for the river to subside or what?" he asked, obviously tired.

She didn't reply but turned and followed Dianne to where the children were.

"Older people are always arguing," Bethany said to Rhys.

"What are you talking about?" Tiffany asked Rhys.

"Mind your own business, bitch." Before he had a chance to finish, Dianne put her hand over his mouth to remind Rhys he was with people he didn't know well enough to be his normal, abusive self.

"Rhys's got a girlfriend!" Tiffany taunted him, as if the past few hours had never happened.

He was about to lash out when Dianne intervened. "Both of you, stop! Grow up, would you? This won't help us get out of here, so I'm begging you both, please, whatever it is you have against each other, shut up. This is neither the time nor place for your quarrelling."

Neither took any notice. "Wish you were still asleep," Tiffany yelled at Rhys.

"And I wish you were dead, you bitch."

Shocked at this vicious bickering, Dianne clutched Bethany and returned to Luke.

"We're heading towards the bridge. As far as I'm concerned, those two can stay where they are. I'm not having them behave like that in front of Bethany. They're a bloody disgrace."

Luke got to his feet, and the three of them started walking back to the smaller bridge. Tiffany and Rhys's verbal stoush faded in the background.

Without warning, the quarrelling stopped when the pair realised they'd be stranded in the fog with dangerous animals around and ran to catch up with the other three.

"Don't either of you say a word!" Dianne thundered.

Luke added, "Okay, Rhys, get up here with me. Now! And you, Tiffany, walk behind with Dianne and Bethany."

"But I…"

"If you or Rhys so much as say one word, I'll make sure you regret it, that clear? I don't need this shit, so shut the fuck up." Luke interrupted, staring menacingly at both of them to reinforce his words, thinking it was probably only the second time he had used that word in his entire life. But he just knew some idiots needed that sort of aggressive jolt.

They dropped their heads and did as they were told, but Bethany looked bewildered. This was the second time in as many hours that she'd heard that word.

After the way Luke said it, she now knew the difference from how it was used by some of the other students at school, who only said it to act tough.

Luke continued to set a slow pace to avoid the rocks in their path, when the moon broke out from behind a break in the fog. This lit up a group of Longhorn bulls and other animals about ten metres ahead of them. Strangely, the animals showed little interest, and all was still and quiet again as the moon disappeared.

As the fog thickened, Luke decided to investigate.

"Folks, can you stay where you are? I'm going to climb down the bank to the river's edge. I want to see how deep the water is."

Up ahead, Ron had recovered except for bruised ribs and an absence of pants. He was glad he'd been wearing boxers underneath.

The temperature was quite mild so he didn't feel cold, but he could see the fog thickening in the river. He stood up and called out quietly, hoping someone was close enough to hear him.

Luke stopped, listened and looked around, thinking he heard something. When he heard it again, he called back quietly so as not to startle the nearby bulls.

"Stay where you are, Ron, if that's you. I've got four others with me. But keep it down. There are bulls around."

"Okay," Ron said.

Luke had gauged the level of the river was now shallow enough for a crossing. He headed back to the others but had difficulty at first in finding them in the thick fog.

When he rejoined them, he said, "I've found a way to get to the other side of the river where Ron is. It's only a couple of feet deep. It'll take us a minute or two to cross as the current's slowed right down."

Interest perked up at this.

"Okay, now listen carefully. Hold hands in pairs and take it slowly. There's a lot of shit in the bottom of the river, so be careful." Bethany giggled at the swear word from Luke.

"Wave your free arms in front of you in case there are any branches, okay?"

Bethany whimpered in disgust after a small dead animal bumped into her and walked close to Luke. The fog seemed thicker than ever

"This is scary stuff, like out of a movie or something," Rhys said in an awed voice.

Dianne remarked, "Wait till you hear what you missed while you were unconscious! You'll be glad you slept through it all, especially getting washed down the river, trapped in your car."

"How did you get into the car after the accident?" Rhys asked.

"We climbed down a branch from the top of the bridge, but that's probably when the snake got into the car too. We were too busy with the rain, and then climbing down, to notice it. We all got in the car except for Luke, and when we got washed down-river, he found us again and got us out."

Rhys looked disappointed at missing the hairy ride, but Tiffany, as usual, couldn't resist further annoying Rhys. "Knowing you, you would have shit yourself, you weasel."

"Knock it off, Tiffany! I'm warning you!" Luke said. Tiffany, knowing she'd again spoken out of turn, stood quite still without saying another word.

But Luke could see on her face there could be more to come unless someone else like Dianne could help him put her in her place.

Together, they might be able to bring an end to all this bottled-up anger. Luke had a hunch it had something to do with her being hurt or bullied in some way.

He was fond of her and hoped he'd soon find out what had happened.

At the embankment, Luke called out to Ron, who responded from nearby. Luke waded to the river's edge and scaled the bank, followed by the rest of them.

When Dianne and Bethany reached Ron, there were hugs all around. Ron winced from the squeezing. Luke noticed Tiffany and Rhys looking distressed and comforted them about their own parents.

"Oh my god, I forgot to get your pants from the roof!" Dianne taunted Ron for his lack of trousers.

"Don't worry yourself, I'll get them when we go back to get their parents, okay?"

Dianne joined Luke in consoling Tiffany and Rhys. A flicker of hope showed on Tiffany's face as she looked across at Luke. For whatever reason, she found strength in him.

Luke turned to Ron. "I'll need your help in getting Tiffany and Rhys's parents from their car down the river."

"Sure thing. Let's do it."

Luke and Ron headed back through the thick fog, climbing down the bank and into the river.

"Hey, Ron, watch out for floating debris and overhead branches," Luke warned him.

As they stumbled carefully along the riverbed, sloshing through the water, Luke gave Ron the lowdown on what had happened since he was thrown from his prime mover.

Ron listened intently and asked, "So you haven't been able to find Bridgette or Stephen, then?"

"No, I've looked just about everywhere. But I haven't seen hide nor hair of either of them."

"Bloody hell! Poor little Bridgette. Where could she be, for God's sake? We need to find her soon. She must be so scared, being on her own." Ron said.

"Yeah, pretty much so. I'm listening to you."

They trudged along in silence, then Ron said, "So we're heading for the smaller bridge."

"Yeah. It's only about another five more minutes from here," Luke said. "But there are some dangerous-looking bulls up top, so let's stay in the river. The car's on the edge of the river, so it shouldn't be too hard to find. Oh yeah, sorry, I forgot to tell you, we can't get them out till we get rid of the snake. It's curled up near David's feet."

"What snake? Great, that's all I need! I'm afraid of snakes. Jesus, mad bulls and snakes! What else haven't you told me, son? I guess we'll have to deal with the snake first."

"Not necessarily. If we can open the door and pull them out quietly, the snake might just slither away or stay asleep, like it was when we left the car about an hour ago." As he said this, the car loomed out of the fog. "Great, here we are."

As they moved closer to the car, Ron became a bit agitated.

Luke got to the car and leaned over into the now-open window to tell Ron what he could see on the inside of the vehicle.

"Now the snake should be—oh shit."

"What d'ya mean, *oh shit*?"

"It's gone."

"Shit," Ron exclaimed. "Where's the bloody thing gone? Thank God there's a break in the fog and the moon's full, so we have a chance to see what we're doing." He looked around for the snake.

"I'll go round the other side and see if I can spot it. Maybe Pearl will know what's happened to it," Luke said.

The men walked slowly around the car to the driver's side. Luke opened the door, and they peered nervously into the interior. They heard a muffled mumble from Pearl, slumped half under David, who didn't seem to have moved since Luke left earlier.

"Are you awake? Where's the snake, Pearl?" Ron said.

Pearl, still clearly in a daze but lucid enough to respond, asked, "What snake?"

"You know, the—"

"Oh, sorry, that's right. It started moving a while ago. It wriggled up and over David's body near my shoulder, then over the left side of my face. I just froze! I think I just passed out with fright. It's probably gone now."

"Hope so," Ron said.

"Did that all happen after I left you here?" Luke asked.

"Yes, is there any news, Luke? You know, Stephen?"

"No, I'm sorry, Pearl. I've looked everywhere I could think of, but no sign yet. I've got Dianne's husband, Ron, with me."

"Hello, Pearl."

"We're going to get you and David out of the car and back to the bridge with the others. Then we'll wait till the sun comes up, okay?"

"Hi Ron. What a night, hey? Are all your family safe?"

"No, we're still looking for Bridgette, one of my daughters. When we get you both back to the bridge, Luke and I will go looking for your baby Stephen and Bridgette."

"Okay," Luke said, "let's get David out of here, Pearl."

Luke and Ron grabbed hold of David's arms, and, after a great deal of pulling and heaving, and quiet cursing from Ron's strained and aching body, they got the top part of David's limp form out of the car and collapsed onto the ground. More straining got him onto the bank. Neither Luke nor Ron had ever thought they could be dealing with a corpse.

Despite this, they exchanged wry grins. Ron gasped in pain again before they both got Pearl out.

"Are you sure you can put up with this? You don't sound that good."

Ron just grunted, motioned weakly with his good arm and said, so Pearl wouldn't hear, "Let's get this over with before I can't do anymore."

Pearl hid her embarrassment by joking about her weight, which was even greater than David's.

"Don't worry about it, Pearl," Ron said comfortingly. "My wife, Dianne, has the same concerns. Let's just get you out of here, and we can see how David's going. Now lift up your arms."

Luke and Ron grasped an arm each, but it was a struggle to even move her.

"Can you push with either or both of your feet on the steering wheel or maybe the gear stick first, then the steering wheel? That will give us a better grip on you. Right, on three, push up on your right leg, and we'll pull at the same time. Okay, one, two, three, go, push hard… That's it! There we go. Got you now. Keep pushing your feet against the seat."

While this was going on, Luke felt quietly relieved that, at last, someone else was making the decisions and dictating the action.

Pearl's body emerged from the confines of the car, and the three of them collapsed on the bank. Unfortunately, Pearl landed on Ron's body, and, again, he gulped in pain, but he was thankful the worst was over. He hoped.

Pearl felt the same. "I'm glad that's over, boys, thanks for that. Now, can we check on David?"

Luke interrupted, not wanting her to see David if he was dead. "Sure, Pearl, Ron and I'll do that. You need to rest a bit, because you haven't moved a lot since the accident, and you might struggle, walking back to the bridge."

Ron said, "Well, we've got two options here. First, we can leave him here or…"

"No, please, we can't do that," Pearl begged, fighting back tears. "Can't we take him with us, somehow?"

"Well, that's the second choice, but I'm not sure how far Luke and I could carry him, with the terrain and all. Besides, I don't think I'm up to it at all with this beaten body of mine. I've done some damage to my ribs."

Luke added, "And there are still those bulls out there, and it took us about twenty minutes to get here. So it would take us twice that at least, then we've still got to find the kids."

Ron backed him up. "Sorry, Pearl, but I think it's better to leave David here till the sun rises. It's not long now, according to Luke, before we could be rescued, hopefully. I don't want to sound heartless, but it's not as if he's going anywhere."

"Besides," Luke said, "we need to get you back to Tiffany and Rhys. They could do with some parenting right now, if you know what I mean."

She sniffed. "You're right, I know. Since Stephens's birth and what's been going on with both of them, sometimes too many things happen at the same time. We, or I should say *I*, have struggled with all of this lately, and I don't have any answers. I don't even know what questions I should be asking to help Tiffany through whatever it is she is going through. I'm just void of anything, like I'm almost numb. Nothing."

Then she remembered where she was and said, "Oh, I'm sorry about that, for going off with the fairies… where were we? Oh, that's right. It just seems hard leaving him here alone. Maybe I should stay with him."

"No, Pearl, let's go and just take it slow, okay?"

Before leaving, they made David's limp form as comfortable as possible on the bank. Nobody wanted to check for a pulse, but he seemed to be breathing, albeit shallowly.

Struggling along, Pearl soon understood how hard it would have been to carry David over the rough terrain.

As they proceeded, they heard mooing from the cows on the far bank. Luke started thinking back to the ordeal inside his brother's SUV and their deaths and reflected that, when he was out of this mess, he'd have a life without constant bullying and harassment.

Everything that had happened since he left home—was it just the night before?—had been violent or tragic, but he indulged in a wry grin as he turned back to look where he was going.

Ron looked across at him. "You okay, son?"

"Yeah, I'm fine."

"You looked like you're in another world."

"Yeah, hopefully it'll be a much better one." Ron and Pearl looked at each other curiously, wondering where that came from.

After their marathon effort in getting Pearl back to the others on the embankment, they reached the spot where they left Dianne and the three children.

"Coo-ee!" Luke called out quietly, to get a fix on where they were. When they emerged from the fog, Pearl hugged Rhys and Tiffany, and a still-wincing Ron enjoyed another gentle hug from Dianne and Bethany.

Luke stood off to one side, glad to be free of any involvement for the moment. But he still couldn't help wondering what it must be like to be part of an ordinary, loving family.

Ron said, "Dianne, it's about time Luke and I went to look for the other two missing children." Turning to Pearl, he added, "We'll do the very best we can. I promise you that."

Turning to Luke, he said, "C'mon, mate, let's go and do what we can. I know it'll be that much easier once the sun comes up, but, as you well know, time is not on our side."

"You're not wrong! Do you want to do a side each or should we stay together? There's not much water left in the river, so it's just the fog we've got to worry about."

"So, what's on your mind, Luke? I get the impression you've been in control pretty much most of the night, so go with your gut, son, and let's keep doing what you've been doing. You're a bloody hero, okay?"

"Nah! Bullshit! Okay then, let's go this way, and we'll see—or not, with this bloody fog—what happens next."

# 42

## Morning

As the fog thickened again, Bridgette leaned against the glass window in the door. Exhausted after her attempts to contact anyone at the radio station via the phone, or anyone nearby with her loud screaming and singing, she sagged into the seat and drifted off into half-sleep, vaguely aware of the low volume of music on the radio. Knowing the sun would be up in a couple of hours, she hoped this would make her discovery easier for anybody searching for her.

"Gooooood morning!" Michael tried to imitate the late Robin Williams from the movie *Good Morning Vietnam*. "It's ten past six here on Crazy FM, and Robyn and I have been on air since six last night. Our night jock has the dreaded lurgy, so we've been standing in for him. We've been focusing on what's been going on around the district in the wake of the terrible floods we've been experiencing. Wayne from the SES joins us again from the command centre. Hello, Wayne."

"Yes, hello and good morning, Michael."

"Wayne, for those just joining us this morning, is there any news to report on what happened overnight?

"Most of the district is underwater, and there's a few people still at their properties as well as those rescued from properties around the area. At this stage, Michael, there's not much more to report arising out of the last hour. I'm hoping everything stays quiet until the sun comes up soon."

"Well, that's good to hear, Wayne. Have there been any severe animal losses around the district that you're aware of?"

"Yes, quite a lot of the animals on various properties have perished, unfortunately, including sheep and horses that are missing. So, over the next few days, there'll be a separate focus on retrieving them. Depending on the condition of the dead ones, they'll probably be taken to the abattoir if that's a feasible option, or we may have to dispose of them in some other way. I'm sure the agricultural guys from the shire offices will deal with that as they see fit."

"Okay, Wayne, that all sounds a bit grim. I'll talk with you in another hour and let's hope it remains quiet, as you say. See ya, Wayne."

"Goodbye, Michael."

"Well, that's the latest news, folks, we still won't know what the extent of the damage is until sun up. So, for now, we'll just keep moving along with music, unless someone wants to ring in to tell us how they survived last night."

Bridgette was now sound asleep, not noticing the fog thickening around her and the surrounding area. For anyone getting there on foot, it was one step at a time.

# 43

## Weather, Will It or Won't It?

Without warning, the weather pattern changed as a small cell rapidly developed into a full-blown storm, guaranteed to wreak havoc as it deepened.

Dr Walter Ahern from the weather services arrived at work in his Melbourne office and climbed the two flights of stairs to his office. In the past forty years, he'd never taken the lift, even if he'd been called to the seventh floor for meetings.

At his desk, he booted up his computers and other electrical equipment and then removed his jacket. The temperature inside the head office was quite cool compared to the humid conditions outside on Queen Street.

Reading the radar with rainfall figures for the past twenty-four hours, Walter was shocked to learn of their intensity, particularly since yesterday's forecast had predicted only half that amount. He studied the statistics dealing with the storms that passed over the Steering district overnight and concluded that the worst was over.

He went back over the previous day's forecast to see where they might have missed anything that could have forecast the flooding that inundated the Steering district.

To his surprise, he saw a new cell developing, and, aware of its potential for further havoc, he called the command centre immediately.

"Weather room, Wayne speaking. I'm head of the SES here in the Steering district."

"Dr Walter Ahern here from the weather services head office in Melbourne. I was hoping to talk with a staff member who could let me know what's been happening in the Steering area overnight, please. I'm also calling about a cell that's just developed on the western side of Steering. Have you spotted that as well, Wayne?"

"Yes, I saw it about five minutes ago, so the weather people are working to figure out why it's turned up and what it's going to do over the rest of the day, Dr Ahern."

Wayne's voice had started to show the strain from the pressure he and the weather people were under, especially now with this new cell.

"As you can imagine, things have been pretty hectic overnight, and this new cell isn't going to help. We've been using the local radio station to broadcast weather reports throughout the night, and I was just about to call them when you rang."

"Okay then, please let them know if they need my help. I'll be right here in my office working to figure out why it's turned up, and what happened last night. So can anybody there help me with that, Wayne?"

Wayne could hear Dr Ahern typing on his computer. He would very much like to get off the phone, but, out of respect for Dr Ahern, he bit his tongue and hoped this call would finish soon.

"Well, I guess I could, but I'm a bit preoccupied with this latest change. Okay if I fill you in later, Dr Ahern?"

"Sure, in the meantime I'll do my own research. Okay, bye."

The doctor hung up, perplexed about what had happened last night and disturbed about this new cell turning up. He checked the rainfall and discovered that the cell was not only a big one, but another slow-moving one.

That was of great concern, as all the rivers ran north over that area, from the Great Dividing Ranges back towards Mildura on the Victorian and New South Wales border.

Wayne's phone rang again as soon as he put it down.

"Robyn here from Crazy FM. That you, Wayne?"

"Yes, it's me. That's weird. I was just about to ring you guys. We may need to put out another warning. There's another storm brewing from the west, and, going by the way it's forming, it looks like it could be quite dangerous over the next hour or so. When I know what it's going to do and when, I'll ring you back with an update, Robyn."

Robyn was on air while Michael caught up on some sleep.

"Thanks Wayne, we'll talk soon. That was Wayne at the command centre on the phone. There's another storm on the way, and they'll get back to us when they know more. We'll keep playing music till he phones us back."

# 44

## A Bloke Can Only Take So Much

At the top edge of the western bank of the river, Luke and Ron were trying to work out a way through the thick fog. Unexpectedly, the wind picked up, carrying away wisps of fog as it strengthened.

They exchanged worried glances.

"I don't like the feel of this. The last time the fog disappeared, it poured rain again. Christ!" he shouted, catching Ron off guard. "What did I do to deserve this? And now this bloody rain again. Shit, I wish I was dead."

Ron now recognised this young man was starting to give up and understood why Luke had been acting strangely.

"I know this is rough, son, but maybe together we can get through it. By morning, you'll look back over all this, and you'll be a stronger man because of what you've been through."

Luke looked at Ron, wondering why he couldn't have had someone like him to guide him through his troubled childhood. Maybe he'd finally found a friend he could turn to.

"Also, we all have heightened emotions at night. We don't generally feel them, as we're usually asleep. But, at times like this, at least we've got each other to get us through it. If you were on your own, it'd be very different. But I'm here with you, son." Ron's face broke into a grin. "But it's only because you know your way around better than I do."

Luke grinned, despite feeling sad and drained, as Ron went on.

"I really need your help to find my daughter and the baby… what's his name again?"

"Bloody Stephen," Luke mumbled.

Ron reckoned if he could get Luke to say the baby's name again, it would change his thinking and get him to focus properly on the job at hand. So he pretended he didn't hear.

"Bloody who?"

"Stephen! That's the baby's bloody name, Stephen," Luke shouted.

Ron was about to reply when something went *plop* on top of his head—either bird shit or something else wet. Then, whatever it was, hit again and again.

"Oh, Christ, no!" Ron cried. "I think it's that rain again. What are we going to do? There's nowhere for all of us to shelter if it's going to be another storm like the last one. Maybe we should head back to the car. Although Pearl doesn't look like she could manage another trip like that again. Do you know where your car finished up?"

"No, I don't. It could be anywhere by now, given what happened to Pearl's car." Luke carefully didn't mention the gory mess still sitting in the front seats of the SUV.

"And you've no idea where the prime mover is either, or the trailer. Who knows where that went?" Luke asked.

"Well, if it's empty and accessible, we might be able to hide in it, if it's safe from flooding."

"Let's go and have a look around the other end, where the accident happened. I guess we'll see what we see."

They climbed cautiously down the bank and began to walk along the riverbed as the rain ramped up to a deafening, torrential downpour. They both cringed at the pounding on their heads and were forced to squint to make out what lay ahead of them.

Luke, leading the way, had his hands out in front to avoid walking into some obstacle. Then he touched something wet and slippery.

"Stop!" He turned around and called out quietly. Ron, not expecting it, nearly knocked Luke over, and he stumbled into an animal in front of him, startling it. Other movements started up all around them, and Luke's worst fear was realised. They'd wandered into a herd of Longhorns and other animals.

Luke yelled, "Run to the bank and don't stop. Just keep going."

They scrambled up the bank, while, in the riverbed below them, the bulls and other animals started running recklessly in the rain towards McKenzie's Bridge.

The two men could just see through the rain as the animals stampeded into the remains of the bridge, then stumbled and bellowed in their panic as they fell over or crashed into each other.

The noise was underscored by bleating and neighing from the other animals from the abattoir. Some attempted to clamber up the slippery banks on either side of the river, but most of them just slid back into those behind them, adding to the pandemonium.

"Gee, I hope I don't come back as an animal," Ron muttered. "Don't know how they cope, carrying on like that, only to get slaughtered and finish up on my dining room table."

As he spoke, one of the larger bulls rolled back down the bank, knocking over three of the following bulls.

"Let's go somewhere safer. Looks like all the mayhem is happening here," Luke suggested.

In fascinated horror, they watched through slight breaks in the downpour as numerous bulls and other animals were dragged down the river towards the smaller bridge. A blinding flash of lightning, then a deafening rumble and roar of thunder.

Several other flashes followed, and their eyes adjusted but not enough to see any sign of the prime mover or trailer, let alone Bridgette or Stephen.

"Doesn't look like we're going anywhere soon," Ron shouted.

"Yeah! What do you reckon we should do?

"Maybe go back to the women and ride it out."

What would they tell the others now?

The four women and Rhys found themselves some meagre shelter under a nearby tree with long, wide branches, hoping it would protect them from this new storm.

A tremendous, deafening crack of lightning flashed across the sky, followed by another vibrating bang of thunder. As they looked skyward, another lightning bolt struck the very tree they were under, sending a large branch crashing down towards them. Luke and Ron were just in time to shove Tiffany and Bethany out of the way.

The rest, on the other side of the huge tree, just looked on, shocked by what had just happened. They hadn't expected to see anyone, let alone Luke and Ron. They were even more surprised to see Ron, especially Bethany.

A dishevelled, bedraggled Tiffany, wet through, clothes clinging to her, grabbed Luke in a moment of heightened emotion and pulled him towards her. She then planted a firm kiss on his mouth, while the others looked on, relieved and happy that Luke and Ron were back.

Following suit, Bethany planted one on her dad's cheek. Dianne was also caught up in the moment and did the same to Ron.

Pearl just hugged Rhys and kissed his forehead, as her son just stood there looking like a stunned mullet.

The rain still fell heavily, and all they could do was to watch the continuing light show. Then, they gathered around each other in a group hug, thankful for the efforts of a still-hurting Ron and a sombre-feeling Luke.

Apart from his mother's hugs and kisses, Luke's miserable life hadn't prepared him for this type of gratitude. But, with Tiffany around, he was starting to believe he could perhaps get used to all this kissing, hugging and love stuff.

# 45

## You've Been Where?

Bridgette awoke from another doze, wiped her eyes and tried to focus again on calling the radio station. Light had begun to filter through the landscape surrounding the river, and she could just make out the shapes of animals along the banks and in the riverbed. She wondered why the river was so low, given the heavy rain that had fallen overnight and what was happening around her now.

Luckily, the back end of the prime mover's chassis had prevented the prime mover from being swept away.

All she could do now was watch, wait and try the phone. She now heard an engaged signal coming from the phone.

Someone at the radio station must have noticed the line was dead! Bridgette replaced the phone in its cradle, picked it up again and pressed redial.

She was amazed to hear it ring and prayed someone would pick up.

"Hi, this is Robyn from Crazy FM, who's calling?" She paused. "Hello, this is Robyn from Crazy FM."

Bridgette was speechless for a second, just gazing at the phone.

Hearing only silence, Robyn was about to hang up when the unmistakable voice of a child said just two words: "Yes, please."

"Hello? What's your name, sweetie, and how old are you?"

"M-my name's Bridgette, and I'm eight years old. And I've been trapped in my dad's truck all night. I'm all alone, and I don't know where I am. Can you come and get me quickly, please?"

Robyn can't quite take this in.

"Just hold on, Bridgette, and I'll put you on to someone else. You can explain to him what has happened and where you might be, okay? Hang on a second, sweetie."

Robyn rapped violently on the studio window, hurting her hand. Michael was resting his head on the bench in front of him. He looked up, half-asleep, annoyed at being disturbed. Robyn pointed to Michael's monitor and talked through their connecting line.

Michael jumped up, now understanding the importance of the situation. He fumbled his headphones on, pressed the button on his panel to receive the call.

"Hello Bridgette, this is Michael and you're on the radio, so what is happening to you, and where are you?"

"I've been stuck inside Dad's truck all night. We were in an accident, and I'm on my own, and I don't know where anyone else is… my mum, Dad or my sister. I'm frightened. I know we were heading into a town, and I think it's the town called Steering. We were all going to stay at the hotel for the night, but we didn't get that far. I'm glad the sun is starting to shine, but can you come and get me quickly, please? It's raining hard again, and I don't want to drown. Please help me."

"Do you know where you are at the moment?" Michael asked, still dazed after being up most of the night. He couldn't process the incredible story she was telling him. He wondered if he was still asleep, having a bad dream.

"What's the last thing you remember, Bridgette? How did you get trapped in your truck?"

"The last thing I remember, I was trying to see where we were going. Dad and I were finding it hard to see out the windscreen. It was raining hard, like it is now, and Dad said 'This is like driving blind', and I think I sort of understand now what he meant. Then, we were going over a bridge, and we didn't see this car. Dad hit it, and it was too late, and that's when I went to sleep. I think."

Michael was now energised at the thought of what he was hearing and concerned about the child. He tried to sound calm as he spoke to Bridgette.

"What sort of truck is it? What load were you carrying? Do you know that, Bridgette?"

"It's a new one. Dad bought it last year. It has everything, just like a caravan. But we were going to a hotel 'cos it's a better place to clean up after a long trip. We've even got a shower that pops out at the side."

This brought a smile to Michael and Robyn's faces as Michael continued, "What's your dad's name, Bridgette?"

"Dad—oh, it's Ron, but I remember him going through the front windscreen of the truck."

"Is that Ron Williams? He has a trailer he uses for carting animals?" Michael was now feeling emotional, concerned for Ron, as he would be for anyone in this predicament.

"Yes! That's my dad, and we were carrying bulls with large, long horns, but I don't remember what they were called..."

"Texas Longhorn bulls, does that sound right?"

"Yes, that's what they call them! There was this big mean one in the back of the trailer. Someone shot him with a dart."

"Do you mean a tranquiliser dart, fired from a rifle?"

"Yes, I think so."

"I remember going out with your dad on a couple of trips. He showed me how many drivers don't really know much about driving, and how it's easy to become lazy. Okay, I've got the police on the other line, Bridgette, and they want to know your dad's phone number, so they can call it, and, while they're talking to you, they can work out where you are. You okay with that, Bridgette?"

"Does that mean you'll have to hang up on me? What if they can't make it ring? What would I do then?" Bridgette began to cry.

"They'll be able to, as they're part of the Emergency Services, and they have the technology if there is little or no signal, so it will be fine, okay? Unfortunately, Bridgette, they have to have a connection to be able to locate you through something called a GPS."

"But what do I do if nobody rings after you hang up on me?"

Michael wasn't sure how to answer. His facial expression told Robyn he needed help with the question, so she took over.

"Hello, sweetheart, this is Robyn, the lady you spoke to first. I have an idea. What if you stay on the line, and you give us the phone number, and we'll give it to the police. We'll transfer you to another line, and then we can help you work out how to answer their call. That way, we can help you press the right button, so you don't get disconnected from either of us. Does that sound like a good idea, Bridgette?"

"Yes, I like that idea. When will that happen?"

"When you give us the phone number, we can then pass it on to the police, and then they'll call you while we stay on the line, okay, Bridgette?" Robyn's voice was calm and reassuring as she switched off the connection so no one else could hear the number.

She wrote down the number and repeated it back to Bridgette.

"Yes, that's it. I can see it on the phone. It says *private*."

"Now, it should say *take call* or something like that, and then *answer*, okay? Press that button and say, 'Hello, this is Bridgette', and someone from the police should answer from where they are calling at their end."

"Are you sure this'll work? I'm scared of losing you, and I'm not sure, and I don't know what to do. Can I keep talking to you, Robyn? I'll wait till someone comes to get me, but can I do that, please?" Bridgette started sobbing again.

"Listen, sweetheart, we're not going to lose you, I promise you! Now, can you tell me how many others were there in the truck with you? And do you know what happened to them?"

"I don't know. I saw Dad go through the broken front window, but the part of the truck that had the beds and other things in it, where Mummy and Bethany were... I don't know where they are either. It's gone."

"The reason why I'm asking is if they need urgent medical care, then we need to get to them as quickly as possible. Maybe there are others, like you said, in the other car, and they might need help urgently. Because you're okay—you *are* okay, aren't you?"

"Yes, I think so, but I'm so scared."

"So, if you're okay, then we need to get help to the others as quickly as possible, just in case they have really bad injuries, do you understand, Bridgette? It's really important that you answer the call from the police, so we can send help for everyone, and not just for you. Can you do that for your mother, father and sister, please, Bridgette?"

Michael made sure the listeners could hear what was happening. The music stopped.

Bridgette had her finger millimetres away from the answer button. For a moment, she hesitated, bringing her hand back to her chest. Then she took a deep breath, hoping she wouldn't lose Robyn and be alone again.

After what seemed like an eternity for all those listening, Bridgette then moved her hand away from her chest and pushed the *answer* button on the truck phone. Then, to her great delight, a female voice answered.

"Hello, is that Bridgette?"

"Yes, this is Bridgette. Who are you?" Excitement and hope now filled her voice.

"My name is Elizabeth, and I'm a senior constable in the police force. Can you hear me okay, Bridgette?"

"Yes I can, Elizabeth."

"You can call me Liz for short, okay? Would you like to say hello to Robyn? She's still on the other line."

Bridgette could hear a big smile in Robyn's voice, even this early in the morning, "Yes, I'm still here. You okay now, Bridgette?"

"Yes, I'm good. I'm so glad this worked, and I'm feeling better now. But I'm very tired though." She yawned.

"So are we," Robyn and Liz said in unison.

"What's going to happen now?" Bridgette asked.

"Well, while we're talking to you on the phone, some people are working out where you are," Liz said. "Do you know, perhaps, where you came from yesterday, and where you were heading, Bridgette?"

"We were at a farm in... I think in the north-eastern part of South Australia. We were heading for a couple of hours in the other direction when it started to rain, that's when it got dark. I remember Dad telling us about white lines, cats' eyes and things on posts that I think we're red and white, and we went over a mountain... Can I ask a question? What's a GPS, and how does it work?"

Wanting to distract the child and keep her awake, Robyn began to explain.

"A GPS is a location device, and it will help the police find you. Now, while you were at school, one of your teachers would have taught your class about the planets in our solar system."

"Yes. I remember them, and they go round the sun."

"That's right. Well, this is how your mobile phone works, so let's pretend for a moment that you are the sun. All the planets are going around the sun. That's you. Now, the way this works with your mobile phone is a bit like when the sun gives off rays. Your mobile phone gives off waves of a different kind. Then, when the sun's rays go to earth, they don't bounce off, they create a warm feeling, right? But, with the waves from your mobile phone, they go to many different satellites around the earth. Just like the sun and the planets, but when they hit any three satellites around the earth, the signal bounces off each of them and bounces back to where you are now."

Bridgette felt a little confused by the explanation, but said, "Yeah, I think so…"

"What happens next is at the police centre here in town, because they have your phone number, it's continually sending out signals to these satellites, and they can track where these signals are coming from. Then, they locate where the signal bounces back, using all three satellites, which are positioned like a triangle around the earth. You know what a triangle is, don't you?"

"Yes. It has two bends at the bottom and one at the top."

"That's right, Bridgette, so thinking about the sun and the planets, where would you be in the triangle?"

Bridgette remained silent for a moment. Those listening in awaited her answer anxiously. Then Bridgette said tentatively, just in case her answer was wrong, "In the middle."

"Well done, Bridgette, that's correct, your teacher will be very proud of you."

Bridgette could hear voices in the background. She heard Liz saying, "It looks like the far north-western part of Victoria."

Then another voice, further away, said, "We've got the coordinates."

Immediately, contact was made with the search and rescue squad and the local police station at Steering. When they realised the town was about five to six hours from the city, they alerted the air wing to send a helicopter.

Elizabeth came back on the phone while Robyn and Bridgette were talking about what happened during the night.

"Excuse me, Bridgette, this is Liz again. We've located where you are, near a town called Steering."

"Yes! That's where we are. We are in a river, and we fell off a bridge called Mack... something, and there was this car coming the other way, and that's when I fell asleep. Do you think it will take long to come and get me? I'm scared I might drown if it keeps raining." Bridgette asked.

"I'm afraid it will take about an hour, sweetheart, but we've been in touch with a policeman in Steering, and he's on his way to where you are right now. He'll tell us how we can best rescue you and your mum, dad and your sister."

"That's good news, Liz. Can we broadcast on the radio about what's been happening with Bridgette?" Robyn asked.

"Yes, that's fine but don't mention the location. Say that a young girl has been found safe and well, but, from all reports, there could be more needing help."

"Will do, thanks Liz. Are you still there, Bridgette?"

"Yes, I'm still here." Bridgette was getting tired, and her voice was slower than before, after all the excitement with the phone call and finding out she would be rescued soon. She wondered how her parents and sister spent last night, and hoped they were all alive, especially after seeing her father go through the windscreen.

"I'll keep this line open for you to talk to Michael again, and you can tell him about what happened to you last night, until the police arrive to rescue you. Is that okay with you?"

"Yes," she whispered, sighing quietly.

"Okay, just hang in there, Bridgette, and Michael will talk with you soon. You're being a very brave girl."

"Michael Scanlon here at Crazy FM, and we've been in touch with the police. They've located a young girl trapped somewhere near Steering. As you've been hearing, we had a call from Bridgette earlier, telling us about her situation, and we were able to get the police involved. They have tracked her down using that wonderful GPS. There's a possibility more people could be trapped where she is.

"We'll keep you updated when we find out who else is in need of help. The police have mounted a rescue operation and should be at the location in about an hour from now. Let's hope all's well with any other people they find there. Now, we still have eight year old Bridgette on the line, and she has asked if she could stay on the line with us until the local policeman arrives. Hi Bridgette, how are you at the moment?"

"I'm feeling frightened, still scared and feeling wet, but I should be all right if you keep talking to me until the policeman arrives."

"Don't worry, sweetheart, we won't lose you. Now, do you want to tell us what happened to you last night?"

# 46

## Look at That

Milo was in a deep sleep.

As he woke, he was at first disoriented by the unfamiliar interior of the coach. Then, when the coach passed a shop sign, he knew this must be the town of Steering. He noticed that Billy and Jo-Anne were still asleep in their seats as they pulled into the kerbside.

Milo and a couple of other passengers stood up and went to the front of the coach then stepped down into the warmth of the morning. As usual, Milo's sheer size attracted a few stares, especially when he stretched lazily, exposing his midriff. Luckily, the others in front of him were unable to see what he was carrying, tucked firmly inside his pants above his large bottom.

Discovering he was being looked at, Milo attempted to cover his protruding waistline and then approached the driver to ask where the men's room was. Before he set off in the direction indicated, he turned in time to see Billy and Jo-Anne getting off the coach. He watched Billy go to the side of the bus to retrieve his luggage, while he kept another eye on Jo-Anne.

He didn't want to lose sight of either of them. Unfortunately, nature's call was urgent, and Milo was obliged to head off to the men's room.

When he returned, everyone, including the coach, had gone, except a few passengers who were being picked up in cars and a couple of dogs looking for scraps. The area was covered in wet, brown dirt, and had a few shabby old buildings. The town, after all the rain the night before, looked completely desolate.

"Fuck!" he said to himself.

A man driving a horse and cart came down the road and stopped almost in front of him.

"Hey! You seen young bloke and pretty girl? They leave me behind. I go to toilet."

The old man looked at this outsized stranger, lifted his hat and scratched his forehead. He wondered what such a person would be doing in Steering.

"Only a policeman, a young man and an overdressed woman sitting in the back seat of the police car," he said. "Why?"

"Was in the men's room and them giving me directions before left. I want to thank, but they gone. I do the same now. What direction they go in?"

"The copper asked me for directions to the old wooden bridges. Said he was new in town. So, I guess that's where they're headed. McKenzie's Bridge, it's not that far. You just take that dirt track off the main road over there and follow your nose, okay?"

"What is follow nose?"

"Don't worry about it. You'll need to get going if you want to catch them at the bridge."

The cart pulled away, and Milo wondered whether he'd gone back a hundred years. He turned in the direction mentioned. He felt around his back again, making sure his insurance was still snug in its position.

Earlier, Scotty had been called to go to the wooden bridge two kilometres outside of town, to investigate a distress call from an eight year old girl trapped in a vehicle in the river. On his way, he'd passed the bus station and, to his amazement, spotted Jo-Anne and Billy standing by the side of the road, looking as if they had only just made one another's acquaintance.

He pulled up. "What the bloody hell are you two doing here?"

"Come to see you," Billy grinned. "You were supposed to be picking me up at the railway station. Only the train broke down and…"

"Never mind that now, I've got an emergency. You'd better both jump in. You can give me your excuse later, Jo-Anne."

As they headed west along a wet dirt road, Jo-Anne tried to strike up a conversation with Scotty.

"I don't want to hear about that now!" Scotty barked. She looked dishevelled and unattractive, nothing like he remembered.

"Didn't have time to tidy up after the five-hour coach journey! I slept for most of it, with my face squished up against a window."

Billy piped up with, "I've never seen so many trees in my life before, Scotty. I reckon it'd be good to live here!"

"Let's see how things pan out over the next couple of months," Scotty said testily, his mind on other things. "Don't get your hopes up. I've got a big responsibility in this town, okay? Let's just enjoy our time together, and we'll see how things go."

As he took an unexpectedly sharp corner, he had to skid the car to a sudden stop to avoid crashing into a fallen tree across the road. This caused everyone to lurch forward. Jo-Anne hit her forehead on the seat in front of her, where Billy was sitting.

"Hey, Billy, can you help me move this tree, please?"

"I can help you, if you like," Jo-Anne said. Scotty gave her a scowl that she interpreted as *Stay in the bloody car, woman.*

"No, thanks. Billy and I will deal with this, you stay put."

As they got out of the car, Billy saw a family of koalas in a tree. He stared, speechless, mouth wide open.

"Close your mouth, Billy, or you'll let the flies in," Scotty told him, trying not to smile. Then he added, "There's lots of wildlife here so you better get used to it, Billy. *If* I let you stay, of course."

A brown snake slithered across the dirt track in between them and the car. Jo-Anne just sat, disconsolate, in the back of the car, trying to avoid Scotty's nasty glances.

Billy couldn't wipe the excited expression from his face. He reckoned he couldn't be in a better place on earth than the Australian bush, first thing in the morning, with bush sounds ringing in his ears.

Out of the blue, some kookaburras started laughing, and Billy was stunned at the incredible noise they made.

"Are they kookaburras? Wow. That's just an amazing sound!" Scotty grabbed Billy to break the spell and led him towards the fallen tree.

Jo-Anne was also mesmerised by the real-life kookaburra laugh resounding throughout the trees. Then, the familiar song from her primary-school days came into her head. *Laugh, kookaburra, laugh.* What a wonderful place to be.

By the time Scotty reached the approach to the bridge, the rain had begun to clear, and the sun was peeking over the horizon.

Milo was literally plodding along in the same direction on a muddy dirt track, the ground squishing under his feet from the overnight rain. He was in the middle of nowhere, but still a long way behind his prey.

He, too, was fascinated by the sights and sounds of the Australian bush and recklessly ignored the warning from the man in the cart to watch out for stray livestock, as well as any wild animals. Without warning, a large brown snake wriggled across the track in front of him. He pulled up, startled. *Probably*, he thought, *it's out looking for food.*

He hoped he wouldn't have too far to go before catching up with the police car, wherever it was heading. He wished he'd found a cab, but there didn't seem to be any around when he'd left the coach at the station.

As Milo rounded a bend, he stopped when he saw his first wild kangaroo, a big old grey leaping over a hedge on one side of the dirt road ahead of him.

Reacting wildly, Milo reached for his gun but quickly thought it was neither the time nor the place for taking pot-shots at the local wildlife. Then, out of the bushes came a second, even larger, eastern grey.

It stopped only a few feet in front of Milo, seemingly mesmerised by the large human. Moments passed as they sized up each other and then came a whole mob of roos, of all different shapes and sizes, hopping onto the muddy dirt road.

The original male grunted before bouncing off after them. To his right was obviously the mother with a joey in her pouch. These two animals also stared at this being before them, and then the mother turned her head and followed everyone else. Her joey was still struggling to look at Milo, its little head peering around the side of its mother's body, as the mother bounded away.

Milo thought to himself, *Good job I live in city... too many strange creatures here in bush.*

As Milo rounded another bend, he saw a police car parked some distance ahead and moved into the bushes to avoid being seen. Keeping to the side of the path hidden by the forest, he continued slowly towards the police car, noticing a familiar figure in the back seat.

He took out his revolver, carefully, so he wouldn't be visible in the car's side-view mirror. He opened the door.

Being confronted by a large man pointing a revolver in her face was not an everyday occurrence, even for a hardened reporter. Jo-Anne was startled and about to scream.

Milo put one finger to his lips to quieten her and beckoned her out of the car with the revolver.

"Where copper gone?"

She was about to speak when they heard voices coming from the river. Milo grabbed Jo-Anne's arm and frogmarched her towards the voices, warning her not to make a sound.

Scotty and Billy, oblivious of what was heading their way, continued to search along the river for the trapped eight year old girl.

Slowly, through the trees, the sun came up and bathed everything in an eerie, luminous glow. The last wisps of fog vanished.

Scotty picked up the sound of voices from the other side of the river.

"This is the police! Can you make your way across to this side of the river, so I can establish what has happened here?"

"Will do!" a male voice replied, and, at that moment, the cab of the prime mover was revealed after the last of the fog lifted.

A little girl climbed groggily out of the cab, only a few metres from Scotty and Billy. She ran towards them as the group from the other side of the river scrambled up the embankment.

Bethany, Dianne and Ron's smiles were mixed with tears of relief as they were reunited with Bridgette.

"My little angel, where've you been all this time?" Dianne asked her.

"I've been in the front of the truck, ever since Dad just disappeared through the windscreen, and everything went black. When I woke up, I could hear someone talking on the phone, but they couldn't hear me for ages and ages, and I went to sleep again. Then, a nice lady talked to me, and she got the police, and they talked to me as well. And then he came." She turned to point to Scotty. They were all standing around listening to Bridgette's description of her adventure when a respectful cough was heard behind them.

They all turned around simultaneously to see who it was.

# 47

## Oh No, Not Again

Every morning, for as long as they could remember, their rooster has awoken the farmer and his wife from their slumber. Not for one minute did they ever seriously consider getting rid of the noisy creature.

Yet, every morning, Katherine said, "I think it's about time we got rid of that rooster."

"What?" John rolled suggestively to her side of the bed, his morning erection signalling his intentions.

"Was it me or did it rain heavily last night?" he asked.

"I didn't know you could hear all that rain with your snoring. It's a wonder I got any sleep at all last night." But she started singing, "It's raining, it's pouring, and the old man's snoring."

"At least I don't sound like a freight train."

"Ya reckon?"

Hearing them, Ziggy, their blue heeler, whimpered outside the bedroom door as the pair of them exchanged their daily, well-seasoned, affectionate abuse. "You're a bitch."

"You're a bastard."

"Bellyacher."

"Charlatan."

"Whinger."

"Shark."

"Swindler."

"Crook."

"Fussy boots."

"Double dealer."

"Gripe."

"What's a gripe?" Katherine asked.

"It's someone who complains about something in a persistent irritating way, like you do, ya fake."

"Moaner."

"Imposter."

"Phony."

"Grump."

"Pretender."

"Fusspot."

"Quack."

"Mongrel."

"Nag."

"God, I love it when you talk dirty to me," she chuckled.

Ziggy had heard all this before and knew only too well what it led to. As the noise got louder, he headed discreetly into the yard, out of earshot.

Sometime later, when the commotion had died down, Ziggy stuck his head through the back door to see if they'd made it to the kitchen for breakfast yet.

Both of them were sitting at the table, stark naked, munching on cornflakes. John noticed Ziggy's head, gave him a whimsical look and said, "What's wrong with you, Ziggy? Cat got your tongue? Looking for some tucker, are you?"

With that, Ziggy slowly entered the kitchen and headed for his brimming food bowl. He got stuck in, knowing they'd soon be off for their morning chores. That meant exercise for him around the property.

John stood up. "I reckon I'll go and have a look over at McKenzie's Bridge. There was a noise coming from there last night. Did you not hear it, Katherine?"

He headed for the door, before quickly returning to take his empty bowl over to the sink and washed it, mindful of the abuse he'd cop if he'd left it on the table or merely in the sink for her to wash.

"If there's nothing there, I'll come back and clean out the fireplace. The nights are starting to get colder now. I should get some fresh logs for the fire tonight, too." He put his rifle over his shoulder, as he'd done every morning for the thirty odd years they'd been living there.

He kissed his wife on the cheek and grabbed her on the bum, before collecting a bag of rubbish to put in the bin on his way to the river. He whistled to Ziggy to join him on the walk across the field, then to the river and bridges a few hundred metres away. Ziggy jumped up, knowing they're off somewhere more interesting than the kitchen.

"Forgotten something?" Katherine asked, looking him up and down.

He looked down and saw, to his amusement, what was missing. "Who's gonna care if I'm still naked?"

She gave him the side-eye, then he propped the rifle against the table and went to the bedroom.

Once dressed, he strolled across the field, Ziggy occasionally at his side, sometimes bounding here and there with all the energy of recently acquired freedom.

John noticed the last wisps of the slow-burning fog, disappearing with the early morning sun. He knew it would be gone completely by the time he reached the river, and he'd be able to investigate what he heard last night, if anything.

Approaching the ground on the other side of the fence, John stopped, wondering if he'd heard the sound of a cow mooing. Ziggy's ears pricked up, and he growled softly.

"Heel," John called, patting him. "Let's wait and see if we hear that again."

At that instant, the unmistakable sounds of sheep and horses came from the same direction as the mooing.

John frowned. Ziggy tilted his head sideways, as if to say, *What was that?* John grinned at his dog, wondering if he'd ever heard these sorts of animal noises before.

Still speculating on where they'd come from, he remembered last night's news on the radio about the flooding of the abattoir. He wondered how many animals there were and stood up slowly, his bones cracking. He moved cautiously to the wooden fence and was shocked to find so many animals scattered around and in the river.

A piece of red cloth hanging on the horn of one of the bulls on the opposite bank snagged his attention.

Ziggy was making strange whining noises.

As he neared the bridge, he saw its timbers leaning at an odd angle. The remains of what looks like a major calamity were scattered around, and, just as he was taking this in, he saw a group of people sitting at the river's edge at the bottom of the bank. He was about to call out to them when he heard more voices coming from the other side of the river.

"Don't shoot, please, don't shoot!" someone yelled. John walked quietly along the fence-line towards the bridge, stepping over broken timbers, making sure Ziggy stayed close by.

He walked onto the remains of the bridge, coming to where a truck had gone through the side-barrier and down over the edge. He still couldn't make out what was going on with the group of people, so stood still for a moment, listening hard.

As he neared the end of the bridge, he heard a voice with a foreign accent. The voice was telling someone in broken English, "Boss didn't like you killing nephew, sent me to take care. For this, you must die. Come here, I put you from your misery. Sit down. Look other way. Don't need to see your face when I shoot."

At this, John quietly walked towards the voice, shocked to see a larger-than-life monster before him.

*This guy must be at least seven feet tall! Have I got any ammo in the rifle?* John wondered, stopped, unsure of his next move.

Someone outside the group saw him and screamed, "Shoot him!"

Awkwardly, Milo swung around, stumbling and catching John off guard. Jo-Anne seized her opportunity and twisted out of the grip Milo still had on her and dropped to the ground.

Milo was about to shoot John before the farmer had a chance to raise his rifle, when Milo's attention was redirected to his groin. He recoiled, screaming in pain as the sensation intensified. He looked down numbly and saw a dog in mid-air, hanging off a large chunk of his trousers and what was inside them. Bumped by Jo-Anne's effort to get away, John fell backwards and involuntarily fired the rifle, hitting Milo in the stomach. The shot just missed Ziggy's head as the giant toppled backwards, Ziggy still hanging grimly on.

Milo was slumped on the ground unconscious from either a bullet or hitting his head.

"Ziggy! Heel!" John ordered. Jo-Anne bent down to pat him.

"Mate! Are you okay?" Scotty asked John. "Think I'd better have that now," he said, taking charge of his rifle.

As the group crowded around, emergency vehicles sped down the dirt track to McKenzie's Bridge, mud flying everywhere, sirens wailing.

The police sergeant climbed out of his car, a bemused look on his weathered face. Before he could ask a question, Scotty said, "I'll explain over a drink later, okay, Sarge?"

# 48

## I Think I'll Go for a Walk

Once the Emergency Services arrived and took over, Billy decided to go for a walk along the river. He didn't bother telling anyone, not even Scotty, because that was how Billy was.

He left after overhearing a discussion about a missing baby called Stephen. He liked babies and didn't think a baby should be alone with all these animals, enormous trees that could fall or men with guns.

He was surprised to see the river so low, given the amount of rain Scotty told him had fallen in the area in the past couple of days, especially the night before. He whistled to himself, pleased to be reunited with his mate the copper.

He was carefully looking for any signs that might lead him to a lost baby, although he had no idea what those signs could be. But he was enjoying the tranquil surroundings, even if the number of dead bodies of animals he'd spotted was a bit disturbing. Some had their bloody insides and guts exposed already, and ravenous birds were enjoying the bonus tucker. Billy had never seen anything like this before, except on television or in a movie.

His attention was attracted by the constant squawking from above, coming from various birds hovering in the trees, waiting to pounce once he disappeared.

He felt his stomach start making familiar rumbling noises. All this eating he was witnessing was making him hungry. He saw a vehicle up ahead on the edge of the bank, with a branch sticking out of its roof. Billy was confused by this, and, as he approached the vehicle, he was startled by a large black bird flying up out of the hole in the car's roof.

He jumped backwards in fright, frozen for a few moments, then said to himself, "No bird scares me! Even if it does have a lump of what looks like flesh in its beak."

He hesitated before poking his head over the hole in the roof. There wasn't much to see, so he went around the vehicle, peering through the windows, wiping away the storm debris for a better look.

He stared through the rear window, accidentally bumping his head on it as he tried to see through the gloom inside. Immediately, he heard a noise from within—like the cry of a baby.

He tried the back door, but it was locked so he walked round to the driver's side. About to open the front door, he tripped over something on the ground. He stood up, checking his head for blood.

He saw he'd tripped over a man's body. He retreated in fright and tripped again, stepping into some fresh cow dung. Back on his feet, he wiped away the cow dung and checked the body.

Then, increasingly loud, incessant screaming from inside the vehicle diverted his attention from the body. Wondering why they hadn't found the baby before, when it was so close by, he removed the key from the ignition and used it to open the back door.

As he did so, the screaming became louder, resonating through the morning stillness—loud enough to be heard by the group back at McKenzie's Bridge.

He heard someone shriek "*My baby!*" Pearl. She couldn't work out where the cries were coming from, so, panicking, she darted off first in one direction, then another, trying to look in several directions at the same time.

Billy had little experience with infants, but he knew enough to pick this one up and try to comfort it. He leaned forward and freed the baby from the insert of the capsule, wedged into its current location by the force of the crash.

The baby had become stuck, behind the container bearing its nappies and other belongings, in a position invisible from anywhere else inside the car.

When the car went over the edge of the bridge, after hitting the semi-trailer, the force of the impact released the inner section of Stephen's capsule from its outer shell. Tiffany's accidental release of the seatbelt allowed the inner section, still carrying Stephen, to fly through the air, before Stephen was released up and out of the inner section. He was momentarily pinned to the roof before gravity allowed him to fall down into the outer shell. When it eventually came to rest, it was completely hidden behind the esky.

Before they'd left her father's house, Pearl had given her teething, feverish baby a sedative, to help him sleep during the journey home and throughout the rest of the night.

This must have left him dead to the world, both during and after the accident.

Back at McKenzie's Bridge, they attempted to calm Pearl, but she became even more frantic waiting to hear Stephen's crying again.

But it didn't come, because Billy had him cradled in his arms. *Beginner's luck*, Billy thought and began rocking Stephen to and fro as he'd seen mothers do.

A particularly rank smell assailed Billy's nostrils. Stephen was clearly in need of an urgent nappy change. *Definitely something for an expert*, he thought.

Forgetting about the body for the moment, Billy turned and walked back towards the others. The change of rhythm started Stephen crying again—a wonderful sound for Pearl.

Scotty looked around, bewildered, and was the first to grasp Billy's absence. He ran in the direction of the crying, with Pearl scampering after him.

The rest of the group, including the emergency workers, watched in growing delight.

Tiffany and Rhys were rooted to the spot until Dianne urged them to join the reunion.

"Go on, you two! They've found your baby brother!" Forgetting their customary hostilities, they ran to catch up to Pearl, helping her over the difficult terrain.

Just about everybody, particularly Luke, had accepted that Stephen had drowned, washed miles away down the river.

As the rest of the group caught up with Pearl and Scotty, they saw Billy clutching Stephen while navigating the riverbed under the partly demolished bridge.

He yelled out to Pearl, "Stay where you are. I'll come to you. It's not safe ground here."

But Pearl was in no mood to obey, and she raced towards Billy, stumbling over a rock and landing on her knees in the riverbed.

"Pearl! Stay where you are and wait for Billy to come to you!" Scotty roared at her. However, Pearl tearfully cried out for Stephen and kept stumbling towards him on her knees, with Scotty and Dianne struggling to hold her back.

Then, in frustration, and exhaustion, Tiffany lashed out at her mother.

"All you care about is baby Stephen, baby Stephen. What about me? Ever since he's been born, it's all about baby Stephen, baby Stephen, I'm sick of it!" She stormed off. "You make me sick, and if I ever get out of this mess, I'm gone, you hear me? Gone!" And with that, Tiffany strode back to the group.

"Bring the baby here, mate, and let's reunite Stephen with his mother," Scotty said quietly to Billy.

Billy walked forward cautiously, making sure he didn't trip too, and handed over the crying baby to Pearl. She hugged his little form to her bosom and crooned, "There, there, darling, you're back where you belong."

She remembered his rescuers. "Oh, thank you, Billy! Thanks, Scotty!" She pointed to the top of the riverbank. "I'd like to go up there so I can breastfeed him. He must be famished, poor little thing, yes you are!"

Scotty and Billy helped a tired, emotional Pearl up the bank and found her a secluded spot to sit down with Stephen in her lap.

"Geez! That was hard work, getting Pearl up here!" Billy commented, unaware he could be heard by all those in the river

Scotty apologised to Pearl and briefly explained Billy's condition to her. "Thank you for finding my baby, Billy. I'm not offended by your comment."

They helped Pearl to sit down. As she placed Stephen on her breast, Billy stood there and scratched his head, curious about what he was witnessing. He'd never before seen a woman breastfeeding a baby up close.

Scotty steered him away. "Listen, mate, I know you don't understand what's happening here, but it's the most natural thing in the world, except that you're not supposed to stand there and gawk. Now, tell me more about the body you found near the vehicle."

They sat and waited for Stephen to finish feeding before heading back to the others.

"I'm going back to the vehicle where Billy found the baby," Scotty told the others. "Someone needs to help Pearl and Stephen. Okay, Billy, come and show me where you found Stephen." He waved to the Emergency Services folks and ordered, "Let's go."

Scotty and Billy helped the Emergency Services retrieve David's body from the riverside, then Scotty went to inform Dianne.

Luke took it on himself to console Tiffany and Rhys, who were in shock at hearing their father was dead.

The fog had now cleared, and, as they were walking away, they found the vehicle with the bodies of Nick and Ryan in it.

Tiffany had recognised the vehicle, and when she looked at Nick's tattooed body, she immediately remembered the first time she saw the distinctive tattoo of a bird of prey, like a hawk, on his neck. That terrifying night flashed back, and Tiffany burst into uncontrollable tears. When they eventually slowed, she explained why she was so upset to Dianne, Rhys and Luke.

"I don't know why I'm crying! I'm glad he's dead. He was the bastard that raped me, that night…"

To Dianne, this now made perfect sense and justified Tiffany's outburst to her mother. But Luke was shocked, although not surprised, that his loathsome older brother would have done this.

He was amazed, too, that Tiffany would still want anything to do with him but felt reassured by the way she was clutching and hugging him now. Glad she didn't blame him, after finally telling those around her about his brothers' actions and her ordeal. They were all relieved at having survived the night. Rhys, especially, was stunned by his sister's revelations and felt a distinct shift in his attitude towards her.

"When I saw stars in the sky, last night, in between the rain and fog, I was wishing you were gone. But you're still here, and I'm glad. I think…" he said, joking awkwardly, yet smiling. Everyone laughed as the tension drained away.

Ron and the girls embraced each other, looking around the now-clear scene of destruction in the daylight.

The ambulance and the SES treated Milo, scratching their heads at his enormous size.

The police and Emergency Services people went to deal with the SUV with Nick and Ryan's remains in it, as well as Bill's body nearby on the riverbank.

Katherine arrived to comfort her badly shaken husband, John.

Despite his familiarity with firearms, John didn't make a habit of shooting humans every day.

Jo-Anne, still in shock, sat and waited in the police car, while others dealt with the dead and the surviving animals.

As Luke stood there, reflecting on his time since leaving home, and on Tiffany's story, a stretcher was about to be carried past him. He turned to see who was on it. They'd found Paul!

He was surprised to find himself feeling so emotional. They had found the one brother Luke thought could have supported him through his turmoil over the years. It never happened, but when Luke saw the remorse on Paul's face, along with a wry smile, he couldn't refuse Paul's handshake. Things might be looking better for the two remaining brothers' relationship, after all.

Luke felt the tears start as the intense emotions of the past twenty-four hours hit home. He nodded at Paul and said, "I'll see you soon."

As the doors of the ambulance closed, everyone gathered around Luke as a final gesture of thanks, and Tiffany kissed him on the cheek.

Luke gazed across the sundrenched, flooded landscape before him and wondered what the future would bring.

# Epilogue

When the dead and injured had gone, Luke was enjoying some quiet time talking about the events of the evening with Tiffany. He turned to look at her directly, compassionately.

"From your affection for me... which I return equally to you, I am a bit troubled as to how to... or whether I should suggest to you about reconciling with your..."

But she pursed her lips, pulled her hand from his and backed away from him.

"I don't want *anything* to do with her, especially after last night, so if you really have any thoughts for me and what might happen to us after today, then don't go there, please."

Although Luke could see how determined she was, he also sensed there could be a glimmer of regret. Perhaps it was just too soon.

"Can I at least ask her to come over? Maybe you could both apologise to each other, so you and your mother can move on from this ordeal. Please."

His warm smile and kindness were too much for Tiffany to ignore, and her face softened.

"Thank you, Tiffany. You won't regret this."

He walked over to Pearl, now quite relaxed as she cradled Stephen.

Seeing a shadow at her feet, Pearl looked up to see Luke smiling at her.

Pearl felt happier but was still in such a confused state that she couldn't remember who was standing before her.

"Sorry! Who are you, again?"

"It's Luke, Pearl. Look, I'd like to bring your daughter over to chat about last night. Is that okay?" He hoped the recent outburst had faded from Pearl's mind, now that Stephen had been found.

She tried awkwardly to get up, and Luke helped her. Tiffany, standing a few feet away, started to understand that her mother had probably been through *her* worst nightmare as well.

"Come here, darl," Pearl said. They put their arms around each other, tears flowing freely. Both mumbled apologies to each other as Luke watched, pleased for both of them.

He took Tiffany's hand tentatively, and they hugged.

"Thank you so much, Luke! You've been amazing, the way you helped us, got us out of trouble. I'm so glad you're not like your brothers." She kissed him firmly, and this time Luke responded and didn't let go.

Pearl wondered, *When did this happen?*

Then, Scotty came over and stood at her feet to get her attention. Pearl recognised his police uniform but not his name, so she asked, "Who are you, and what have you done with my husband?"

# The Steering Times

Many criminals assume they are above the law.

Mario Sculini (alias the Boss) was one of those. He is now dead after many years of iron rule in the underworld. Last night, during a shootout between members of the Federal Crime Task Force, the Boss and a number of his bodyguards were killed. A single bullet ended Sculini's reign.

A young girl, believed to be a family member, was found in a wine cellar with a young male. Police are releasing neither of their identities at this stage.

A tip-off about the whereabouts of the Boss was received by the Task Force a few days ago, after an alleged attempted murder in a small north-western country town called Steering, about five hours drive northwest of Melbourne near Mildura. The town recently had major flooding.

A man of Ukrainian descent was captured by police while holding a journalist and a policeman at gunpoint on the outskirts of the town. Reports are unclear at present; however, rumours are that it all stems from the journalist's investigation into underworld dealings. The senior constable, who had been under threat from the Ukrainian, spoke of the heroic efforts of a farmer and his dog, who together disarmed their assailant, allowing the officer to handcuff him.

The accused was reported to be a huge man, well over 200 cm (over seven feet) tall and weighing about 130 kilos.

It has also been revealed that a serious accident occurred that night at the scene of the arrest. It is unclear whether the two incidents are related.

# Coronial Investigation

## Victim 1

David Lockwood was driving a 2011 Mercedes station wagon on 3 February 2011. His wife, Pearl, was a passenger, along with their three children: Tiffany, 17; Rhys, 15; and Stephen, 6 months.

The point of collision was at McKenzie's Bridge which carries a single lane in each direction. The Lockwood family entered the bridge outside the town of Steering around 7.30 p.m. The roads were wet from heavy rain, which began two hours earlier and was still intense at the time of the accident.

At the same time a Kenworth prime mover carrying the owner/driver, Ron Williams, 40; his wife Dianne, 38; and their twin 8 year old daughters, Bridgette and Bethany, was pulling a cattle trailer and approaching from the opposite direction.

The prime mover crossed onto the westbound lane and was not seen by Mr Lockwood until it was too late for him to take evasive action, due to the intense rain.

A collision occurred between the front passenger side of the prime mover and Mr Lockwood's station wagon, causing the latter to crash through the bridge's railing and into the river approximately ten metres below. None of the surviving occupants suffered serious injuries except for mild concussions, from which they all recovered later in the evening.

Unfortunately, Mr Lockwood died during the night from a snake bite to the neck.

The snake had reportedly followed the family into their car, where they were sheltering from the fierce storm. He had also suffered a broken wrist.

## Victims 2 and 3

After the initial collision, an SUV, driven by Mr Nick McKenzie and carrying his brothers Paul, Bill, Ryan and Luke, arrived on the scene and collided with the trailer of the prime mover.

In circumstances to be described later, Nick, Ryan and Bill all died after being gored by a Texas Longhorn bull.

Paul McKenzie was seriously injured. He is badly concussed and has a periorbital hematoma (black eye) on his right side and some minor cuts and abrasions on his chest and back. Luke McKenzie escaped virtually unscathed and was instrumental in providing assistance to the remaining survivors.

The Crash Unit Forensics investigated the circumstances of the crash.

The prime mover was the subject of a mechanical inspection, and the opinion produced was that it was in good condition, with efficient braking systems. There were no suspension faults in the trailer.

The Road Transport Authority (RTA) also prepared a detailed report concerning the surface friction of the bridge at the scene, as well a safety analysis of the suitability of the bridge. Concerns in relation to both of these matters were expressed.

Mrs Lockwood requested that an inquest be held, as, at the time of the accident she was in no state to comprehend what had happened. Given there were some considerable uncertainties in relation to a number of issues, a decision was made to hold an inquest.

Issues to be established:

- The identities of the deceased persons. When, where and how they died, what caused their deaths, and the circumstances leading to their deaths.

- The conduct of the prime mover driver involved in the collision and the mechanical condition of the prime mover.
- The condition, layout and engineering of the bridge and road surface at and near the site of the collision.
- Whether similar deaths at the site could be prevented from occurring.

The scope of an inquest goes beyond merely establishing the medical cause of death. An inquest is not a trial between opposing parties but an inquiry into the cause of death or deaths. The focus is on discovering what happened, not on ascribing guilt, attributing blame nor apportioning liability.

The purpose of an inquest is to inform the families and the public of how the deaths occurred with a view to reducing the likelihood of similar deaths.

As a result, the Act authorises a coroner to make preventive recommendations concerning public health or safety.

A coroner must not include in the findings any comments, recommendations or statements that a person is, or may be, guilty of an offence or is, or may be, civilly liable.

## Autopsy Results

An autopsy examination found multiple traumatic injuries suffered by Nick and Ryan McKenzie in the front seats of the SUV. These included crash injuries to the chest with multiple rib fractures and a ruptured diaphragm, an extensively ruptured liver, multiple face and arm fractures, and a non-displaced cervical spine fracture.

The cause of Nick McKenzie's death was the heart being pierced by the horn of a bull, which had partially released itself from the crashed semi-trailer. The multiple rib fractures may have been caused by the motor vehicle accident, with other injuries contributing. Pneumothorax, the presence of air or gas in the cavity between the lungs and the chest wall, causing the collapse of the lung, was also present.

Ryan and Bill McKenzie died from similar injuries, also attributed to attacks by one or more bulls.

Mr David Lockwood died from the effects of a snake bite. A significant quantity of the snake's venom was found in his system.

The Crash Unit Forensics (CUF) provided a report to the coroner, detailing the type of venom, and it was requested that the information not become public.

The lead investigator was Senior Constable Scott Taylor, who was also the first response officer on the scene. SC Taylor had completed basic Forensic Crash Unit Training, as well as having had significant practical experience. Sergeant Bert Logan also assisted.

SC Taylor reported that the bridge has rarely been used since the decline of the local economy during the 1980s.

## CUF Report on Scene Observations and Conditions

It was estimated that Mr Lockwood had less than a second to take evasive action. Having regard to the closing speeds between the two vehicles of about 10–20 k.p.h., SC Taylor stated that, realistically, Mr Lockwood had no opportunity or option to avoid the crash.

The truck driver and his passengers all suffered minor injuries. The unusual position and angle of the prime mover that collided with Mr Lockwood's vehicle suggested to SC Taylor that the intense rain caused the crash.

The prime mover entered from the western side of the bridge, and its trailer was wedged against the light pole after tumbling into the river and landing on top of Mr Lockwood's car but not squashing it, as the trailer was wedged against the bridge.

SC Taylor was able to confirm that the RTA Road Rules provide that it is legal for a motor vehicle to enter the bridge when it is occupied by another vehicle.

The investigation revealed that, as the bridge was rarely used by more than one vehicle at a time, this was a case of the three vehicles being in the wrong place at the wrong time.

The driver of the prime mover submitted to a roadside breath test, which was negative for alcohol. No traces of drugs were found. Each of the three deceased brothers had blood readings of more than 0.10.

Senior Constable Taylor concluded there were four major contributing factors to the accident. In order of significance, they were:

- the intense rain and suspect road surface,
- the decayed condition of the bridge,
- the flushing of the road surface by rain, and
- the lack of visibility for all involved.

SC Taylor, in talks with the relevant authorities, has concluded there should be flashing lights set up at either end of the bridge to warn any approaching drivers that another vehicle is occupying the bridge and to wait for this vehicle to exit before entering.

## Conclusions

When Mr Lockwood saw the prime mover ahead of him, he had no opportunity to take any evasive action. A number of factors that contributed to the accident were identified by the CUF investigations.

It is difficult to apportion these factors in percentage terms, and I find they all contributed in some parts.

Certainly, the wooden bridge's configuration, combined with the slippery surface and decaying structure, played significant roles.

I will be recommending Luke McKenzie for a bravery award for his actions in helping to rescue those involved in this terrible accident.

Mr John Meadows and his dog Ziggy will also receive my recommendations for recognition of their bravery in overcoming the assailant in the latter stages of this matter.

## Comments and Recommendations

It is recommended, if not already being implemented, that the RTA proceed with the redesign and re-construction of McKenzie's Bridge, and a flashing light system be connected to the police station for regular monitoring.

I intend to provide the information gained from the investigation and inquest to the relevant authorities forthwith.

I close this inquest.

State Coroner
25 February 2012

# Appendix

Most animals slaughtered for food in Australia have had their throats cut with a knife (referred to as "sticking") so that they can be bled out.

Prior to this, they are typically meant to be unconscious (though, as of 2011, abattoirs in Australia have permission from state governments to slit the throats of fully conscious animals, as part of the religious practices of halal and kosher slaughter).

There are three main methods of stunning intended to make animals unconscious before slaughter: captive bolt, electrically and gas chambers.

# The Art of Road Use

Most drivers have a reasonable understanding of their approach to driving, anywhere around the world, especially in trying conditions. However, even the most dedicated and professional drivers (like me, the author) will at times revert to the age-old saying, "I'm only human." So, knowing well the ins and outs of driving in all weather conditions, I have a reasonable grasp of the law, and I understand the road rules.

I thought I would provide you with the following insights that could serve you well while you are manoeuvring your way around Australia, on its many and varied roads, on your journey from point A to point B.

In anything we do in life, there is an inherent art or a developed skill that we have accumulated over time, which gives us the ability to do whatever we put our minds to. But, sometimes, these abilities can come undone for various reasons, as I will endeavour to explain in the following examples.

## Drive to the Conditions

If you have been driving on dry roads for a long time, because there hasn't been any rain during that time, you might want to think about your abilities when driving in unfamiliar conditions, combined with the added risks involved.

As you're confronted with more issues than you're used to, you should plan your journey and then drive to the conditions—especially if the road will take you through hills and fog-filled valleys.

In severe conditions, it makes perfect sense to take pride out of the equation and slow down.

Remember, you're only human, and you will eventually get to where you are going. Alive.

## Overtaking

Regardless of whether it is day or night, you must be aware of a couple of things that will make your overtaking manoeuvre much safer than just "pulling out and planting it".

First, you must be a reasonable distance behind the vehicle you're overtaking, and you must be extra mindful if you're towing a trailer or caravan.

Once the road ahead levels out and your vision is good, make sure you are a minimum of fifty metres behind the vehicle in front of you, then time your passing manoeuvre by slowly building up speed.

As the oncoming vehicle passes you, you have a better and safer opportunity to pass unimpeded. This also takes less time than if you were not to perform this manoeuvre properly.

## Flash Flooding and Driving in Water

Fifteen centimetres of water under most family cars will cause a loss of control and stalling.

Thirty centimetres of water will float many vehicles.

Any more than sixty centimetres of water, whether flowing fast or slow, will move most vehicles, especially heavier ones like SUVS and utes, along with the current.

Never drive into water over the road unless you know how deep it is, but, even then, you must take into consideration what type of vehicle you are in.

When in doubt, don't go in as, in the end, it will cost you to be pulled out, and some insurance companies don't cover this.

## Mirror, Mirror Intimidation

If you find yourself continually looking in your rear-view mirror because a vehicle is too close to you, then this other driver has control over you.

Instead, you should be watching what happens in front of you, to control them.

You can tilt your rear-vision mirror to night vision at all times, even during the day. That way, they can't see you looking at them if you need to.

Don't let anything distract your driving; focus on what's ahead and stay in control. And take all distractions out of the equation.

And your mobile phone: if a phone call is urgent, they will call again, unless you have Bluetooth in your vehicle.

## Motion Disorientation

Imagine you've been travelling at a high speed for a long distance, like on a main road or freeway.

Suddenly, you have to slow down to half or a quarter of that speed, for school zones, roadworks, etc.

What happens here is that your brain tries urgently to adjust, and that can take more time than you imagine.

This will vary with every driver.

Take your foot slightly off the accelerator, and the rest will take care of itself. Do the same when approaching traffic lights if you're not expecting a traffic-light change, especially if you're towing or carrying a heavy load, even a small trailer.

Remember: you're driving from point A to point B. You must concentrate on that, not what you're doing when you reach point B.

## Back Roads and Dirt Roads

Again, drive to the conditions, take pride out of the equation, and you'll get there eventually.

Back roads and dirt roads are narrower than main roads and treacherous at the best of times. Those with bitumen may have wide or narrow dirt shoulders. If you're faced with any oncoming vehicles, slow down, keep half of your vehicle on the shoulder and pass each other at the same speed.

If it's a larger vehicle passing you, then come to a stop. Then, the stones in the dirt won't possibly hit your car or, worse still, the windscreen.

With dirt-only roads, there are two important thoughts here.

First, you have minimal control at the best of times. You should stay, at best, in the middle of the road, except when you are slowing down or are confronted with another oncoming vehicle.

Second, braking suddenly provides you with absolutely no grip whatsoever. None. Nil. So slow down well before another approaching vehicle.

Again, drive to the conditions.

## Light Changing

If you're driving all night, as most interstate truckies do, have a sleep/break at sun-up or sunset, as they do.

Same goes if you're driving all day. And that's for ordinary motorists as well.

When you're yawning or your eyelids start to flutter or want to close for longer periods than normal, that's basically telling you that your body is tired, and it's time to pull over or change drivers. Especially if you're travelling interstate or for a long distance that you haven't done before.

With all the freeways being built around most countries, there's less hassle than in stopping or going through smaller towns now, but you can always turn off and visit one if you're tired or hungry rather than stopping at one of the bigger truck stops.

It's becoming more attractive to drive, whether on your own or with others (i.e., when you can share the driving).

But you need sleep if you've been driving all night or all day. If you don't get even as much as a powernap, you'll nod off or have a microsleep. This can cause you to fall completely asleep at the wheel.

That's why many drivers often crash first thing in the morning, because they haven't slept all night or have had too little sleep.

Most interstate and local truck drivers have fatigue-management training nowadays and are taught to have regular breaks. It is better-policed than it used to be, so there's no excuse for trying to beat the system.

Depending on where you drive in the world, you might not have some or all of these regulations.

Nowadays, you can see trucks of all shapes and sizes parked on the side of the road around lunch time. As it is the law now, in Australia, it's now compulsory for truck drivers to have a regulated break.

They may only drive for no more than five and a quarter hours, and then must have a fifteen- or thirty-minute break during or at the end of that period.

Two fifteen-minute breaks must be taken before seven and a half hours are up.

It varies in most countries, as do the rules covering livestock transport.

## Driving in Severe Conditions

You may continue on if you know the road, especially in conditions such as fog.

If you don't know the road, you should wait it out, or you should drive to the conditions and take your time from point A to point B.

Fog is claustrophobic at best, and, if you think you know better, you are only asking for trouble.

Depending on the various locations around the world, sleet, snow and whiteout conditions are even more treacherous.

If planes don't fly in these conditions, then you shouldn't drive either if you're not comfortable with what's in front of you.

## Going through a Tunnel for the First Time

Speaking with a few people about going through tunnels for the first time, I was surprised at how many were critical of road authorities for failing to provide instructions on navigating the tunnel, regardless of where it was located.

Most professional drivers, including taxi drivers, couriers and the like, who do it every day, know how to work a tunnel, as it's just second nature to us.

But, for the average motorist in a car, van or towing something, my best advice is to stay in the left lane, except in single-lane tunnels.

Either way, once you're in any tunnel, you're subject to the conditions, regardless of how you feel at the time. Then, just go with the flow until you become more confident.

Apart from the morning and afternoon peak times, it will always seem like a long trip if there is traffic congestion.

But there are those who feel claustrophobic in a tunnel and are anxious to get out as quickly as possible. This can create more congestion because of the way they are driving. They try to go too fast or too slow and end up causing accidents. Sometimes, the run is quite short, but it can feel like ages. However, you can double or triple that in peak times.

As you will start to become more confident about what to do, you might start to use another lane or just decide to stay to the left.

Do not change lanes continually, as it causes a domino effect and eventually makes it worse and slows everyone else down.

Here are some valuable hints about entering and going through any tunnel.

- Check and understand the signs above and on the roadway.
- Use your normal headlights.
- Put your radio on for emergency announcements.
- Check your fuel.
- Don't use sunglasses in a darkened tunnel.
- If you see a breakdown or accident that has just happened, or if you are stuck for a short time, put your hazards on until you can indicate to get past, if possible. Or you'll have to wait until you are told to proceed by someone authorised. Use your car's air-conditioning on low only on very hot days, as it can get much hotter inside a tunnel when congestion occurs.
- Stay in the vehicle if the traffic is fast-moving and you've been in an accident or broken down—unless a vehicle is about to catch, or is on, fire.
- Turn off the engine, also, if stopped for any period longer than expected.
- Pull off to the side if you can. Note your vehicle's location.
- Assess your vehicle's operating problem. Call the emergency number located in the tunnel and tell them your situation. Wait calmly for an incident vehicle to arrive.
- When you exit the tunnel, wait until you have adjusted to the change in light conditions, especially during sunny days.
- Turn off your headlights if it is sunny.

## Road Hog

Many people don't like trucks hogging the road and sitting in the fast lane.

Depending how you look at it, trucks are a necessary evil.

But many motorists don't realise that, if they cut in front of a truck, it can't slow down or stop as quickly as smaller vehicles can, especially if they're loaded.

Cutting in can cause an accident, as well as slow other vehicles that are following on behind the truck.

Unfortunately, some drivers believe that the fast lane is always the fastest lane, but if you look closely, it's not.

## Merging

Here is another unwritten law.

When you come down or along the on-ramp to merge with traffic already on the freeway, or any road, then it's *your* responsibility to merge with them, not the other way round—regardless of whether you have ramp signals or not.

Vehicles already on the freeway have priority, so you should give way to them and merge with them by looking earlier, rather than waiting until the last second to merge. By then, it's too late, and you could cause others behind you to have an accident.

Unfortunately, at peak times, it is everyone for themselves. With the number of vehicles in peak times and with under-developed roads, there is no quick fix.

Many drivers enter freeways at speeds that are slower than the flow of traffic on the freeway, often forcing a vehicle already on the freeway to slow down and brake suddenly. This causes accidents and frustration for everyone.

Most vehicles can travel at a reasonable speed, so you need to look at who is merging with whom to determine who is going to be in front at the point of merging, especially if it's a large semi-trailer or someone towing a trailer or caravan.

## Obeying Speed Limits at All Roadworks

Speed limits are important, and, on the odd occasion, you will hear protests about a certain speed.

In a suburb near me, parents forced the roads authority to reduce the speed limit near a school, and they won.

As for roadwork speed limits, the problem here is the lack of uniformity from the road authorities, regardless of where you live.

And just as much intolerance from motorists, especially when there are no workers around.

Or signs were left on the side of the road, forgotten, after the works were completed.

Workers are entitled to protection at all times. Sometimes, there is no consistency from either side about whether all the protocols have been implemented for their safety.

This is annoying, and it will only get worse, due to the ever-increasing population, with not only new roads, but also increasing lanes on current ones.

There is a simple reason for these limits. But not a lot of thought has gone into the dynamic of the real-time effect on the continued flow of vehicles and, more importantly, the safety of road workers.

## So, There is a Need For...

One thing drivers don't often realise is that you could be caught flouting the law at any time.

But most drivers have become used to not being caught, so they continue on as if they are doing nothing wrong.

The same can be said about using mobile phones or drink-driving.

## Who Owns the Road? We All Do

If you're following another vehicle, and you're too close to them because you don't want other drivers to push in front of you, then you could miss vehicles on the side of the road, for example, a cyclist.

If cyclists are taking up most of the lane, or the entire lane, if they are continually doing that every day, and if you believe this shouldn't be allowed, then you have the right to complain to the relevant authorities.

Before you think about the inconvenience they are causing you, ask yourself whether you are paying attention, as you should be.

## Know Your Vehicle's Height

Always check if there are any bridges that you need to go under on your way to point B.

Unfortunately, most (if not all) apps/GPSs do not have any information regarding bridges or their heights.

I would urge every driver to measure the height of their vehicle, be it a car, caravan, trailer or a loaded-to-the-max car roof. Most importantly, measure the height of your load.

Just before a bridge and at the bridge itself, well positioned signs tell you what the height limit is.

It's your responsibility to know the height of your vehicle plus its top load.

## How to Deal With Big Trucks

Like many things in life, trucks are a necessary evil, and there will only be more of them in the future.

But one thing is paramount: don't get anxious about these massive mobile monoliths. Treat them the same as any other vehicle around you and don't ever cut in front of them, even if you think there is a space for you. They cannot stop like a car can, and, if they are loaded, then their stopping distance is quantified by their speed and load.

For example, if a loaded truck is travelling at 60 kph, it will take at least 100 metres to stop safely, whereas a car can stop in less than 15 metres.

So, respect the trucks, go with the flow of traffic, and you'll get to point B in about the same time.

Bees, surprisingly, are a perfect analogy for how things work in nature. Like worker bees, truck drivers are a necessary element to allow society to function as a whole.

Somebody has to deliver your items without delay, so don't badmouth all trucks and their drivers. We're not all to blame for someone who did something wrong. A little bit of understanding and knowledge on your part goes a long way towards bridging the gap. Respect goes both ways.

## Damaged Roads and Road Funding: Who to Contact

Contact your local council about damaged roads, and they should tell you if it is their road or what the road authority is in your state.

## APP/GPS

Regardless of the app you're using, there is no quick fix to accurately calculate the time you'll take to go from point A to point B. An app can only give an estimate.

Accidents and road hazards are common these days. Nothing is as it seems.

However, there are exceptions to this, no matter what app you use or where you're driving.

Simply double the time you think your journey will take, to counter the unexpected, especially at peak times.

It doesn't matter whether it's day or night, city or country—shit happens.

Good luck.

## Killing a Human vs. Killing an Animal

First, it's better to hit an animal rather than to swerve or brake hard to avoid it.

Most people have no wish to kill an animal, but a human life is always more valuable.

Missing a human and killing an animal is socially acceptable, but killing a human just to miss killing an animal is not.

If you do hit an animal, especially a large one, the problem you face is it could find its way through your windscreen and do horrific damage to your vehicle, to you and any passengers.

And an animal that's still alive will kick more than you'd expect.

## Distance Travelled With Your Eyes Off the Road

There's a simple way to figure out how far you've travelled while you're driving along any road.

Nowadays, a lot of drivers calculate distance travelled using mobile phones—when they should be watching the road.

But they don't understand the distance their vehicle travels while their attention is diverted. Every second their eyes are off the road, they're moving closer to a disaster, such as running off the road or hitting and killing someone.

Distances travelled at any speed are easily calculated at twenty-five percent of the speed you are travelling at.

For example, at one hundred kilometres per hour, you travel twenty-five metres in one second. That's the length of a B-double semi-trailer.

At a slower speed of sixty kilometres per hour, you will travel fifteen metres—the length of a normal semi-trailer.

Believing that it's okay to look away for what is only a second is really stupid. Someone could be dead by the time you read this sentence. Most people would do well to be a little bit more thoughtful about their driving habits.

## Too Close for Comfort

When you're parked behind another vehicle, make sure you can see its rear tyres, especially if it's another car, as some trucks do not allow this.

The reason is that if the vehicle in front of you breaks down or runs into the vehicle in front of them, then you cannot turn to your left or right to move around them, especially if you have another vehicle too close behind you as well.

If you find you are in this situation, please make sure you look at the oncoming traffic before you leap. Getting out of your vehicle, you could be struck and possibly killed.

For your own safety, consider the consequences of your actions.

## Cut Out Cutting In

Annoyed at drivers cutting in front of you because they're in a hurry, only to find you're next to them at the next set of traffic lights?

What you may not realise here is that no matter how many vehicles do this to you, you'll still get to where you're going in much the same time as it's always taken.

How it comes about is like this: when these annoying drivers do this to you, there are many more doing it way in front of you to other drivers like you, but who are leaving your lane and moving into another lane further up the road.

So, you can see that, no matter how many do this to you, there are just as many leaving your lane.

As for blasting your horn or giving them the bird or abusing them, they don't care about you, and it's too late anyway.

So, take your time, and you'll get where you're going safely.

**Last Word**

Drive smarter, not faster.

# Thoughts from the Author

I've been a driver for more than forty years and been in the transport industry for about two-thirds of that time. I've seen a lot in my lifetime, and it all helped me write this story. You can't avoid hearing or seeing incidents such as I've witnessed on our roads over that time.

It's my belief that we all change every five to ten years. It's the life skills that we learn that determine our future. Not just in everyday situations, but also as road users of all types.

Experience beats youth hands down, because, as we get older, taking risks takes a back seat, and I can vouch for that.